RUSSIAN AND EAST EUROPEAN STUDIES

Jonathan Harris, Editor

NOT A HERO

A NOVEL

IGNATY POTAPENKO

TRANSLATED BY MICHAEL R. KATZ
WITH AN INTRODUCTION BY OTTO BOELE

UNIVERSITY OF PITTSBURGH PRESS

Published by the University of Pittsburgh Press, Pittsburgh, Pa., 15260
Copyright © 2021, University of Pittsburgh Press
All rights reserved
Manufactured in the United States of America
Printed on acid-free paper
10 9 8 7 6 5 4 3 2 1

Cataloging-in-Publication data is available from the Library of Congress

ISBN 13: 978-0-8229-4698-4
ISBN 10: 0-8229-4698-X

COVER ART: Illustration from *Satirikon*, no. 13, 1908.

COVER DESIGN: Alex Wolfe

CONTENTS

—

—

Ignaty Potapenko

PORTRAIT OF IGNATY POTAPENKO, CA. 1885

NOTE ON THE TRANSLATION

Potapenko's *Ne geroi* **was originally published in the journal**
Vestnik Evropy, 1891, nos. 9–12. I have chosen to translate the
slightly abridged version that was published later by A. F. Marks
in *Petrograd* (no date), in volume 5 of I. N. Potapenko's ten-volume
Sochineniia (pp. 343–512).

INTRODUCTION

—

Otto Boele

To call a nineteenth-century Russian writer "prolific" amounts to saying nothing at all about him. In the second half of the century, writers were prolific by definition, such were the demands of a rapidly expanding literary market and the ambitions of an increasing number of writers trying to live by their pen. As students of Russian literature know only too well, Anton Chekhov and Fyodor Dostoevsky were, at least partly, in it for the money. Their financial hardship left them simply no choice but to regard literature as an important (if not their only) source of income. Leo Tolstoy and Ivan Turgenev were exceptions in this regard as they did not depend on their writing for their livelihood, but this did not prevent them from being quite productive too. Writing was a way of life in the late nineteenth century, or rather a struggle for life that made one occasionally forget about such romantic notions as inspiration and artistic integrity.

While high productivity was the general norm, some authors reached a level of literary output that was considered uncommon even by the standards of their time. One such author was Ignaty Potapenko (1856–1929) who after abandoning an array of academic pursuits in Odessa and St. Petersburg, eventually settled in the capital to become one of Russia's most widely read authors of the 1890s.[1] Before the end of the century his ever-expanding collected works already counted eleven volumes with an average page count of 500. Later editions of individual volumes were published throughout Potapenko's career on top of new work that continued to appear right until his death in 1929. At some point his output acquired such legendary proportions that a satirical journal speculated about Potapenko's ability to write novels "using his hands and feet."[2]

Why read Potapenko now? Why introduce an author who even at the peak of his fame was sometimes criticized for the shallow portrayal of his characters and the rushed nature of his writing? *Not a Hero* is an intriguing attempt to engage with the legacies of nineteenth-century Russian literature by simultaneously perpetuating and challenging them. On the one hand, the novel presents a fictional portrait of a new type of *intelligent*, an updated "hero of our time" who anticipates the direction in which society is heading; on the other hand, the title seems to subvert that concept head-on.[3] *Not a Hero* reads as a classical *roman à thèse* promoting a political program, the so-called theory of small deeds, but it is also the product of Russian literature's often bemoaned commodification. Finally,

---

1. For a more extensive discussion of Potapenko's earlier novels, see Otto Boele, "'New Times Require New People': The Demise of the Epoch-making Hero in Late Nineteenth-Century Russian Literature." *Dutch Contributions to the Fourteenth International Congress of Slavists* (Amsterdam: Rodopi, 2008), 133–149.
2. "A Graphic Review of Ivan [*sic*] Potapenko," *Satirikon* 13, 1908, n.p.
3. Derived from Mikhail Lermontov's eponymous novel (1841), a "hero of our time" became a standard expression in Russian literary criticsm signifying the "typical" representative of a specific generation of the intelligentsia.

while Potapenko himself increasingly enjoyed the reputation of a commercial scribbler, it is precisely the ascent of the hack writer that *Not a Hero* both signals and laments. Owing to its contradictory nature, *Not a Hero* offers a unique perspective on the changes and continuities in nineteenth-century Russian literature and society at large.

Potapenko's novel deserves to be read for yet another reason. It introduces us to a debate that is as relevant for Russia today as it was in the 1890s: how to bring about social change within an oppressive and ossified political system without resorting to or provoking violence. In contrast to his colleague and friend Anton Chekhov, who was often criticized for merely signaling problems, but not offering solutions, Potapenko did provide an answer by introducing the "non-hero," an unspectacular, but effective role model who, in Potapenko's view, would help face the challenges at hand.

To put the novel in its proper context and make it more digestible for the twenty-first-century reader, this introduction discusses both issues, the novel's political agenda and its position vis-à-vis Russian literature's "commercialization." Occasionally it touches on the author's relationship with Anton Chekhov as this will allow us to gain a more nuanced understanding of how Potapenko earned the dubious reputation for which he is still known.

A Tendentious Novel about Literary Bankruptcy

Not a Hero is a peculiar amalgam of topical statements on the perceived degradation of Russian literature and political ideas about the need for social reform. In terms of composition and character constellation, the novel closely follows the conventions of the tendentious realist novel that thrived during the reign of Alexander II (1855–1881). Pushing a radical left-wing agenda or, on the contrary, taking up a more conservative, "antinihilist" stance, tendentious novels usually lack a proper plot, thus allowing the characters to engage in lengthy monologues and discussions on the social and political issues of the day.[4] Often these discussions are dominated by some charismatic, slightly mysterious outsider who, even when he eventually dies or is proven wrong, for some time inspires or unhinges the community he has entered. Evgenii Bazarov, the iconoclastic protagonist in Ivan Turgenev's novel *Fathers and Children* (1862), is a paradigmatic example.

The "community" is usually an upper-class family running an estate or a group of like-minded people (friends, acquaintances, colleagues) in some unnamed provincial town, but *Not a Hero* is situated in St. Petersburg, more precisely in the capital's literary circles, which include both successful writers who have their work published in sumptuous book editions, and unscrupulous hacks dashing off sensationalist feuilletons for the penny press. These two extremes are represented by the fashionable writer Nikolai Baklanov, the author of idealistic stories about the countryside, and Anton Polzikov, a quarrelsome alcoholic who has sold himself to the *Secret Word*, one of the "vilest" newspapers in the country, as he admits himself.[5] Yet despite the difference in standing, Baklanov is just as much a captive of the literary rat race as his miserable colleague. To keep up his expensive lifestyle and satisfy his wife's every whim, he too has no choice but to compromise on the quality of his work when he threatens to miss a deadline for a particularly lucrative contract. Although he eventually succeeds in submitting the manuscript on time, he does so at the expense of his health and good name. For anyone involved in the literary business, then, the danger of hitting on hard times is always lurking, tempting even the serious writer to lower his standards and "sell out" when the need arises.

The outsider in this story of greed and crash materialism is Dmitry Racheev, a former friend and university classmate of Bak-

---

4. Nikolai Chernyshevsky's infamous novel *What Is to Be Done* (1863) and Vasilii Sleptsov's *Hard Times* (1865) are generally regarded as belonging to the left-wing branch of the genre. Ivan Goncharov's *The Precipice* (1869) and Fyodor Dostoevsky's *Devils* (1872) represent the other side of the political spectrum and are often referred to as "antinihilist" novels.

5. The name "Polzikov" can be translated roughly as "he who crawls."

lanov's who, after an absence of seven years, unexpectedly returns to St. Petersburg for the sole reason of "find[ing] out for myself what's going on here." Level-headed and oozing self-confidence, Racheev cuts a striking figure among the stressed-out literati of St. Petersburg who have grown accustomed to measuring any intellectual endeavor not by its intrinsic value, but by the financial gain that can be derived from it. Much to Racheev's bewilderment, Baklanov's reason for introducing him, a married man, to the attractive and wealthy Evgeniya Vysotskaya, turns out to be entirely "mercenary": to provoke a love affair that he could then use in his next novel. The routine-like way in which Baklanov judges anything he encounters from the point of view of its suitability for a literary plot frightens even himself, a sure sign that he begins to doubt the moral soundness of his craft: "Here I am, it seems, waiting for an old friend [Racheev]; and I relate to him sincerely, genuinely, but the first thoughts occasioned by his arrival—would there emerge a social-psychological novel, of, say, some twenty printer's sheets?" It is not so much the habit of constantly searching for useful material, as the reflex to quantify the potential output that indicates how much of a commodity literature has become.

As we will see, the character of Racheev performs a more important function in the story than merely to awaken Baklanov's conscience, and yet indirectly his righteousness and healthy pragmatism serve to indict the literary milieu with its incessant pursuit of money and cheap recognition. It is this indictment that makes *Not a Hero* a "novel of literary bankruptcy," as Abram Reitblat has called it, a genre that purported to warn the reader of the moral decline of Russian literature, but echoed the intelligentsia's anxiety over its own marginalization and the growing popularity of cheap popular fiction in the so-called thin journals and the penny press.[6] Potapenko clearly shared this anxiety, which is not only suggested by Baklanov's behavior and Racheev's indignation but also explicitly

---

6. A. I. Reitblat, "Roman literaturnogo krakha," *Novoe literaturnoe obozrenie* 25 (1997): 99–109.

expressed by Tomilov, a young and still unspoiled writer who in a "vehement speech, uttered with passion and sincere feeling" implores his colleagues "to adopt a tendency" (that is, to write socially meaningful literature). An example of Potapenko's weakly motivated happy endings, this scene wants the reader to believe that the serious writer, the man of letters "with a mission," will eventually prevail in Russian literature.

The irony is, of course, that Potapenko was intimately familiar with Baklanov's predicament, especially in the 1890s, as he was struggling to meet his financial obligations toward his wife (whom he had left), his mistress Lika Mizinova, and their illegitimate daughter, Khristina, who would die in infancy. By the mid-1890s his financial situation had become so desperate that, apart from appealing to Chekhov's benevolence to help out in the short run, he was forced to increase his literary production even further and subject himself to the scathing criticism that would permanently tarnish his reputation. Already around that time, reviewers were complaining that his "realism never reaches its full force," the "narration is too rushed and artificial," and important events in his characters' lives are simply relayed without detailing their emotions.[7] The widely shared assumption that Chekhov used Potapenko as the real-life prototype for Trigorin, the trendy, hyperproductive writer in *The Seagull* (1896), shows that his public image was growing increasingly similar to the figure of the hack writer that he himself had helped expose. By the time *Satirikon* made fun of him for churning out novels "using his hands and feet" (1908), few critics were prepared to take him seriously anymore.

No More Heroes

Among Soviet scholars who studied his work at all, Potapenko was invariably regarded as someone from the "Chekhov school." Both

---

7. N. Strakhov, "Povesti i rasskazy I. N. Potapenko: Tom vtoroi," *Kriticheskie stat'i*, vol. 2, (1861–1894) (Kiev: Izdanie I. P. Matchenko, 1902).

writers made their debut in the early 1880s and developed a genuinely warm relationship that started in 1894 and lasted until Chekhov's death ten years later. Most importantly, they were "men of the
1880s," intellectuals who supposedly could not muster the fighting
spirit of the previous generation, the radicals of the 1860s, and easily
succumbed to the political pressure of Alexander III's reactionary
regime (1881–1896). Contemporary critics and Soviet scholars were
nonetheless convinced that one cardinal difference set the two writers apart. If Chekhov was a more thoughtful and melancholic author,
a "pessimist," then Potapenko was initially hailed as a "fresh talent,"
an "optimist," albeit with a limited grasp of the political reality.[8]
"Whatever horror is depicted in Potapenko's work," the authoritative
critic Aleksandr Skabichevskii wrote, "the reader will be overcome
by a stimulating feeling of joy. His soul becomes light and he is even
prepared to cry out: no matter what, how good it is in this world!"[9] It
was this "naive" optimism that would ultimately discredit Potapenko
in the eyes of Soviet historians because it smacked of conformism
and an unsavory willingness to accept the tsarist regime as a given.
Chekhov's "pessimism," on the other hand, testified to a genuine
concern for the well-being of the Russian people even if this did
not translate into concrete political action. In *Plot for a Short Story*
(1969), a film by Sergei Yutkevich, this "difference" is exploited for
dramatic effect with Potapenko featuring as Chekhov's conceited
"other."[10] He childishly prides himself on producing an entire page
when his friend manages only a line and he prefers to stay in St.
Petersburg or live it up in Paris while Chekhov travels to Sakhalin
to study life in a penal colony. Although Potapenko acknowledges
that Chekhov is more talented, he cynically remarks that it does not
make much difference since Russian readers and critics are incapable

---

8. M. Protopopov, "Bodryi talant," *Russkaia mysl'* 9 (1898): 165–166.

9. A. M. Skabichevksii, *Istoriia noveishei russkoi literatury, 1848–1908,* 7th ed. (St. Petersburg: Izdanie F. Pavlenkova, 1909), 377.

10. *Plot for a Short Story (Siuzhet nebol'shogo rasskaza)* / *Lika, le grand amour de Tchekhov* (Soviet Union / France), 1969.

of appreciating good literature. In comparison to pensive-looking Chekhov, well-groomed Potapenko appears to be nothing but a shallow hedonist and a bad patriot.

It is not my intention to redress the balance in Potapenko's favor, but we should be aware that his popular image as a superficial and "unduly" optimistic hack writer is rooted in a political dispute to which *Not a Hero* contributed in no small measure. Apart from warning his readership about the moral bankruptcy of Russian literature, Potapenko also used his novel as a vehicle for the promotion of the "theory of small deeds," a program that called for social improvement not by bringing down the existing order by force, but through constructive work and gradual progress. To provide the common people with medical care, raise their educational level, or be actively involved in local administration was considered infinitely more productive than to confront the regime openly by assassinating its main figureheads, as the terrorist organization the People's Will had done in 1881, killing Tsar Alexander II. The theory thus introduced a new behavioral model whose ideal adherent was the pragmatic "nonheroic" *intelligent* who shunned political violence but contributed his might by working as a doctor or teacher in Russia's backwaters. In the words of Yakov Abramov, the theory's spiritual father: "Our intelligentsia considers itself to be either too heroic or incapable of doing anything. [In this country] everybody is either a hero or a wimp. Isn't it about time that a middle type started to emerge—a man capable of doing simple, honest work? We need such a man very badly and the future belongs to him."[11] Abramov even discovered a worthy role model in Doctor Astrov, one of the main characters in Chekhov's play *Uncle Vanya* (1897), whose genuine dedication to his profession and his considerable human shortcomings made him an entirely plausible figure.[12]

While no one could deny that "men capable of doing simple, honest work" were useful to society, it was the very concept of grad-

---

11. Ia. V. Abramov, "Stoit li rabotat' v derevne?" *Nedelia* 41 (1885): 1412.
12. Ia. V. Abramov, "Nasha zhizn' v proizvedeniiakh Chekhova," *Gospoda kritiki i gospodin Chekhov: Antologiia*, ed. Stiven Le Flemming (Moscow: Letnii sad, 2006), 17–23.

ualism as well as the absence of any political demands in Abramov's program that radical thinkers found disturbing. To the influential Marxist critic Vatslav Vorovskii, Astrov was just one of Chekhov's proverbially disillusioned heroes whose pedigree ultimately led back to the superfluous men of the 1840s.[13] Vladimir Lenin regarded the theory of small deeds as a reactionary phenomenon that threatened to distract society's progressive forces from the revolution.[14] Not surprisingly, this became the standard Soviet view of the theory of small deeds, which negatively affected the perception of anyone associated with it. Writing in the early 1980s, one Soviet scholar contended that for all their commitment to performing small deeds, Potapenko's heroes only demonstrated the "infeasibility of such cultural patchwork."[15]

In *Not a Hero* we never learn what "patchwork" Racheev is actually involved in, but it is hard to miss the similarities between Abramov's "middle type of man" and Potapenko's mouthpiece when the latter starts explaining to Evgeniya Vysotskaya how he has arrived at his philosophy of life. Note how Racheev has learned to scale down his ambitions and now rejects any masterplan that would miraculously and instantly transform the whole country:

> During a time of restless impulses [when he was a student], I imagined how I would make the entire Russian people happy, if not the whole world. But once I had acquired a practical base, I modestly limited the area of my activities to the small neighborhood where my estate is located. . . . And if you are going to ask me now about my program or my system, I

13. V. V. Vorovskii, "Bazarov i Sanin: dva nigilizma," *Estetika. Literatura. Iskusstvo* (Moscow: Iskusstvo, 1971), 229–255.
14. V. I. Lenin, "Chto takoe 'druz'ia naroda'? i kak oni voiuiut protiv sotsial-demokratov?" *Polnoe sobranie sochinenii* (Moscow: Izdatel'stvo politicheskoi literatury, 1967), vol. 1, 135–346.
15. V. B. Kataev, "Chekhov i ego literaturnoe okruzhenie (80-e gody XIX veka)," in *Sputniki Chekhova*, ed. V. B. Kataev (Moscow: Izdatel'stvo Moskovskogo Universiteta, 1982).

won't be able to give you any answer. I don't have any kind
of program. I'm trying to get to the bottom of all the details
of life in my small region, and try to relieve and improve its
existence.... And so, you see, Evgeniya Konstantinovna, that
I'm by no means a hero.

This emphasis on the "nonheroic" character of his activities does
not so much testify to Racheev's modesty, as it serves to convince
Vysotskaia to follow his example and make herself useful in a sim-
ilarly unspectacular way. Unwilling to give up her comfortable life
in the capital, she could still make a difference, not by toiling in
the provinces, but by using her beauty and social respectability in
St. Petersburg "to enlighten the upper class." As Racheev puts it in
one of the novel's most programmatic phrases: "Work can be found
everywhere; enlightenment is needed in every corner."

Racheev's words may strike us as naively optimistic, especially
if we consider that revolutionary activism and violent resistance
would soon gain in popularity again, culminating in the anarchy and
bloody events of 1905–1907. Partly for this reason Soviet historians
would dismiss the figure of the nonhero of the 1890s as a chimera,
the sorry product of Potapenko's "petty-bourgeois optimism," which
had prevented him from understanding that "good intentions" were
not enough.[16] From the point of view of Soviet historiography, the
theory of small deeds would always remain a failure, a dead end of
wishy-washy populism.

In reality the practical successes of the theory of small deeds
were considerable. Between the mid-1880s and World War I thousands of young men and women flocked to the countryside to work
as doctors, nurses, teachers, and agronomists, making an important
contribution to the improvement of life in the provinces. Potapenko
may not have been the most eloquent spokesman to disseminate
the theory of small deeds in his writing of an engaging, but often

16. M. Klevenskii, "Potapenko," *Literaturnaia entsiklopediia*, ed. A. V. Lunacharskii
(Moscow: Gosudarstvennyi institut sovetskaia entsiklopediia, 1935), vol. 9, 179–180.

rambling *roman à these*-cum-novel of literary bankruptcy, and his protagonist certainly did not become an epoch-making hero such as Turgenev's Bazarov towering over the decade he was believed to represent. Yet the ideas expressed in *Not a Hero* offered an alternative path of development, as well as a more or less defined program for action that appealed to large groups of educated Russians making the revolution look somewhat less inevitable than it would eventually appear from the vantage point of Soviet history. Now, after more than a century, the theory of small deeds is occasionally invoked in the context of Russia's civil society by moderate bloggers and opinion makers preferring the "quiet," steady work of a "conformist" such as Anna Federmesser over the "loud," confrontational course of the opposition leader Aleksei Naval'nyi.[17] At least for these opinion makers, the theory of small deeds today "is alive as never before."[18]

---

17. Anna Federmesser (1977–) is an activist and the founder of VERA (Faith), an organization that has actively supported nursing homes and homes for the elderly since 2006. Aleksei Naval'nyi (1976–) is widely regarded as the most influential leader of Russia's nonparliamentary ("nonsystemic") opposition.

18. Georgii Bovt, "Apologiia konformizma: pochemu 'teoriia malykh del' i segodnia zhivee vsekh zhivykh," *Snob*, May 22, 2019, accessed June 21, 2021, https://snob.ru/entry/177284/.

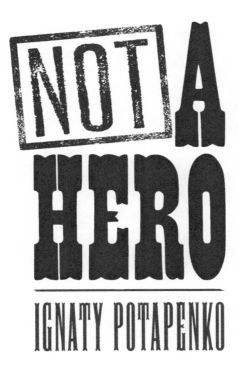

NOT A HERO

IGNATY POTAPENKO

PART I

—

Baklanov was coming down the iron staircase from his apartment on the third floor. He appeared as he always did: not bad looking, and although it couldn't be said that he was well built, handsome, or elegantly dressed, he was rather agreeable. Everything he wore sat easily on him, even looked a bit baggy; in any case, it wasn't fashionable: his coat was long, although the dandies on Nevsky Prospect were sporting short ones; his trousers were wide and striped; meanwhile the latest fashion was checked and narrow; his hat was soft, and light-colored, which didn't match his dark-gray coat at all; but all of this suited his handsome face with its rounded light-brown beard, his ruddy cheeks, and his very kind gray eyes, which regarded the whole world in friendly fashion and continually said, "Never mind, never mind; of course, not everything on earth is splendid: there are many imperfections, injustices, and insults; nevertheless—never mind—I still live well enough and I love God's world!" When he reached the last step, the respectable gray-bearded doorman, in spite of his height and weight, bustled about, quickly pulled open a drawer of an ash-wood table, took out a small packet, and handed it to Baklanov.

"This is for you, sir, Nikolai Alekseich! They just brought it and I didn't have time to deliver it."

Baklanov took the packet, raised his eyelids and brows pleasantly, as if asking, "For me? Who could it be from?" He slowly began to unseal the packet, at the same time continuing his way along the footpath of Furshtadtskaya Street. He really couldn't imagine from whom and for what purpose he would receive a telegram.

"Ah, that's who it is! That's who!" he muttered aloud, having torn it open and first read the signature. It said: Racheev. The telegram briefly announced his arrival tomorrow morning at eleven o'clock at the Nikolaevsky Station.

"Racheev, Racheev! An old friend, a sincere friendship, from school . . ." thought Baklanov, continuing his way along Liteyny Prospect in the direction of Nevsky. He himself didn't notice how his own steps had become faster and firmer, and how agitated he'd become. He hadn't seen Racheev in seven years or so, and hadn't thought about him during all that time. The last time he'd visited from Moscow he'd stayed only two weeks. He'd been gloomy and angry about everything. Baklanov remembered the heated scene in Palkin's Restaurant, when the two of them, together with Polzikov, were drinking in a private room. They were all flushed with drink, Racheev most of all, because he drank not for pleasure, but for the sole purpose of getting drunk, and, as he said, "seeing the world turned upside down." At that time Racheev was suffering from the usual illness of decent Russians—not knowing where to apply his strengths so they wouldn't be wasted. Baklanov and Polzikov were having a conversation about some beginning author; Baklanov was arguing that he undoubtedly had talent while Polzikov, with his usual Mephistophelian malice, was saying that all persons lacking talent were once beginning authors. All of a sudden Racheev banged his fist on the table with such force that a bottle jumped and fell onto its side; red wine poured onto Polzikov's light vest.

"Devil take your talents, your lack of talents, and all your literature, with all your noble ideas on paper! It's no good, no good, no good! It's good for nothing!" he shouted in an agitated, trembling voice, and he ran his fingers through his thick dark hair with a kind of despair.

"Let's assume that it's not worth a brass farthing; but why break the furniture?"[1] Polzikov observed, shrugging his shoulders, swiftly moving his chair away from the table; he set about urgently wiping his vest with a napkin. "You've ruined my vest!"

"Yes, that's so!" Racheev continued in a tone of irritation, bitterness, and mockery: "It's a pity, since your vest was not to blame. . . . Your vest. . . . It's perhaps more honest than all the rest of us taken together! It's without any feelings or a soul, while we have intelligence, abilities, strengths, and aspirations. . . . And we waste all this on drink, food, and friendly conversations . . . for nothing and no one! No, let there be no more of this!" once again, with even greater force, he banged his fist on the table. "I'll either take the bull by the horns, or—I'll put a bullet through my head!"

He shook himself off, stood up, and extended his hand to his interlocutors. He seemed to have sobered up completely; his feet were planted firmly, his eyes looked simply and sensibly.

"I'm leaving tomorrow. Farewell!" he said affably. "You can keep your Petersburg . . ."

"Where are you going?" asked Baklanov.

"To my own estate. I shall remain there in solitude, rest my head on my hands, and ponder the Hamletic question. And you will hear something about me in the future."

The next day the friends saw Racheev off on his train. For about a year Baklanov didn't hear anything about his friend; then rumors reached him that Racheev was living on his estate, not far from Moscow and in the vicinity of the estate of Baklanov's aunt, almost without leaving. Rumors were divided: the Moscow correspondents who'd been his schoolmates portrayed Racheev almost as a hero, who'd devoted all his strengths to good deeds, which they, the correspondents, also loved, even though they didn't devote their own

---

1. A variation on a famous line from Nikolai Gogol's comic play *The Government Inspector* (1836): "Of course Alexander the Great was a hero, but why break the chairs?"

energy to the cause; the aunt wrote (at that time she still had use of her right hand) that Racheev was simply a madman. Baklanov, of course, didn't believe his aunt, and regarded the views of his correspondents as some of those ennobling exaggerations that generous people offer so readily, because it doesn't cost them a thing. Racheev himself didn't write a word and all of this taken together helped Baklanov completely forget about his friend. During this time he'd managed to get married, firmly establish himself in a literary career, and become close to the rank of a favorite writer, a rank that the capricious public does not bestow all that easily.

Then, all of a sudden, a telegram from Racheev! At once all the decent, even sometimes tender feelings, which he had long nourished for his school friend, rose to the surface. What a fine fellow! Genuine, by no means stupid, sincere, easily carried away. He had no particular talent, but isn't that a talent in itself—to be a good man, who attracts public approval? And the main thing was whether perhaps he might be bringing with him something new, some characteristic of the present that would be useful for refreshing his own observations. This was very important.

Baklanov got as far as Nevsky Prospect and then turned in the direction of the Admiralty. "Where shall I go?" he wondered. He had gone out for a walk before breakfast, which he did every day. "Here's what: I'll go to see Evgeniya Konstantinovna! This will give me a chance to tell her about tomorrow's event. Racheev, of course, will be introduced to her, and she will fall upon him, as an interesting hero. She's always looking for something novel, something that doesn't resemble reality. And this will give him a chance to be of use to her."

He took a cab and headed toward Nikolaevskaya Street. But before he arrived at the entrance, he saw a carriage harnessed to a pair of black horses and recognized them. The carriage rolled out of the gates and smoothly approached the entrance. The door opened and there emerged a graceful woman of average height, wearing a long fashionable gray blouse, embroidered with glass beads, with a small gray cap adorning her light golden hair, with a tiny green bird on it that perfectly matched her pleasant, cheerful, lively face, more slender than full, with clear, somehow unusually direct eyes.

"Nikolai Alekseich!" she called in a melodious voice, which was somehow lacking in gentleness. Her eyes opened wider; a welcoming smile appeared on her rosy, full lips, but at the same time it was a sly smile, as if it contained some secret thought. The expression of her eyes, which now looked not so simple and honest, deviated from this smile. "I'm glad to see you. Come here!" and she motioned to the door, which was still open. "I was on my way to the Shopping Arcade, but I'm in no hurry!"

"No, no, please! I knew that you were leaving, and I stood up just so, almost automatically!" he replied, squeezing her small gloved hand that was just extended. "Let's go down.... I only wanted to see if you were well!"

"Oh, I am, though I'm bored because all my friends have forsaken me."

"Your friends? Which ones?"

He asked with an apparent grin; she blushed slightly, her smile becoming even more expressive, almost sarcastic.

They walked slowly down the stairs.

"You still can't forgive me for this, can you?" she asked.

"Our splitting up? Oh, my goodness! What wouldn't I forgive you for? You know, Evgeniya Konstantinovna: there isn't anything like that on earth.... Don't you know that?"

"I do, unfortunately!"

"Unfortunately? Why unfortunately?"

Evgeniya Konstantinovna signaled to her driver that he should follow them as they walked along the sidewalk.

"As if you didn't know?" She asked, casting him a sidelong glance. The smile had already disappeared from her lips. "Because everything's all the same and there's nothing of interest to me, nothing instructive; all of you are the same in this regard, and everything resembles ... all the rest.... All of you, more or less ... how can I say it more gently ... you don't tell me the truth and by not doing so, you offend me!"

Baklanov burst out laughing.

"In general the truth is a bitter pill—I'm not saying this as applied to you—and I'm not used to upsetting my friends. Ah, yes, here's what: I can offer you the chance to make the acquaintance of a certain person, who is, if not something new, then at least not too ordinary. . . ."

"Some literary talent, young, and inspiring hope?" she asked in the same lighthearted manner as his.

"Oh, no, this time I'll spare you from that. Besides, that sort of person is not unusual in your living room. It's even noted that if a young man appears in your house, he lays all his talents at your feet and reserves for himself the title of a man inspiring hope."

"My goodness, these literary figures who have managed to justify those hopes are so wicked and merciless," she observed with a humorous sigh. "But who is it—your unusual person?"

"He's my old schoolmate and friend, by the name of Racheev, Dmitry Petrovich. . . ."

"You've never said anything about him. . . ."

"Yes, I'd lost sight of him; I considered that he, so to speak, had vanished from the earth. But he's suddenly returned, and how? I received a telegram from him—he's arriving tomorrow and, of course, he'll put all of us to shame and disgrace us. . . ."

"It's high time! But how's this friend of yours different from Baklanov, Polzikov, Mamurin, and the others?"

"Evgeniya Konstantinovna!" Baklanov said pretending to be hurt, and even paused for a moment. "Is there really no spot in your heart for Baklanov, apart from Polzikov, Mamurin, and *tutti quanti*?[2] That's painful. . . ."

"Ha, ha, ha! We were talking about your friend. . . . Go on!"

"If you please!" Nikolai Alekseevich muttered with a look of sad submission. "My friend Racheev has been searching for a long time and rather energetically, so to speak, for a genuine way of life, and has found it in the countryside. . . ."

---

2. "All the rest" (Ital.).

"There's nothing unusual about that so far. . . ."

"Wait a moment, there will be. . . . He lives in the country not for the cool temperatures, nor for the fresh air, but rather for the implementation of his wide-ranging humanitarian ideals."

"Now that's interesting, but there's still nothing unusual about it. . . ."

"Well, perhaps there won't be, I don't know. . . . There's nothing that can astonish you, Evgeniya Konstantinovna, because you've been around. But I'll add that my friend is an intelligent fellow, educated, passionate, and unusually convinced of his own views. To finish characterizing him, I'll say that he's thirty-two years old, a brunet, and very handsome. . . ."

"What's that addition for? To offend me?"

"No, but that's so important for a woman: youth and beauty. Not one eminent and ecstatic prophet can move her in the least if he has a face full of wrinkles and is missing his front teeth. That's my opinion. . . ."

"It's a rather repugnant opinion and besides, it's not original! Nevertheless, you've got me interested in your friend. Bring him to meet me. . . ."

She extended her hand and then hurried toward her carriage. Baklanov lifted his hat and with his eyes followed the carriage, which turned onto Nevsky Prospect. He headed home because the breakfast hour was fast approaching. His wife didn't like it when he was late. All the while a barely visible smile played on his lips and he thought: "If Racheev isn't stupid, some entertaining episodes can occur on Nikolaveksaya Street." And in his head, which, on the basis of some two or three scarcely noticeable situations, was used to creating entire novels, there already flashed an outline of a broad picture with a beginning and ending, a multitude of beautiful and interesting episodes, the heroine of which was Evgeniya Konstantinovna Vysotskaya. For a long time, almost from his first meeting with her, he'd imagined her as the heroine of a novel. Her history and her present life, her appearance, her views and habits—all these so suited this goal and inscribed themselves in his notebook. There was only one thing missing from this novel: the heroine didn't reveal herself by some definitive step, at least not in his presence, and he couldn't guess in advance, what sort of turn this original, independent, supple nature, would take, which time and time again evades a positive identification with the help of the usual psychological judgment. And for some reason it seemed to him that Racheev was fated to cause a crisis in this nature, which then, as he thought, would unfurl in all its powerful breadth.

"However, the devil knows what this is!" thought Baklanov, stepping onto Furshtadtskaya Street and approaching his apartment. "What a foolish habit—to regard the world from the point of view of its suitability for a work of literature! Here I am, it seems, waiting for an old friend; and I relate to him sincerely, genuinely, but the first thoughts occasioned by his arrival—would there emerge a social-psychological novel, of say, some twenty printer's sheets? The devil knows what direction my brain's taken! They say that a cobbler, when he meets a new person, first of all looks him not in the face, but examines his boots, and a tailor, his jacket, and they judge people from that point of view. It can't be said that this is a flattering analogy for a writer!"

II

Baklanov went to his study first, but since the small clock over the fireplace was chiming one o'clock, he returned and walked through the hall to the dining room. In similar circumstances Katerina Sergeevna demanded punctual precision, and when he was late for breakfast or dinner, she knew how to ruin the two meals. She would become stern, and even reply to his questions unwillingly, wouldn't laugh or even smile when Baklanov made a witty remark or recounted amusing things, and when it was really necessary to laugh, she generally took on the appearance and tone of voice of a guiltless, offended woman, and this depressed Nikolai Alekseevich and spoiled his appetite. She considered that the punctual arrival of all family members at the table was an essential condition of orderliness, which she upheld assiduously in the household.

But Baklanov was not late and found her fresh, cheerful, content, and interesting in her white dressing gown, with her lovely and carefully arranged coiffure of thick, dark hair, and with a rosy color on her usually pale cheeks. He kissed her and she met him with a polite, welcoming smile. He also kissed his pretty, four-year-old daughter, who was sitting next to her mother on a wicker high chair, and he merely nodded to the young woman with a pretty pink face with little freckles, with two heavy golden-red braids, who was sitting at the end of the table. This was his sister; they were on amicable terms, but without tenderness.

"Did you sleep well? When did you wake up?" he addressed everyone at once in a tone of humorous substance, as he sat down at the table and poured himself some reddish vodka from the decanter.

"I just got up, and Liza got up with Tanya, as is appropriate, very early this morning!" Katerina Sergeevna replied with a little laughter. She was cheerful for no reason at all, simply because she woke up after a good sleep, felt healthy, strong, and lovely, and she didn't expect anything from the day ahead but a series of calm and more or less pleasant impressions.

"Very early, for you—that means around eleven, isn't that right? Well, by that time I'd managed to write almost four printer's sheets."

"I should think so! You get up at an unseemly early hour! Have some of the mushroom sauce. It's the creation of our new cook, Aksinya. . . . And are you writing something again?"

"Of course, how could it be different? We always eat something and wear something. . . . Well, that means it's necessary to write something."

"And once again something rural?"

"Not especially, but the action takes place for the most part in the countryside."

"What a bore! Aren't your readers fed up with that by now, and you, too?"

Nikolai Alekseevich raised his eyebrows slightly.

"I've asked you more than once, Katya, not to raise this subject," he said with badly concealed dissatisfaction. "It's precisely that point where our agreement ends and there begins. . . ."

"Our disagreement? Ha-ha-ha! So what's so bad about that or . . . dangerous? If people agreed about everything, it would be very boring!"

Nikolai Alekseevich furrowed his brows even more and regarded his wife sullenly.

"Well, it turns out too merrily when intimate people, living, apparently, a life in common, disagree on the most basic principles," he said, and once again he looked at his wife almost with hostility.

"Oh, my goodness!" cried Katerina Sergeevna in her previous cheerful tone of voice, apparently, paying no attention to her husband's mood. "But I can't profess my love for your countryside, when I can't stand it and even simply despise it from the bottom of my heart! I'm merely being sincere and nothing else. I find the countryside with its residents, your beloved heroes—boring, stupid, crude, vile, and worthless; I'm saying this in all honesty, and I'm surprised that you have the desire to write about it, and that your readers want to read about it. . . . However, I'm deeply convinced that if you, a countryside-lover and a populist, were settled in the country and forced to live there with those Pakhoms and Akulinas for two years, and if you were deprived of everything that you do here, you'd howl like a wolf. . . ."[3]

"That's a completely different question," Baklanov remarked in a softer tone.

"That's just the point: for your own convenience you make two questions out of it, one for the soul, and one for the body. . . . But I have a question. That's all there is to it."

During this dialogue the young girl was looking at her parents with an expression of obvious misgiving. At home, and especially with his wife, Baklanov was always even-tempered, moderately cheerful, genially lighthearted, and very concise in those instances when a serious question was under consideration. He knew how to subordi-

---

3.   Pakhom and Akulina are typical Russian peasant names.

nate his mood to necessity; and necessity consisted in having peace and quiet predominate at home, and having a family life that was not disturbed by disagreements or tumultuous scenes. Disagreeing with his wife about many things, even very many things, he almost never argued with her, and if he did, it was gently and meekly, yielding point after point. Katerina Sergeevna didn't know how to argue objectively; taking every disagreement as a personal insult, she very quickly adopted a hostile tone, began throwing out caustic remarks and reproaches, and frequently wound up with tears in her eyes, and somehow a saucer or a plate would get broken. Why allow things to reach that point? There was no hope of convincing her of anything; meanwhile, several hours would be spoiled for him, for his sister, for Tanya, for the servants, and the guests who happened to drop in on them at that time. Therefore, Nikolai Alekseevich maintained a rule of retreating, and in every instance he practiced that until, under the specious excuse of wanting to smoke a cigar, he could manage to withdraw to his study and there consider himself the winner.

But the young girl always looked frightened when conversation turned to the countryside or to her brother's literary works. It seemed that in these cases Nikolai Alekseevich was incapable of controlling himself; these, perhaps, were the only questions that compelled him to argue and defend his position passionately. After a whole series of squabbles, which ended when Katerina Sergeevna, trembling, with flashing eyes, declared herself to be the unhappiest woman in the whole world and, of course, refused food, drink, and other earthly things, and Nikolai Alekseevich had retreated to his study and was pacing energetically from corner to corner, sighing deeply from time to time, running his fingers through his hair tragically—Baklanov triumphantly asked his wife never to raise these questions. Therefore, Liza awaited the storm, all the more so since there appeared on Nikolai Alekseevich's face a malevolent sign—his brows were furrowed, something that she had occasion to see very rarely on her brother's face.

But on this day everything turned out happily. Katerina Sergeevna rarely felt so hale and hearty as she did then. Constantly complaining about her nerves and becoming easily upset for the most insignificant reasons, rarely socializing on other days, she seemed to be a completely different person, and the world seemed to be not that bad a place; in her soul there prevailed a desire to see the pleasant and cheerful side of everything. Today was just that sort of day, and she could utter her tirade about the countryside in a completely serene and kindhearted tone of voice. Having noticed that her words affected her husband not quite favorably, she stopped in good time and ceased entirely. Thus a family squabble did not ensue, and the look of alarm disappeared from Lizaveta Alekseevna's face.

Katerina Sergeevna busied herself with Tanya, who was insistently demanding attention, since her pinafore was covered with mushroom sauce. Nikolai Alekseevich took out a small cigar, cut off its end, and started smoking; they served him a miniature cup of black coffee.

"Here's what I wanted to tell you, Katya!" he said in a completely calm and kindhearted tone: "I received a telegram from my friend Racheev. He's arriving tomorrow; I don't know if he plans to stay with us; in all likelihood, he won't; but I still consider it my duty to invite him here. . . ."

Once again a look of alarm appeared in the young lady's eyes. She was even surprised at how her brother had dared to make such a proposal. Nothing upset Katerina Sergeevna more than the presence of an outsider in her house. There was the time when one of Baklanov's friends came from Moscow and spent four days with them, and those four days were blighted for the entire household. Katerina Sergeevna used to say that in such circumstances she felt that an outsider's eyes were constantly looking into her soul, and that she felt uncomfortable even when she was left alone in her own room. And at those times her look always becomes stern and hostile toward all the members of the family, and in particular toward the guest; it's impossible to please her, everything seems unfortunate and everyone finds it difficult to be with her.

But such was the good fortune of that day. Katerina Sergeevna didn't say a word in protest. She merely expressed the doubt that the guest would be comfortable in the corner room, and she expressed surprise that Baklanov had friends about whom she'd never heard a thing.

"There was never the chance to tell you!" remarked Nikolai Alekseevich. "Racheev is not only an acquaintance, but my friend . . . and an old friend!"

"Ah! I don't believe in old friendships, when you haven't mentioned him once in the past five years!" said Katerina Sergeevna. "Where is he coming from and what for? Is he a man of letters?"

"Not really. I recall two or three articles of his, not at all remarkable, by the way. He lives on his small estate not far from Aunt Marya Antipovna."

"Then what do you have in common with him?"

"What do you mean? In the first place—our past. We were at the gymnasium together and then at university. Next—our convictions, our views. . . . He's a convinced populist, moreover—on practical grounds. I've heard that on his country estate he's actually implemented his convictions."

"So that's it? For the first time in my life I'll see a man who not only expounds on his convictions, but actually implements them!" Katerina Sergeevna remarked with gentle irony in her voice. "That's intriguing. . . . However, this Racheev must be a very boring person."

"I can't promise anything in advance!" Baklanov replied goodnaturedly, sitting down on the wide, soft sofa and enjoying his cigar.

"Perhaps he can serve as a source of discovery for Liza—she's also quite a populist in a fashionable hat!"

These words were uttered, however, not at all in an offensive tone. Katerina Sergeevna frequently made jokes at Liza's expense. They lived amicably and never quarreled. Perhaps this occurred because Liza was able to put up with it and concede. When Katerina Sergeevna was subject to an uncontrolled nervous mood, sometimes resulting from some insignificant reason, and began carping about trifles with a cruel and agonizing enjoyment even for her, seeking in them a new cause for her irritation, Liza, clearly noticing that protests in such circumstances would achieve the opposite aim, regarded all of this in silence, with a slight smile. Katerina Sergeevna valued this, and the two women, so much alike, got along with each other. Nikolai Alekseevich also appreciated this. When three years ago, Liza expressed a desire to settle in Petersburg and live with them, he, naturally, hastened to write to her with the warmest invitation, adding that his wife would be very pleased. Katerina Sergeevna, for her part, also expressed her pleasure. She considered that her husband's sister had the right to do so. But in the depths of his soul, Baklanov concealed the apprehension that this would upset their quiet family life. He had almost no conception of his sister. She grew up in the provinces under her aunt's care, and that's where she attended school. He left when she was a little girl, unattractive, round-faced, and ungainly; and he was very surprised, when, arriving after this marriage, he visited his aunt and beheld a grown young woman, well brought up, who met him simply and naturally, and began talking about his works with enthusiasm. She was his admirer, sharing his views, for which her aunt called her a "little fool," while her brother looked at her with affection. However, he issued the invitation to her to come to Petersburg in passing, incidentally.

"Why would you want to stay here, sister? You could come and live with us, really!" he said in passing during one of their conversations.

"What for?" she asked. But he was already speaking to his aunt, didn't hear her question, and didn't return to this subject.

A year passed, Liza turned twenty, and the aunt began talking about her marriage.

"You, let's say, are not bad looking; you're a redhead, and men like redheads, especially with your golden red hair. . . . Nevertheless, it's difficult to make a good match here. There are no suitable people; they're all boors. . . . You should write to Nikolai; let him invite you to live with him. There are many suitors in the capital, an overabundance of them!"

Liza wasn't planning to get married, but she didn't have anything against moving to the capital. An exchange of letters took place, and Liza was now in Petersburg. Her brother met her with restrained joy;

up to the last moment he was hoping that something might prevent her, or that she would reconsider. He valued the peace and quiet of his small family circle, and he related to his sister more with formal, brotherly affection, than with love. Meanwhile, he had rarely heard that two young women could live amicably under one roof.

But Lizaveta Alekseevna managed to make her presence in her brother's house pleasant and very quickly dispelled all of Baklanov's fears. She had a special skill of getting involved in everything concerning the running of the household and in so doing, relieving the lady of the house of her domestic role, while also remaining entirely outside the Baklanovs' exclusive family matters. In such a manner, her presence was viewed as that of a useful and pleasant helper, and the inner, personal lives of the Baklanovs were not affected in any way. During arguments between the spouses, accompanying Katerina Sergeevna's capricious outbursts, she would disappear unnoticed and not reappear until the sky had cleared. When they turned to her with some complaint, she always delicately, but very decidedly took up the wife's cause, which earned her the wife's good favor and the husband's gratitude. More than anything on earth she loved her little room, where, sitting in her armchair or lying on her bed, she became engrossed in books, of which her brother had a large collection. But of everything she had occasion to read, in the forefront she placed the works of her brother Nikolai Alekseevich, considering them the height of perfection.

Liza smiled at Katerina Sergeevna's remark.

"What sort of populist am I, really . . ." she said in a gentle, weak voice. "You do me too much honor, Katya! I don't know Racheev very well. I've seen him only twice. Once he came to visit my aunt when our warden seized the peasants' livestock. He made efforts to get them freed. . . ."

"That's exactly what constitutes the implementation of lofty ideals," Katerina Sergeevna observed ironically.

"No, it's a long story!" Liza continued and her face, usually cold and serene, came to life and her voice became sonorous. "He says to our aunt: you demand three rubles from each of them, but for a peasant, three rubles is a week's work. Besides, the cows didn't ruin anything, they merely trampled the grass. And our aunt laughs and replies: if you sympathize with them, then you pay the money for them, and I don't intend to waive my rights. Racheev didn't say a word in reply; he took out his wallet and paid the sum of twenty-four rubles for the eight cows."

"Extremely generous!" Katerina Sergeevna muttered with her previous irony.

"That's not all. About three weeks later an unfortunate incident happened to our aunt. Racheev's men rounded up our cows and their calves, around fifteen head altogether. They informed our aunt, and she became indignant: how dare he? It wasn't neighborly and not what gentry do! But Racheev never had the habit of rounding up others' cattle. Our aunt wrote to him: a misunderstanding has occurred, but I trust that you will behave honorably and release the cattle. But he replied: I'm also not inclined to waive my rights. Be so kind as to pay me three rubles for each one. She had to pay! Since then our aunt can't stand the sight of him. . . ."

"Well, so, all I can say is: he's not a milquetoast, and that's good! By the way, we'll get to see him tomorrow, this hero of yours! I imagine how angry he'll be!"

"At what, Katya?" asked Baklanov, regarding her in surprise.

"What do you mean? At life and the setting of a populist writer, his frivolous wife, who loves her comforts and who dresses decently. . . . For heaven's sake—we have six rooms, when we could all live in one: I would sleep on the bed, you on the stove, Liza on a sleeping bench, and Tanya in a hanging cradle. . . . We spend three rubles for dinner every day, when we could be satisfied by a pair of Dutch herrings, three pounds of bread, and a bottle of kvass; we go to the theater, arrange receptions, oh, Lord! I think that when he sees all of this there'll be a quarrel on his first day here, if not a real fight."

All of this was said in a half-sarcastic and half-joking tone, but without any malice. Liza, naturally, had already folded her napkin, inserted it into a napkin ring, and anticipating the possibility of a more or less major discussion between the spouses, she sensibly returned to her own room. But Baklanov said not one word in reply to his wife's outburst. He leaned his elbow on the back of the sofa and smoked his cigar as if Katerina Sergeevna's words hadn't offended him in any way. But there occurred to him a series of thoughts and comparisons. It seemed to him that his friend really would be very surprised. If Racheev read his works in which he so intensely and eloquently preached the simplicity of life and mocked the empty, meaningless passion for the temptations of comfort—then, of course, this contradiction would be immediately apparent.

And what an anxious feeling stirred in his heart. Why? He himself couldn't explain it. What's this? Was it really remorse or cowardice before a friend's reproaches? But he'd earned all this by his honest and hard work and his God-given talent. This thought, however, didn't provide much comfort, and when he went back to his study, and took out from his desk drawer a notebook half-filled with his small script, he felt at once that he wouldn't write anything sensible. A feeling of vague anxiety hampered him.

III

Baklanov took up a position near the exit from the railway platform and looked unhurriedly and carefully, without any noticeable rush, at all the passengers who were passing him with their suitcases and bundles. "Did I really miss him?" he asked himself after the crowd had significantly lessened.

Just then a tall, broad-shouldered man who was approaching, wearing a dusty gray coat, under which peeked the pointed collar of a blue cotton shirt. Baklanov looked at him and thought: "Could that be him? But when did he grow such an enormous beard?" In spite of the fact that his long, broad black beard was unexpected, he recognized his friend at once; he knew him primarily by his restrained smile, which played on his lips somewhere under his thick mustache.

"My, my, my! When did you grow such a gigantic beard? I could hardly recognize you!" Baklanov said in astonishment, while at the same time exchanging kisses with his friend. "It's amazing!"

"It grew in the fresh air!" Racheev replied in a rather strong, loud, and distinct voice. "Thanks for meeting me! I dispatched the telegram on the off chance, thinking that perhaps you were no longer in Petersburg. . . ."

"Well, where else would I be and how could I not meet my old friend?" Baklanov answered with genuine warmth in his voice. "Do you have any luggage? Give me the ticket; the porter will fetch it quickly. . . . I've summoned a cab already. . . ."

"Where to? I don't need a cab. . . ."

"What do you mean? We'll go together to my house! There's a room ready for you! I live some distance from here: on Furshadtskaya Street. . . ."

"Thank you, but I won't need it."

"What are you saying? What nonsense! Do you want to offend me?"

"No, I don't, but I won't stay with you. I'll live here on Znamenskaya Street. Is the old woman still alive?"

"She is, but she seems to have gotten younger, and she's no longer on Znamenskaya Street, but on Severnaya. . . . Listen, I won't allow it; I'll take you by force to our house. . . ."

"Oho! Well, this Petersburg is a fine place! I've hardly set foot in it, and already there's a threat of violence! No, my friend, I have my reasons. . . ."

About ten minutes later the two friends were standing in a small room on the third floor of the Severnaya Hotel. Baklanov stared at his friend, trying to observe the changes that had taken place in him. He had gained in strength and power. Seven years ago he had been a thin, weak-chested young man, who looked very much like a boy, with pensive, shining eyes, and a sickly pallor to his face. His eyes had reflected a kind of uninterrupted fatigue and indifference. Only at a time of strong agitation, for the most part artificial, did fire appear in those eyes, and some indestructible energy come from his glance. But the agitation passed, the temperature fell, and once again—there was his cold, sickly exhaustion, as if this man didn't care whether the world existed or not, whether it was beautiful, and whether life was worth living. Now he was a completely different person. Every feature of his face exuded profound and persistent energy, every movement, every word. This man undoubtedly had achieved a balance between his aspirations and his strengths, and perhaps, he represents a solution to that puzzling, psychological problem that many people have attempted to solve without success.

"What are you staring at? Is there really anything surprising about me?" asked Racheev, washing and changing his traveling jacket for a lighter, brighter one.

"Everything's surprising about you, Dmitry Petrovich, everything!" replied Baklanov thoughtfully. "One has only to look at you and an entire poem is born in my brain."

"Ha-ha-ha! And you've remained the same. Just as before, do you still think in poems, novels, tales, sketches, and stories?"

"The same, but not quite. Besides, you'll see for yourself. I've gotten married, my friend. . . ."

"Yes, that changes a man. You're right. For better or worse, but it definitely changes him. But you'll be surprised when you learn that I married, too!"

"You? Whom did you marry?"

"Well, it makes no difference to you, let's assume, because you don't know her. . . . But that's not important. Tell me what you're doing now, how you are, what you're writing; I've heard about your literary successes. . . . Tell me about Petersburg, what people are doing here, and what trend is prevailing. . . ."

"The trend is quiet. We live from day to day, we do no evil to anyone, nor any good either!" Baklanov replied with a melancholy mien. "God preserves us from every disaster. As for me, I'm writing well, working a great deal, because I need a lot of money; I'm being published and read eagerly. . . . That's everything."

"Everything? Is it really?" Racheev asked with a slight surprise. "Is something troubling you? Are you concerned with some problems? Are you trying to put forward some ideas? We, living in the provinces, are used to regarding Petersburg as the factory that produces ideas, tendencies, and generalizations of varied questions and aspirations, and then puts them into circulation. Well, then, what have you worked out in the past seven years, tell me about them! Don't think that I'm interrogating you," Racheev comforted him. "And don't think that I'm completely ignorant on this account, I've followed some of it and read your work a great deal and approved it very heartily. I like your manner: passionate, picturesque, persuaded, and persuasive."

"Ah!" sighed Baklanov. "Enough about me; let's talk about you. That's much more interesting! Why have you come to Petersburg? It seems to me that I have the right to ask this of a man who hasn't done us the honor of a visit in seven years and then all of a sudden. . . ."

"How you express yourself!" his friend interrupted him. "I'll take this into account. I've grown completely unaccustomed to the refined way of speaking used here. Why did I come? What do you mean? It might be just to have a look at what's going on here. To learn some good sense from you and finally, to amuse myself. I'll spend two months here. . . ."

"That's all?"

"Is that too little? Do you have so much of interest? Well, I'm in no hurry. I can stay another month, if it's worthwhile. . . ."

"Hmm. If it's worthwhile! Why . . . that depends. . . . You say to amuse yourself. What exactly do you mean by that?"

"Probably the same as you do. . . . I see that you're looking at me rather strangely: as if I'm not the same sort of person as you and everyone else. . . . Everything clever, diverting, lively—interests me, just as it does you, I hope. Lively society, an interesting play, good music, a smart book. . . . We have so little of all that; I like all of it and if you can present it to me, you'll be doing me a great service. . . . I see that you're surprised, disappointed. . . . I can observe from everything that you met me with preconceptions. Had someone told you about me? Portrayed me as a man who had become stale, grown coarse, fossilized, isn't that right? And suddenly I ask for music and lively society! Isn't that so?"

"No, it's not like that at all," Baklanov replied in earnest. "The point is that you're asking for the impossible. That's what I mean!"

Racheev raised his eyebrows with a look of astonishment.

"What does that mean?"

"Well, take, for example, the lively society you desire. God have mercy! We don't have it and you won't find it no matter what you sacrifice for it! Here you'll meet large groups, but. . . . I can even afford you that opportunity. . . . Every other Friday I host a reception at home. Thirty or forty people gather at my house. And I can report to you that it's so terribly boring, even so dreadfully that I'm sure you'll run away from it the very first evening. No matter how people try to adapt, nothing comes of it. They try to sing—then give up; they try to dance—and give up; they try to argue about intelligent things, but they give that up, too. Except, perhaps, they do partake of refreshments in friendly and harmonious fashion, but everything else they only try. . . . And it's like that everywhere, wherever you go. . . . Then: show you an interesting play. . . . But, my friend, there aren't any, none at all. They aren't being written. People don't even want to write plays that they can write. They act out only childish fables on the stage. . . . Good music? Well, that must exist somewhere, but I don't follow it. . . . And as for smart books, that's all in vain. . . . In that regard, the cupboard's bare. . . ."

Racheev regarded his friend in silence.

"That's not good, my friend, Nikolai Alekseevich, not good!" he said with a tone of polite, friendly reproach. "Not good at all!"

He said not another word of explanation and began to pace the room pensively. Baklanov still didn't understand what that thrice-repeated phrase referred to, nevertheless for some reason he suddenly felt uncomfortable. He couldn't dispel the distressing sensation that his "fresh" friend would discover in him some defects of contradiction, no foundation for his hopes. . . . And this "not good," said so simply and gently, and his subsequent pensive pacing around the room definitely upset him. "Devil take it, such simplicity comes out of him, such assurance, such freshness!" he thought, looking at Racheev's stocky, stately figure, "and how much generosity, even naiveté in him, and in his glance!" But still the "not good" troubled him.

"What exactly does that refer to? Explain, please, Dmitry Petrovich!" he said with a smile, barely concealing his distress.

Racheev replied, while still pacing the room:

"It refers to the fact that you, Nikolai Alekseevich, are beginning to grow old! However, it's too early for that."

"How's that?" Baklanov asked with sincere astonishment.

"Here's what: you mumble and grumble about absolutely everything. There's no lively society, no one's writing good plays or clever books—the cupboard is bare! Really? What hard times these are! Saying this, it turns out that here in Petersburg you suffer from such boredom, a clever man finds it very difficult to live here. Meanwhile—you, a smart man, live here as well as many other clever people.... And precisely here, in Petersburg, and no one wants to live anywhere else.... How can this be? What you say is not true! Not true, I'm telling you my honest opinion. You have convivial society, and you probably spend many evenings pleasantly and sociably; well, confess: you engage in long, interesting conversations, laugh heartily, and return home reluctantly.... Doesn't that happen? And you attend openings at the theater. And there you watch attentively and follow the actors, laughing frequently, and at times your heart beats faster. ... And you run to bookstores, and you spend time looking through the new arrivals, and you frequently carry away some fresh copy of a new book under your arm. Well, confess, isn't this true or almost so?"

"Perhaps!" said Baklanov in a tone indicating that he was about to voice a fundamental objection. But Racheev didn't wait for him; he merely wanted to complete his thought.

"That's exactly the truth, my friend," he said, after sitting down at the table and looking at his friend with his affectionately smiling eyes." I came to this conclusion a long time ago and I'm very glad that you support it: namely, that the residents of Petersburg are such kind and simple folk, just like the rest of humanity, but for some reason they assume a pessimistic air. And what a strange pessimism it is. They don't miss a chance to criticize themselves, their society, their theater, their books, and their ideas.... Yet they themselves know all too well that interesting people can be found in every society; and in every person, even the most ordinary, if you dig deep enough, you'll find something interesting, original, particular; in every play once in a while—there's some new word, a lively scene, a draft. . . . And in every book there's something clever. . . . And of course they know full well that nowhere else in Russia does intellectual life seethe or is it so advanced as it is in Petersburg. . . . They constantly grumble and berate themselves. . . ."

"Hmm," said Baklanov in the tone of a man who's made a discovery: what you say, perhaps, is close to the truth! So help me God! Only one thing isn't accurate: that we try to affect some kind of pessimism. We don't try anything of that sort, but simply . . . how shall I put it? We're fed up with all these blessings so abundantly sent us by fate; we want something better, but we can't create anything of that sort. . . . Yes, yes, that's true!"

"Well, that's the same pessimism, just not from its head, but from its tail!" Baklanov remarked with a laugh. "You also like to ascribe to yourself some kind of moral weakness, flabbiness, powerlessness. . . . Well, the hell with it! What made us get into an argument right away? Here's what, Nikolai Alekseevich: I'm a curious fellow; I don't want to waste time in vain and I wish to find out for myself what's going on here . . . and I'm very much relying on you. Introduce me to as many people as possible. . . . You understand: as many as possible. I want to see as many people as I can and to feel them, so to speak, with my own hands. . . . I have a few acquaintances here, but they're of a different kind. . . ."

"That's possible, as many as you wish!" replied Baklanov. "Meanwhile, you'll make an extremely interesting acquaintance. . . . A certain lady. . . . She's a widow, young, wealthy, clever, and the main thing, she's original and, so to speak, remarkable. If you like, one can even say, she represents something new, a new type. . . . She has a salon where you'll meet people of all possible intellectual professions. . . . But I warn you, there's a risk: she's beautiful and you might be attracted to her. . . ."

"Well, don't worry on that account. Fortunately I've passed the time when it's necessary to warn me about similar risks. Besides, I'm married. . . ."

"Oh, friend, that doesn't mean a thing!"

"In your opinion, it doesn't, but in mine, it does!" Racheev remarked in a serious voice, and once again Nikolai Alekseevich, as before, experienced a vague feeling of awkwardness. "He's simple, very simple, but there's something in him that sets him apart from the rest of us," he thought and at that moment he was unable to specify what exactly that quality was.

Racheev stood up.

"Here's another thing: advise me where I can purchase some dress clothes, a pair of black pants, gloves, and so forth. After all, without all that I won't be able to take a step here. But, something simpler, naturally, and cheaper. I need all this for about two months here, and then I can throw it all away. . . . And now, take me to your place to meet your family. That's where we should begin. But I hope that, for old friendship's sake, you'll permit me to wear a jacket, right? Don't worry, it's all decent and proper. . . . I'll just change my clothes now. . . . I'll strip from myself all traces of a provincial man and make myself over into a man of the capital! I've grown unaccustomed to these clothes, but I don't want to fall flat on my face. . . ."

Baklanov smiled at his friend's remark, but Racheev set off to wash and to "strip away all traces of a provincial man." About ten minutes later he returned from behind the curtain separating his bed; smiling broadly, he said:

"Well, then? What do you think? I hope that I'm completely proper and that not one of the residents of the capital will point at me and say, 'There he is—that boor!'"

Baklanov looked his friend over, praised his striped trousers and dark-blue jacket, and in general found that in terms of his appearance, he couldn't wish for anything better. . . . They took a cab and headed to Furshtadtskaya Street.

IV

It was breakfast time, but Baklanov and his friend weren't there. Liza was sitting in the small living room, hurrying to finish some journal article; Tanya was jumping around her, constantly running up to her, pushing her and interfering in all sorts of ways. The lively, happy girl with her short-cropped hair, resembled her mother, and even the color of her cheeks, still rosy, bore a matte shading; her little dark eyes cleverly and slyly looked out from under her long, thick eyelashes.

When it struck one o'clock, Katerina Sergeevna came out of her bedroom and entered the dining room.

"Why don't you go in to breakfast, Liza?" she asked loudly.

It seemed to Liza that there was a barely perceptible note of irritation in her voice. Katerina Sergeevna, who usually went to breakfast wearing her dressing gown, now was dressed as if she was about to leave the house. She was wearing a black cotton dress, which charmingly covered her stately, portly figure. She loved the color black, which suited her well, and readily dressed in it. Liza came in, leading Tanya by one hand, and in the other hand, she held a half-opened book, and she began to search for a place to leave it.

"Choose one of the two: either have your breakfast or read!" remarked Katerina Sergeevna. "Nanny, put Tanya's napkin on her! Tanya, do you want a cutlet or an omelet?"

Liza put the book down on a small round table and silently sat down in her place. Katerina Sergeeva was cutting and eating a cutlet with extreme seriousness, a businesslike expression. For Liza this was also a sign. She now solved the question of the source of today's irritation, how serious it was, and how low the barometer could fall. The first puzzle was solved all by itself.

"I'm surprised at Nikolai!" said Katerina Sergeevna. "Will he really bring this gentleman here after breakfast? That means, it will be lunchtime and then it will be dinner. . . . I can't stand it when people in the house eat all day long, as if at an inn. . . . Why, the train arrives at eleven o'clock. . . ."

"In all likelihood, Racheev put up in a hotel and Kolya stayed too long with him!" said Liza.[4]

---

4. "Kolya" is a diminutive form of the name Nikolai.

"It's all the same to me, where he stopped. . . . But I'm unable to receive him after breakfast. . . . After eating my fill, I can't entertain guests—it's not even healthy. . . ."

"He's an unassuming fellow, Racheev. . . . You don't have to entertain him at all."

"However, you won't have me receive him wearing only a smock!"

"Believe me, he wouldn't accord it any meaning!"

"Very possibly. . . . But I can't allow myself to do that! What for? Is it because he's my husband's old friend? I'm convinced that this old friendship will lead to a situation where these two friends, after two hours of conversation, won't know what to say to one another. . . . Tanya, if you allow yourself to pick up the meat with your hands one more time, I'll have you removed from the table. . . . I can't sit for three hours strapped into a corset!"

Tanya meekly wiped her fingers on her napkin, and without any objections began eating with the assistance of her fork. She also felt that she should submit and remain silent as best she could. And Liza thought: "Thank heaven that Racheev is staying in a hotel. God forbid he should arrive here with his suitcases."

Just at that moment a bell sounded in the hallway.

Katerina Sergeevna stood up.

"Please, tell Nikolai to leave me in peace. I won't come out. . . . I just can't now!"

Impulsive wrinkles appeared on her forehead, and in her voice there sounded a restrained tragic note softly, as if this woman had just been gravely offended. She withdrew immediately to the bedroom, without even finishing her cup of coffee.

Liza didn't stir from her place. Her face assumed a look of worry and gloom. She found it extremely unpleasant that Racheev happened to arrive on such a disastrous day.

She could already hear footsteps and voices in the living room. Liza was sure that her brother would be escorting the guest into the study. He would never dare bring him directly into the dining room after arriving so late for breakfast. Before everything, he would inquire about his wife's mood.

And instead, they proceeded to the study.

Nikolai Alekseevich loudly invited his guest to sit down for a moment; he only wanted to warn his wife and then to introduce them, if she was feeling well. A moment later he entered the dining room.

"Where's Katya?" he asked.

But he had only to glance at his sister, so that he could answer his own question correctly. However, today he didn't want to believe it at once and his face assumed an inquisitive expression.

"Katya asked me to say that she would not come out and you shouldn't disturb her. She was expecting you for breakfast, and was dressed accordingly.... It would have been better if you had arrived on time!" she added with a slight trace of reproach.

"Ah!" said Baklanov with a quiet, but deep sigh. "How unpleasant! Is she in there?" he asked, casting a glance at the bedroom.

Liza nodded her head. He carefully opened the door to the bedroom and went in, firmly closing the door after himself.

The bedroom was large, divided by a curtain. In the front half of the room, which had windows overlooking the courtyard, there was soft, low furniture, covered with cretonne, a dressing table, and a miniature writing desk with an elegant writing set. The other half of the room served as their actual bedroom.

Baklanov moved the curtain and saw Katerina Sergeevna lying on the bed face up, with her hands behind her head.

Nikolai Alekseevich hoped that it wouldn't take much for him to persuade his wife to come out. But when he saw that she was wearing only a white skirt and a white nightshirt, and that her dress lay in disarray on the chair, his hope was seriously shaken.

"Katya! What is it? I was delayed because he wanted to change his clothes in his hotel room.... I couldn't possibly abandon him the first moment after his arrival.... You'll come out, of course?"

He said all this in an extremely soft voice, trying to avoid any rough notes. His tone expressed the simple conviction that Katya would emerge to greet the guest; one couldn't even hear the suspicion that she was irritated and feeling hostile.

"I have a headache!" Katerina Sergeevna uttered abruptly and turned onto her side, her face toward the wall, on which hung a small Caucasian rug.

"But come out at least for a minute.... Then you can leave and lie down! It's awkward. I said that I'd introduce you...."

"Just think how important this is and how it really matters to him," she said, still not turning to face him.

"Yes, it's very important.... He's very interested in you!" Baklanov uttered with conviction; but it was said counting on a woman's weakness—her vanity; in fact, Racheev had provided no reason to state this.

"Interest in me?" asked Katerina Sergeevna and turned over again on her back; her face expressed some malevolent irony. "Your friend is a very kind fellow.... But I'm not interested in him at all.... I'd be very content if he passed me by and I didn't have to make his acquaintance.... He's simply not likable, your friend, even though I don't know him at all....":

All this was said with the sole aim of saying something unpleasant to someone, offending someone, angering someone. Katerina Sergeevna felt the need to do so at that moment. Baklanov had become accustomed to these inexplicable moods and in such cases he concerned himself with only one thing—how to moderate and scatter the clouds as quickly as possible. But his task was further complicated by the circumstance that his friend was waiting in his study, and he couldn't be left alone; that meant he had to hurry; he lost his equanimity and his temper.

"Ah, my God, this is ultimately unbearable!" he cried in strong irritation. "Constant contrariness always and in everything. Can't you take control of yourself, even just for propriety's sake? We're behaving like children—playing some game.... I'm making all sorts of concessions for your serenity, but you can't even make a trivial one for me! You want an outsider, who's just entered our house for the first time, to know that we had a quarrel...."

Katerina Sergeevna raised herself, sat on the bed, and straightened her body.

"You want to force me to see him?" she asked with a gloomy voice, knitting her brows spitefully.

"I want you to gain control of yourself. . . . You can sit there for a few minutes and then leave under some plausible pretext. Perhaps it would be difficult for you, but not altogether impossible!"

"I don't do anything under a plausible pretext. . . . I'll come out, if you demand it. . . . But excuse me—I can't smile, when I'm feeling miserable!" she said in her previous tone, and stretched her hand out toward her dress. She continued and all of a sudden her voice began trembling and tears could be heard. "I know. . . . You didn't say anything to your friend . . . didn't even hint. . . . But you sighed twenty times saying the word 'wife. . . . ' 'Understand,' you said, 'how happy I am. . . . ' Well, of course you're not happy. Everyone thinks and says that I am to blame for everything. . . . But what's to be done? I can't change. . . . I know—I'm a nasty woman and a very bad wife. . . . But. . . ."

And her eyes filled with tears. Another few words and she would have started crying. . . . But Nikolai Alekseevich couldn't tolerate this tone. As much as it annoyed and even angered him when his wife, under the influence of irritation, was unjust and capable of deeply offending for no good reason at all the first person she encountered, it affected him to the depths of his soul when Katerina Sergeevna was feeling depressed, abased herself, and was reduced to tears. At such times he was overcome with compassion; his heart filled with tenderness for this helpless creature, because he knew that at this moment she was in fact suffering, feeling herself to be a nasty woman and a bad wife, and to blame for everything, and for a minute before, when she hated all people and the whole world, she was also being sincere and also helpless. At such moments he felt how infinite was his attachment to his wife, and he understood that those concessions that he was making to her, and with which he had just reproached her, were nothing at all compared with those sacrifices that she was able to make, if only he could offer her a serene life.

Nikolai Alekseevich approached her and seizing her hands, he began kissing them.

"Katya! Enough! Katerinochka! Dear! Nothing of the sort! Forgive me my outburst—it was stupid, foolish. . . . It's not worth your tears. . . . Really, it's not worth it," he said in a tender, heartfelt voice.

Katerina Sergeevna nervously bit her lower lip and tried to pull her hands away, but he didn't let them go and kept on kissing them tenaciously. Finally, as if weakening in the struggle, she allowed him to do so. Then he took her head in his hands, lovingly looked into her face, and tenderly kissed her warm, moist eyes. But with a weak gesture of her hand she pushed his head away, and looked intently into his eyes, as if trying to determine whether these caresses were genuine, or he was simply trying to appease her. But it was clear that in his eyes she could read his sincerity, because her face suddenly blossomed into a merry, joyful, lovely smile; a heavy flush appeared on her face; she trembled and pressed her entire body against his. . . .

A moment later she was already laughing; she dressed quickly and said:

"I don't care about your views. . . . Really, I'm ready to support you, if you like. . . . But love me as enthusiastically as you do now, and not with that empty, dumb, formal love, with which husbands usually love their wives. . . . Oh, I don't want anything more and you see—there is a medicine for my ailment. . . . I want you to cower before me a little, even just a drop or two; to lie at my feet and offer me small sacrifices. . . . I know this isn't good, but it will make me happy. I want you always to feel guilty before me. . . . Ha, ha, ha! Is it true that I'm a little insane? What do you think?"

The flushed, lively, laughing face with shining eyes that she showed Nikolai Alekseevich was such a lovely one that he rarely saw. He admired her and her black dress, which, when lying there, was so gloomy and unremarkable, but on her, now looked so handsome and even elegant. He said he agreed to everything—to cower before her, to lie at her feet, to offer her sacrifices, and to be the one to blame all the time.

"Well, now go back to your friend. I'll just comb my hair and be right out!" she said. "You'll see how charming and kind I'll be to him. Well, kiss my hand and go away! If you like, I'll even become a populist! Ha, ha, ha, ha!"

She extended her hand to him—he kissed it, smiling. He was glad that the incident had concluded so with such an unexpected and favorable outcome, and that he had such a charming wife, and that she loved him so very much, and finally, that he himself was experiencing such a warm, heartfelt, and joyful feeling.

"Are you to blame?" she asked with comic seriousness.

"I am!" he replied with the same expression, placing his hand over his heart.

She began laughing. He returned to his study.

V

Liza didn't stay in the dining room for long. She realized at once that the conversation in the bedroom would hardly be brief. Tanya finished her breakfast; nanny took away her napkin and wiped her lips and hands. The little girl looked lovely in her blue sailor suit with an embroidered gold anchor on her chest. When they were dressing her, they kept in mind that there would be a guest.

"Let's go into the study, Tanya!" Liza said to her.

"But isn't a guest in there!" the girl objected.

"Well, we'll go and entertain him. After all, you know how to entertain guests!"

"I'll say, I do!"

Lizaveta Alekseevna went into the study, leading Tanya by the hand; the girl walked carefully and hesitantly, as if afraid of some danger. But, of course, this was merely her flirtatiousness, because Tanya looked everyone in the eye boldly and was afraid of no one. Racheev, turning over the pages of some book he was holding in his hands, having picked it up by chance from the table, stood up and politely, but with great restraint, bowed to Liza like someone he was meeting for the first time.

"We're somewhat acquainted!" said Liza, replying to his bow.

She always had the ability to behave confidently with everyone and to speak simply, quietly, and without embarrassment. In this respect, provincialism had not imprinted its stamp on her because it was counteracted by her natural spiritual equilibrium, which so surprised everyone in this young lady.

"Excuse me, please ... I don't remember!" Racheev replied, staring at her face.

"At Aunt Irina Matveevna's.... I'm Nikolai Alekseevich's sister!"

"Ah, Lizaveta Alekseevna! Yes, yes, forgive me, please.... I didn't expect to meet you here, which is why I didn't recognize you immediately.... I remember you very well, although I saw you only twice.... Of course! Back then, just as now, your golden hair made an impression...."

She smiled at his remark.

"Sit down, Dmitry Petrovich. My brother will be here in a minute.... In the meantime, I'll entertain you somehow.... Won't you tell me something about my aunt?"

She sat down on the sofa, and Tanya stood next to her. Racheev occupied his previous place.

"I don't know much!" he replied. "I haven't been there since she got angry with me.... Besides, your aunt considers me insane."

"Yes, that's true. She can't reconcile herself with your activity."

"That is, the fact that I'm not amassing wealth.... That's really all my activity. For her, at least. But a majority of our landowners don't amass wealth.... Or, at least, they haven't...."

"No, it's not that!" the young woman objected in a very serious tone, "It's not that they haven't amassed wealth, but that they've *spent* it all. And then there are also those who have neither spent it nor amassed it. They merely sit there with their arms folded. But you're not like that, you neither sit around doing nothing, nor acquire.... That's the difference!"

Racheev was listening to the young woman's words with curiosity, and even with some surprise. He thought that she was reasoning logically; while by her manner and her way of speaking he determined that she was a "well-read young woman." He never expected to encounter all this in someone brought up by Irina Matveevna, an old woman, literally incorrigible in her ignorance.

While he was reflecting on these matters, there occurred a brief period of silence, during which Tanya approached him unnoticed.

"Why do you have such a black beard? Do you dye it?" she asked, carefully examining his beard and mentally comparing it to her father's light beard.

"No," Racheev replied, drawing the girl to himself, which she didn't resist. "I don't dye it. That's the way it grows. . . . What a sweet niece you have!" he added, addressing Liza. "I also have a little girl, only younger and darker. . . ."

"I didn't know you were married!" said Liza.

"Yes, I got married almost two years ago."

Liza had another question prepared: to whom? But for some reason she thought that question would be inappropriate. Meanwhile, it very much occupied her thoughts. She knew every single one of the eligible women in their district, but decidedly she couldn't think of anyone suited to be Racheev's wife.

"I'm ready to bet that I know what you're thinking about!" he said, looking her straight in the eye with a slight smile on his face.

She blushed, which rarely happened.

"Really?" she said with obvious embarrassment.

"Really. You're thinking, who would marry him?"

"You guessed!" replied Liza, now regaining her self-control. "I was thinking about that."

"You knew that young woman. You saw her frequently. . . ."

"It's very possible, but I can't imagine who it is."

"Do you remember Sasha Malinova?"

"Sasha Malinova?

Saying this her eyes opened wide and expressed unspoken astonishment.

"Yes, I remember. . . . So it's she?"

"Yes, she's the woman I married!" Racheev confirmed simply and stood up, because just then footsteps were heard in the room; he thought that the mistress of the house had entered together with Baklanov. But seeing that Nikolai Alekseevich was alone, he said to him: "Lizaveta Alekseevna and I have been chatting; it turns out that we're old acquaintances and that she knows my wife. . . ."

"Ah, yes, yes! She has spoken about you. Please forgive me for taking so long. My wife will be here in a moment. She's very glad you've come. Your reputation as a hero precedes you," Nikolai Alekseevich said cheerfully and lightheartedly.

"Ah, is that so? Excellent!" replied Racheev in the same tone. "Well, you can be sure that I won't fall in the mud and will try to live up to the reputation that precedes me!"

But soon her bewilderment dispersed. Katerina Sergeevna appeared, flourishing, pretty, and welcoming.

"Here's my wife, and this, Katya, is Dmitry Petrovich Racheev, my old friend from school and everywhere else!" said Nikolai Alekseevich.

Racheev and Katerina Sergeevna shook hands.

"I've hear marvels about you!" Katerina Sergeevna began at once, with some unusual vivacity in her voice.

"Really? What, for example? You're frightening me!" said Racheev.

"For example, that you're a totally consistent man: you do what you say you'll do. . . ."

"That's true. I do have such a habit, or, at least, I attempt to carry through. . . . But is that trait really so rare?"

"In any case, it's not so common. But I also belong to that same group of consistent people. I always act in such a way as I say I will. Except that I speak foolishly and act foolishly! Don't think I'm joking; it's the pure truth! You can ask Nikolai Alekseevich." She looked at her husband with slyly squinting eyes. Nikolai Alekseevich looked at his wife with a smile, enjoying her mood.

"However," she continued in the same playful tone, "I'm not a wicked person and I will feed you breakfast. . . . Let's go! You're probably hungry, aren't you, Dmitry Petrovich?"

"Yes, I am rather hungry!" he replied with a bow.

"You see, Liza, you didn't take good care of him, but I will!" she tossed at Liza.

They went into the dining room and sat down at the table. Breakfast was already warmed up, and in general it was apparent that Katerina Sergeevna was in fact "taking care" of him, something that Liza hadn't expected at all.

"But I have one weakness, a very little one," continued the mistress of the house, offering her guest a plate of cutlets and mustard. "I don't like it when people are late for breakfast or dinner, and as a result I'm capable of making a violent scene. I must tell you this because you'll be having breakfast and dinner with us every day! However, there are all sorts of other trivialities about which I can make a scene."

"I'd like to learn those trivialities by heart, like the grammatical exceptions in Latin, so that I can refrain from committing any of them for the next two months," said Racheev.

"Unfortunately, it's impossible to foresee them because they're constantly changing. It depends on the weather, the cook, the seamstress, and so on."

"Oh, that's terrible!" cried Racheev. "It means that your life is an undertaking based on risk!"

"Alas! And not only my life, but the lives of everyone whose fate is linked to mine."

Their dialogue in this cheerful and lively mode lasted all during breakfast. Liza looked one moment at her sister-in-law and the next at the guest with astonishment, while Nikolai Alekseevich applauded both of them in his heart: his wife because she so charmingly kept her word and was so splendidly disposed, and Racheev because he seemed far from boring, and even a clever and resourceful conversationalist; consequently, he was making a favorable impression on Katya and she was getting to like him. Decidedly, Nikolai Alekseevich had to regard this day as one of great success.

Katerina Sergeevna persistently pressed food on Racheev, while he, afraid to offend his kind hostess, ate everything she offered.

"You eat so well that I feel like having breakfast again," said the mistress of the house and in fact she broke off a piece of cutlet with her fork and ate it.

"Well then, if I've succeeded in teaching Petersburg residents how to eat properly, that would be no small accomplishment!" Racheev replied.

"Do you think that Petersburg people suffer from a bad appetite?

You're mistaken. Here some people with the most innocent appearance consume six or eight courses. . . ."

"Nevertheless, they don't know how to eat!" repeated Racheev. "Just look, I ate four cutlets before your very eyes, and perhaps, if you don't consider it inappropriate, I'll eat one more. . . . I don't doubt that Nikolai Alekseevich, too, and every other resident of Petersburg, is able to consume the same amount of food, but to do so, he'd need five changes, five variations, and five deceptions. In addition, he'd need a setting: a dining room table, with various accoutrements, not only the necessary ones, such as plates, forks, knives, glasses, but also completely unnecessary items, such as: three different goblets, a vase of flowers, and so on. And in addition, he'd need everyone to be gathered at a certain hour, or else they wouldn't have an appetite. Whereas we eat, like Sobakevich;[5] if lamb, then an entire lamb; if piglet, then an entire piglet; if beef, then a quarter of beef. Sobakevich was a healthy man, and although Gogol didn't say anything about it, I'm certain that he didn't care at all where and in what setting he ate, and also he didn't much care whether everyone had gathered for breakfast or not. He wanted to eat and set about consuming the side of lamb. . . ."

"Do you regard all other matters just as simply?" asked Katerina Sergeevna, who had begun to be seriously interested in her husband's friend, who had declared himself so abruptly.

"Yes, also in all other matters. We try to use life's blessings in the simplest, and therefore, most straightforward form, without complicating things cunningly and without wasting time and effort on this philosophizing. And you—that is, not you personally, Katerina Sergeevna, but residents of Petersburg in general and townspeople—you try, on the other hand, to complicate, to confuse, in order to make it more . . . well, how to put it . . . more intriguing. . . ."

"You must be interesting people, and it's worth getting to know you better."

5. One of the landowners in Nikolai Gogol's novel *Dead Souls* (1842).

"Oh, enough! What's so interesting about us? You merely glance at us and we're like an open book! I came here to have a look at interesting people."

"And do you know, Katya," remarked Nikolai Alekseevich, "to whom I intend to introduce him first of all, as an interesting example?"

"Why of course, your Vysotskaya!" said Katerina Sergeevna with a rather noticeable expression of irony. "She's the new idol, one before which everyone here, who claims to be clever, bows down."

"Oh, but not me! It's impossible to say that I *bow down*," said Baklanov. "But that she is a very interesting person, that I can confirm."

"And do you, Katerina Sergeevna, disagree with that?" asked Racheev.

"No, I don't; on the contrary—I find that she's very, very interesting . . . to men. In the first place, she's beautiful and clever, which traits are not often combined in a woman. She's wealthy and she can display herself in elegant settings. . . . That's also very important to men. Besides, she's very experienced and knows how to keep all her admirers on a leash, so that not one of them ever loses hope. . . . Moreover, she acts according to her progressive principles and in addition she knows one secret, which progressive women of recent times didn't know or didn't wish to know. They rejected elegance on principle and deprived themselves of it; while she does just the opposite, combining progressiveness with elegance and thus, of course, only gains from it. Those women of bygone days soon tired the men and caused them just to smile, but she vanquishes whole hoards of clever people."

"However, Katerina Sergeevna, you're being rather wicked!" said Racheev.

"Not at all. This is all true. Just wait and you'll soon find out that I approve of her. She wants to reign and enjoy lasting success, and men love this, and it merely pays honor to her subtle intelligence and knowledge of the human heart. . . . I confess, I regard her with great respect, but I don't acknowledge her as some new social type, while all the men do. . . . In certain respects I even agree with her: for example, she can't stand the society of women; nor can I. I find that the society of the most awful men is still more interesting than that of any ladies, even the most progressive. Therefore, we see each other only once a year.... But I'd definitely urge you to have a look at her. She's the latest word in feminine guile."

When breakfast ended and everyone had risen from the table, Katerina Sergeevna repeated her invitation to the guest to come have breakfast and dinner with them every day.

"We," she added, "will order a lamb, or a piglet, or a quarter of beef specially for you. You won't find that anywhere else."

Racheev thanked her, and said that he wouldn't be able to spend every day as pleasantly as he had today, but that he would try to take advantage of this invitation as often as possible.

After he bid farewell to everyone and departed, Katerina Sergeevna returned to her husband in the study, and, placing both hands on his shoulders, began laughing in the most cheerful manner:

"Well, Nikolka, are you pleased with me?" she asked.

"Yes, indeed! You were so charming and agreeable!" Baklanov replied.

"I like your friend. I even find him handsome. There's something determined and self-assured about him. He must have a strong character."

"Yes, he does."

"Did you notice that I didn't say a thing about the countryside? That was just for you.... Did you feel it?"

"Thank you!"

"But sometime I'll come to grips with him on that subject!"

"He'll crush you! He's not like me—a theoretician. He experiences the country in practice."

"We'll see if he crushes me!" Katerina Sergeevna replied merrily and went to change her clothes.

VI

Dmitry Petrovich went outside. It was a gray day, but quiet and warm. Having arrived immediately on Nevsky Prospect, he sensed the crowd at once, the bustle, and this aroused a pleasant nervous agitation in him.

He stopped in front of the shop window of a bookstore and methodically examined the new arrivals. A splendid small volume of Baklanov's latest novel occupied a prominent place. On it, by the way, was indicated: "Third Edition." Racheev thought to himself: "This means that Nikolai Alekseevich is very popular."

Next to him at the shop window stood a gentleman—tall, thin, rather stooped, wearing a long, dark coat with a raised collar. The collar was covering his face from below, and from above, a hat was pulled down over his forehead. The only thing one could see was his nose and the gold-rimmed glasses resting on it, and from the slit in the collar, one could see the end of a long, narrow, reddish beard. Dmitry Petrovich wouldn't have paid this man any attention, but it seemed to him that he was looking at Baklanov's book with unusual attention. Racheev found this very interesting. Perhaps he was just one of Baklanov's readers, an admirer, of whom there were many, and he might even be an acquaintance in common. The tall gentleman took a step back, and was about to proceed farther, but he suddenly paused, as if struck by an unexpected sight. He looked at Racheev through his glasses with his blinking, squinting eyes, Racheev looked at him, trying his best to remember something. Suddenly they simultaneously rushed to each other and began to kiss each other firmly and to shake each other's hand.

It was Polzikov; but Racheev, although he recognized him, couldn't accept the fact that it was really he—he'd changed so much.

"My goodness! Is it really. . . . Really? You and me?" cried Baklanov, and regarded his old friend with an astonished and uncertain look.

"Ha, ha, ha, ha! I don't know about you. . . . But as far as I'm concerned, then, it's really me, I. . . . The real, original me!" Polzikov replied in a hoarse and, at the same time, shrill voice. He laughed, but with some kind of pitiful crease on his lips and his entire face; when he opened his mouth wide, one could see that he was missing many teeth, and those that were left, thanks to the fact that they stuck out peculiarly and in disorder, made an impression of some rapacious fangs.

"What is it?" continued Polzikov with the same apparently forced laugh. "Didn't you recognize me? Ah? Where did my youthful power, proud strength, regal valor go? Ah? Hey, friend, the hell with it! It happens to all of us! I know, my friend, you look at me and think: What is it that so crushed that poor fellow Anton? Ah? Have I guessed correctly? Ah? That's it! Well, just wait, I'll tell you everything. . . . But I am unbelievably glad to see your face. You don't believe me? You see, I'm asking because around here it's not acceptable to believe Polzikov. . . . Ha, ha, ha! Polzikov said it—that means it's a lie! But you should believe me, I swear, I'm glad. And what brings you here? Whom did you see? That scoundrel Baklanov? Ah? Are you staying with him? No? Why didn't he, that swine, tell me? I would have met you. . . . I would have met you appropriately. But wait, friend, why am I pouring all this out to you in the Arcade? Let's go somewhere. . . . Well, to Maloyaroslavsky? Agreed?"

Racheev was so astonished at his friend's appearance, speech, tone, and gestures that he didn't object to anything, and followed him.

They came to Bolshaya Morskaya Street, climbed the stairs and occupied a deserted room in the Maloyaroslavksy Tavern. Polzikov ordered vodka and some snacks, and took off his long coat. They sat down opposite each other. Polzikov leaned over the table, supported his head on his hands, and took a good look at Racheev, all the while blinking as though holding back tears. Racheev could now study his friend's face in detail. It had never been handsome. But good health, which had breathed in every one of his features and covered his cheeks with a bright, fresh flush, had hidden its defects before. But his alert, bright eyes, at a moment of oratorical eloquence, had conveyed to his face even a kind of distinctive beauty. Now it was gaunt and pale. A long face, it looked even longer as a result of its leanness; his large nose seemed larger than before or it had grown longer; his pointed beard, which turned up at the end, conveyed a nasty expression to his entire face; only his eyes remained the same;

their perspicacity had become sharper, and his frequent blinking kept them moist and added to their brilliance. His thick red hair had become thinner, forming deep furrows over his temples.

"And you, my friend, Dmitry Petrovich, you've also changed!" Polzikov said at last. "But you've changed for the better, while I've changed for the worse. . . . Yes! Well, why are you so silent? Say something!"

"Hey, Anton Makarych, wait, let me collect myself!" said Racheev. "You've really surprised me! Where did everything go? Your health, what about your health?"

"Everything, my friend, has gone into the struggle for survival! Everything's fallen with a thud! Hey, but what's health? Is it really only health? And everything else that was, has all been wiped away by that damned law! Well, let's celebrate your unexpected arrival and our marvelous meeting! Well, then!"

He poured two glasses and pushed one toward Racheev. They clinked and drank.

"It's all gone away, Dmitry Petrovich, everything!" Polzikov mumbled, snacking on some dried fish.

Thanks to the problem of missing teeth, he somehow managed to maneuver his jaws, which gave his face and old man's look.

He poured again and offered a glass to Racheev.

"No, I won't have any more!" he said.

"What?"

"I won't. I never drink more than one. . . ."

"Well, friend, how dare you? We haven't seen each other in a hundred years, I'm unbelievably glad, and you—you drink only one glass! What's that about? Your principles? To hell with your principles! Hey, you wanted to astonish me! We, my friend, have disregarded even more important ones! We had such principles! Enormous in size! Well, drink, drink, don't worry!"

Racheev resolutely shook his head.

"Damn it, you! Well, what if I were dying and my whole life depended on your glass of vodka. . . . Would you also refuse to violate your principles? Huh? You wouldn't drink? Huh?"

"If you were dying, I would drink, but thank heavens, you're not dying. . . ."

"Ah, in other words, there's a concession! That's consoling! Because we have such principled men, that even if you're dying, they wouldn't give in! So strict! They all have principles, but even so, their heads and hearts are vacant. . . . That's what kind of people they are. So, you won't drink up?"

"If I really have to. . . . Listen," Racheev said, addressing the servant: "Bring me half a bottle of white table wine!"

"Hey! A compromise! Wine—that's a compromise with vodka! Well, isn't it all the same? Now, to business. So, as I was saying, it's all gone away, into the struggle for survival. . . . Into the belly of the beast! As you like, but I will have a drink. . . . If you'll allow me. . . . And I don't understand why you don't! What sort of principle is there in drinking vodka?"

"It's unnecessary, Anton Makarych, and I avoid everything unnecessary!"

"Unnecessary? Ha, ha, ha! You avoid the unnecessary? While I do just the opposite: I avoid everything that's necessary and accept only the unnecessary. . . . That's what contains all the sweetness of life. . . . Yes. . . . So, I'll drink up, if you permit me. . . ."

He drank a third glass and, forgetting to snack, began to pour himself a fourth.

"I'm afraid of an empty glass!" he explained.

"Tell me, please, are you well-off?" asked Racheev, who wanted to hear a coherent account before Polzikov managed to get drunk. He already saw from all indications that he loved to drink and would soon get drunk.

"Completely. Even excessively so. I earn about seven thousand!" replied Polzikov.

"And, as far as I can recall, you were a good family man!"

"Yes! I was, I was, I was!" Polzikov sang, rather than said, and suddenly burst out laughing unnaturally.

This grated upon Racheev.

"What a fellow you've become, Anton Makarych!" he said, shaking his head.

"A bad one? Huh? Oh, friend, I've really degraded myself in all respects! That's for sure. . . . And it's especially painful to see you, such a proper man, proper in everything! Especially, if you think about it carefully, a man should be that proper. . . . You're healthy, and you stand up straight, your constitution is well put together, neither too light nor too heavy, and you regard things directly, your views are open and firm; clearly—you don't miss a thing. And clearly your conscience is clean, yes, that's obvious. . . . And where did you find such polish? In which delightful location? I look at you with envy! While I, you see what I am! I'm a person 'completely opposite,' so to speak. Damn it! I see discontent on your face. As though you are saying, I'll never get any sense from you; you just keep talking nonsense. . . . Wait, I still haven't gotten to the point. If I'll drink a fourth glass and a fifth, then it will be a different matter. . . . Then I'll become a clever man. . . ."

They served Racheev's wine.

VII

"Do you remember Zoya Fyodorovna?" Polzikov asked unexpectedly, leaning against the back of his chair and adjusting his glasses twice in a row.

"Of course, I remember her. She's your wife, right?"

"No, not my wife, but Zoya Fyodorovna!" Polzikov interrupted him abruptly, distinctly drawing out the syllables. "What the hell sort of wife is she when she's cohabiting with a noble doctor, Kirgizov? Huh? Do you understand what I'm saying? Exactly! And so, friend, for no apparent reason. . . . Openly, one might say, out of the blue. . . . Well, if one could say that this Kirgizov is a genius, he's not . . . just a simple fool. . . . Only you see, he has some sort of humanitarian idea, something like poverty is no vice, for example; and he stole that idea from some clever fellow, someone like you or me, because he himself could never come up with it on his own. But what's the secret? You and I know very well, for example, that poverty is no vice, but we keep quiet about it because who doesn't know this? But not him; he has this radical idea because he's never managed to steal another, a better one. Therefore he goes around with his head held high, his eyes aflame, with a mysterious look. . . . It's apparent at once that this fellow is not without reflection, and that he has something astonishingly majestic in his soul. Women feel this, especially if he has a Roman nose, a well-developed chest, and well . . . other attributes, just as it should be. Right away in her heart, or elsewhere, I don't know, where a worm starts gnawing. . . . Right away she arranges to be his 'one and only,' a tête-à-tête, in other words. . . . Well, he informs her in a sonorous voice, 'Madame, poverty is no vice!' But that makes no difference to the lady, if they're alone and he has a Roman nose, and so on. . . . And if he makes eyes at her, as it should be. . . . First, her hand, then her foot, and then all the rest! She leaves a note for her husband: I can't live with you, because you don't have an idea, while he's brimming over with a great idea. Or else, without a note: take a cab! And that's the end of it. . . . That's what Zoya Fyodorovna did, and many other women, too. That's the fashion here, my friend. Today it's also fashionable to slander the eighteen sixties.[6] That's to no avail. There, as a matter of fact, there was an idea, foolishly grasped, but still it was an idea. . . . They seized upon freedom, you see, because they hadn't seen it before and didn't know how to deal with it. And they thrust it in everywhere, this freedom. . . . And today, this is how it's done . . . it's like changing a restaurant, where one's sick and tired of dining there. Just listen, Dmitry Petrovich, to their conversations. Now and again you'll hear: do you know that Telyatnikova has separated from her husband and is living with Porosyatnikov! And a year later you hear: Do you know that Telyatnikova has separated from Porosyatnikov and is living with Bugaev? Huh? And the men also don't stand there gaping. . . . She's separated, is living with someone else, he's sepa-

---

6. A decade when radical thinkers were much in fashion.

rated, and is living with someone else.... This is all so simple and ordinary, just like the horse-drawn trollies along Nevsky Prospect: they came together at the station and then separated again! Freedom of feeling! Ha! What kind of crazy feeling is that? What does feeling have to do with it? This, friend, is the freedom of excitement, and nothing more! Drink your damned wine at least! You're not drinking at all.... I'll drink up the vodka.... Don't worry! You think I'll get drunk and begin to spout rubbish? You're wrong! I get close to the truth only when I'm drunk!"

"And the children?" asked Racheev. How do they deal with the children?"

"Children? Good question! In the first place, they rarely have children, and if there are any, only a few! Today there's a theory: people who do intellectual work, who provide a tone to social life, so to speak, are not obligated to increase mankind. They're occupied with higher considerations, and children would hinder them.... Let the lower folks engage in that, they say.... Well, in a word, it's left to the peasants.... Do you understand? It adds to the peasants' work. Before they had to locate the raw materials and feed the chosen ones of humanity; today, besides that, the obligation to increase human kind is also laid upon him.... And if by some miracle there are children, they shuffle them around: this one's for you, this one's for me, and that's that.... One is lacking a mother, while the other has no father...."

"Do you know," he said after a short silence, a malicious grin on his face: "He deserted her...."

"Who?" asked Racheev, whose head was spinning after all these bitter words uttered by Polzikov.

"Doctor Kirgizov deserted Zoya Fyodorovna! He received an appointment somewhere: either in Batumi or in Vladivostok.[7] Well, he said to her: 'My dear, it would be uncomfortable for two people to travel such a long distance. They will pay me a small salary; the

---

7. Batumi is the second largest city in Georgia, located on the shores of the Black Sea. Vladivostok is the largest Russian port on the Pacific coast.

traveling allowance has also been reduced nowadays; in a word, I'm not well-off, and poverty, as I already told you at that memorable moment when I said all the rest, poverty, I say, is no vice. And therefore: farewell.' And this chaste pauper departed, while Zoya Fyodorovna remained out in the cold. . . . I thought she'd come back to me; but no, her pride didn't allow that. She came to her senses, and she became keen on the art of dentistry. . . . Now she's languishing in poverty, while I earn seven thousand rubles and don't give her a kopeck. . . . I have nowhere to spend the money, but I don't give her any. . . . That's what!"

"And your son? You had a young son?" asked Racheev, recalling that he had even participated in the celebration at the birth of Polzikov's heir.

Polzikov shuddered and dropped his glass.

"You're a swine, Dmitry Petrovich, and nothing more!" he said in a tragic voice and suddenly fell silent.

His eyes began to blink horribly, and it seemed that in fact he was almost about to cry. This lasted not more than a minute, after which he extended his hand to his friend and said in a simple, even voice:

"Excuse me, friend. . . . I've lost sight of the fact that you just arrived and couldn't know. . . . My son, Antosha, died. . . . It was the same year you left. Damned diphtheria. . . . Doctor Kirgizov was treating him. . . . The ignoramus. . . . He destroyed him. . . . And she could join her fate with that man! Phew! I don't even like to remember these events!"

He fell silent again. He silently poured himself another glass, drank it, and didn't say a thing. Then he poured Racheev some wine, and with a nod of the head, invited him to drink. Racheev did so.

"Where are you working now?" he asked.

"*Secret Word*! It's a literary newspaper, economic, political, and immoral," replied Polzikov, without raising his head and painstakingly chewing a snack.

"What? You're writing for *Secret Word*?" Racheev exclaimed with genuine astonishment.

"Yes, indeed!" replied Polzikov, with a smirk. "What of it? Don't you like it? Ah?"

"No.... It's just that I'm surprised!"

"Yes! At first I myself was also surprised, but then I grew used to it.... Never mind, I got used to it! And you keep saying nations—nations!" he began again, but now raising his voice. "Everything surprises you, everything.... But why? Because you don't want to understand it. But try to.... You put your fingers into my sores, pierced with nails. For example, I work at *Secret Word*. It's a vile newspaper, that's for sure. But then—where should I work? I'm a writer—therefore, I have to write. There's nothing else I have to do or know how to do.... Well, sir, where are our good newspapers, honest ones, that is? Well, just count them: one, two ... and that's it! But here we have many good people; it's a prejudice that there are so few of them. We have a large number! And they write a lot and have taken all the places at the good newspapers.... Wherever you turn, a good person sits and writes a good article! I moved around for a long time, endured considerable hardship.... Even though I acquired something of a name for myself, still I wasn't earning any real money. You write something sensible and you think: where do I send it? There—it's embarrassing, here—it's shameful, so where?—it's a disgrace! And there, where I would like to send it, there's no place for it, and you'll have to wait two months.... Well, and you're poor.... We have lots of vile places; you receive a large sum there and they pay a great deal. And then there's that woman, Zoya Fyodorovna, who ran away.... I agonized, I did, and suffered, and I thought and thought, and reflected, to hell with it, my friend.... I took it, dashed it off, and sent it to *Secret Word*.... And there at once: Welcome! If you please! Seven thousand a year, write whatever you wish, even about *The Lay of Igor's Campaign*, if you want, as long as my name appeared under it![8] What do they need? Do you think they needed Polzikov? Not at all.

8. *The Lay of Igor's Campaign* is an anonymous epic poem. While some have disputed its authenticity, the current consensus is that it is authentic and dates to the medieval period.

They had enough of their own young fellows, all passionate young fellows, more skilled than Polzikov. But the point was that Polzikov was an honest name, and they wanted to show the respectable public: here they are, they said, your honest men of letters! We threw seven thousand at him, and he came over to us. . . . You see, they wanted to discredit an honest tendency, that's all! Therefore, they know their own worth. . . . I don't give a damn about anything on earth, for I understood that honest men are just the same kind of rogues as the real scoundrels! That's what, my friend!"

"Does that mean you've changed your convictions?"

"What for? Not at all. My convictions have remained the same. . . . You must be joking, friend, that for seven thousand I would change my convictions. Convictions are my inviolable holy of holies."

"But do you write in the same key as *Secret Word*?"

"I write in my own key. How can I explain it to you? It exists in music. For example, the maestro is conducting in some key, let's say F major. . . . And he has to transition to D minor. Thus he begins to modulate. While he's doing so, it's impossible to determine what key he is changing to. Perhaps some minor key, and perhaps into some even more major key, or perhaps he won't change at all. Well, I'm modulating; I just keep on modulating. I don't go this way or that; or, as they say, I remain above the fray. That's what! But to change my convictions for the sake of those splendid eyes of the passionate young people at *Secret Word*? Not a chance! Just consider this: in some five or six years they'll say good-bye to me. What use am I to them? My name is slandered, and that's enough. . . . The goal is achieved. That's how I'll resolve my modulation into a different key! Yes, friend, that's the struggle for survival!"

Racheev stood up and began pacing quickly about the room. Never before in his life had he seen a man who, not even noticing it himself, so deeply despised himself as Polzikov did at this moment. And it was hard for him to figure out how to relate to this man: he was unhappy, pitiful, vile, and there was much calumny in his words, but also a great deal of truth, toxic, burning truth. And is a man's downfall really so simply accomplished, as Polzikov had narrated? Is there not really in the human soul, in the man himself, one reliable hook, which he can grab hold of, even just to hang above the abyss?

"You're telling me terrible things, Anton Makarych! I didn't expect this. I didn't think that such changes could occur!" Racheev said in a fervent voice, while Polzikov grinned somehow plaintively and blinked his eyes.

"Get used to it, friend, get used to it. . . . And that's not all," he said. "At least I didn't betray anyone; sometimes it happens that people do."

"But there's no law that this is necessary! Why, many people stand firm! Take for example, Baklanov; he hasn't betrayed anything!" Racheev continued heatedly.

"Why, yes! Baklanov! I'll say! Why betray him? Ha, ha! Baklanov! He has some talent! Baklanov's much in demand! They publish him here and there! His books sell impressively. . . . There—I saw printed 'Third Edition!' So why should he change? Why change when he's fine as he is?"

"Only because of that? It's not true, not true at all! I don't believe it!" cried Dmitry Petrovich; but Polzikov didn't listen to him.

"Take Baklanov and me. He's fortunate in all things. He has a brilliant talent, while I have only limited talent; he's handsome, his wife is beautiful, clever, loves him, his family hearth is inextinguishable. . . . And me? What do I have? I have a stable instead of a family hearth. . . . Ha, ha, ha! Nothing works for me. . . . I've grown hunched, wrinkled, my hair's thin, my teeth have fallen out. . . . He has everything in place. . . . Phew! Damn it! What a vulgar thing life is! Why? It's incomprehensible! Well, don't listen to me anymore, Mitry, because I've crossed the limit. . . . I've become tipsy. . . . You can go to hell, and I'll stay here and fall asleep. . . . Don't be embarrassed: they know me here; I feel at home. Give my regards to that swine Baklanov and his lovely wife! What a splendid woman! Only she's a lunatic. . . . Yes, she is! But, you know, she has these shifts from despair to joy, from rage to kindness. . . . It's a miracle, it is! There's only one woman even better than she is. Do you know who it is? Evgeniya Konstantinovna . . . Vysotskaya! She, my friend, is really special.... With a social-political slant.... Have you been to see her? No? Go there, Baklanov will take you to her abode.... She despises me.... Yes.... But I adore her! Because she's a ... phenomenon! Do you understand? She's an epoch unto herself! Well, get lost, go ... to hell with you!"

He placed his head down on the table and, it seems, was already fast asleep.

Racheev quietly walked into the hallway and called the waiter.

"Is he often like this?" he asked.

"It happens at least once a week.... But don't worry about it. He's fine here. He'll stay that way for an hour or so, have a little nap, and then he'll go on his way as if nothing happened.... He's fine here.... We'll lock the door so no one will go in....

Racheev paid the bill and left. His mood was unbearably grave. At first when he revived in the fresh air, he almost regretted that he had yielded to temptation and accompanied Polzikov to a tavern. But then he recognized that this was faintheartedness. After all, he wanted to get to know what today's Petersburg was all about, so there was no way to avoid painful sensations. He had to see everything that presented itself to him. He felt sorry for Polzikov, but it was hardly possible to save him. He had endowed his own position with too many eloquent sophisms, as a result of which he would not be able to see the truth. And the truth wouldn't change him!

But what sort of "phenomenon" was this Vysotskaya, about whom he had already heard so much in the course of the past few hours? An "epoch," Polzikov had even said. He definitely had to take a look at her.

He headed toward the Winter Palace, and then proceeded to the embankment, hoping to disperse the painful impressions of the conversation with his friend.

VIII

He stopped across from the island where the Peter and Paul Fortress stood, and looked at the Neva. The view of boats moving in all directions, as it seemed, ready to collide with one another at any moment, distracted him somewhat. The wind blew from below; the Neva heaved. He looked for a boat and got in it, to go for a ride along the river. The boat started moving downstream; along the way all the familiar buildings became visible along both sides. Nothing had changed, everything stood in its former place and looked as majestic as it had before.

But then he turned his face to the right and his heart fluttered and began beating faster before he managed to orient himself fully. Yes, there it was—that building every corner of which was as familiar to him as those corners in his own apartment. And it, too, had remained the same as it had been—not seven, but fifteen years ago, when, as an eighteen-year-old youth, he'd first entered it with humility and, at the same time, enthusiasm, with a palpitating heart.

Here Racheev ordered the boat to tie up to the shore and let him off. He wanted to walk around the university building, to walk through the courtyard from one entrance to another, and to see if this courtyard seemed as unusually long to him as it had then. And as he walked step by step along the university gallery, more and more memories overwhelmed him. In his imagination there arose an image, shrouded in fog, which was becoming clearer and clearer. . . . Polzikov! Yes, it was he who was still pursuing him: he—today's Polzikov, who was so different from that tall, clean-shaven youth with whom he had arrived from the provinces and with whom, with timid steps, he had entered under the roof of that building on the embankment in order to submit an application. He was a youth with a high forehead, under which stern, but at the same time slightly sarcastic, small clever eyes regarded God's world. At that time the sarcasm in them was still hidden; somewhat later, it began to appear more clearly in his glances and his speech; then it began to predominate in all his actions, gradually filling with venom, but never ceasing to be noble and always directed at those objects that merited his biting laughter.

Yes, there was a great deal of foolishness in those groundless passions, in the eager chase from one shining point to another, when each spark flying accidentally out of some smoky chimney was seen as the sun. . . . There was a great deal of noise, excitement, theatricality, but guided through all of this by the passionate aspiration to find the truth, no matter what, to discover the true path. Had all this really changed, wondered Racheev, in the same way Polzikov had changed?

No, that couldn't be. How was it then that Polzikov had reached the condition in which he'd just seen him? And was it only Polzikov? Perhaps such an attitude dominates here and is simply considered in the order of things? Racheev wanted to find out in a hurry, because it seemed important to him and since the impression of the recent meeting was so strong; he was ready to return to the Baklanovs a second time and begin a conversation about this.

He went back, crossed the Neva on the Dvortsovy Bridge, and boarded a car of the horse-drawn tram. When it had reached Liteiny Prospect, it seemed to Racheev that some familiar figure, shaking his stick, was making his way across Nevsky heading toward the station, maneuvering among the masses of cabs on the street. After taking a closer look, he recognized Baklanov. "Where's he going? Is he perhaps coming to see me?" flashed through Racheev's head. He hurriedly jumped down and caught up with Nikolai Alekseevich.

"Where are you off to?" he asked, grabbing hold of his friend's sleeve.

"And where are you coming from?" Baklanov asked in turn, smiling: "I thought that after your trip you were going to get some rest; I didn't expect that if I came to see you, you might not be at home."

"I was introducing myself to the city of Petersburg!" replied Racheev. "Who can sleep when you have such things happening here? I'm glad that I met you."

"What sort of things?"

"I met Anton Makarovich and sat with him in the Maloyaroslavsky Tavern for an hour and a half," said Racheev instead of giving a direct answer.

"Ah! Yes, that's another matter! An edifying meeting."

"That meeting put me in a bad mood and induced the most awful thoughts."

"That's too bad, Dmitry Petrovich. If you're going to be upset at every kind of nastiness, you won't last through it all. However, it's understandable—you're a fresh, young person, and as such, you're generally more impressionable about such things. As soon as they see something, they immediately get upset. While we, natives of Petersburg, have grown accustomed to such similar surprises that we don't even pay them any attention. Our nerves have become blunted."

"What strange things you're saying! How can you relate to things properly and appreciate them—you, who stand above and guide public opinion, when your nerves have become blunted?"

Baklanov smiled again.

"Ah, Dmitry Petrovich! I like looking at you, I simply do!" he exclaimed, taking his friend by the arm. "You remind me of a bird who's just been caught and placed in a splendid, spacious cage. Next to it sits another bird on a perch that's already spent many years in the cage. And this bird quietly pecks on seeds and bathes in its cup of water, cheerfully flying from place to place and even singing its songs. And the new arrival huddles and frowns, shuddering at every sound, and can't understand how the first bird can fly other than in wide-open fields, but in a cage, even though it's so luxurious and spacious; how she can bathe not in a stream, but in a cup of water, and how she can still sing her songs. . . . But days pass, then weeks and months; she'll get hungry and thirsty, feel a need to stretch her wings, and she'll start flying, eating, drinking, and singing, and then, at last, she'll consider all this natural. . . . May this not happen to you, Dmitry Petrovich; spend a little time in our cage, and then fly away to your open fields. . . . Yes, so you ask: how can we relate correctly to things and evaluate them, when our nerves have been blunted? How can I put it? Once again I'll resort to a comparison—forgive me that I have this bad habit of a fiction writer. Take a Russian, a genuine one, who has spoken Russian all his life, spoken correctly, even though he's never studied the rules of grammar. And he hears a foreigner speaking Russian, distorting words. Every error grates upon his ears because he feels it, this inaccuracy, with his whole being. Now take a true classic, a virtuous Latin teacher. Assume that he is solemnly making up an examination. He is also grated upon, yet he doesn't feel it with his whole being, but knows it in his head. He knows the rules, which he's learned, learned fundamentally, and he sees that this contradicts some rule or other, in such and such a paragraph, and therefore he has to assign a low mark. Excuse this long comparison, but do you understand the difference? It's just like you and me: you feel, with your fresh nerves when something disgraceful happens in front of you, but we—we know, on the basis of our principles, of which we've accumulated a large quantity—that it's disgraceful and that here one should protest.... Well, naturally, it's not at all like that; we still don't have a complete result and are outraged; and there are cases where we can also feel it with all of our being.... But the line has stretched out so long, that it may lead to this.... So, what were we talking about? About Polzikov? Yes, yes! I tell you that Polzikov is still rather a comforting case...."

"What's so comforting about him? God help us!"

"The fact that at least he's always castigating himself.... And that at least he still has a God, only he's hidden Him far, far away. Then again, friend, there are those who've never had any God at all. These people were born with an empty place in their chest; they never felt anything sacred there; and these people, my friend, are really ready for anything at any time of night or day: to sell, to betray, to drown, and to cut throats.... Polzikov just sold himself and betrayed, if you like ... but he won't sell out his nearest and dearest or betray them, I can stake my life on that.... Oh, but what do you think, Dmitry Petrovich," Baklanov added suddenly with some hint of sadness in his voice and a loud sigh. "Polzikov, of course, is frankly an unsightly creature, so to speak. But in many of us, who in reality behave correctly in everything, so to say, there's a swine in the depths of our soul.... Sometime, at the right moment, I'll make a confession to you and you'll see what sort of beast that is.... Let's leave this topic.... Don't go home.... Let's go to Peski, shall we? I feel that I'm also overtaken by a sort of melancholy.... Listen, Dmitry Petrovich, what's happened to you? This morning, when you arrived and we were sitting in your room, you made an impression on me of such a fine fellow that I started to envy you, and now you've gotten so worked up, you've also infected me...."

"Wait, Nikolai Alekseevich, wait a moment.... Let me get the feel of my surroundings; let me come to myself.... *Homo sum*, my friend, *et nihil humanum*, you know, as it stated somewhere, *mihi alienum esse puto.*...[9] And whatever you want, I can't become a fine fellow, as you call it.... No, no, recollections have overpowered me.... Well, let's walk along Ligovka, shall we, to the Tauride Garden.... Is it true that we three, you, me, and Polzikov, arrived here from the provinces with such pure hearts, with the most innocent intentions? Do you remember that time?"

"How could I not? A splendid time!" Baklanov cried with genuine enthusiasm.

"And consider this: you and I were materially well-off, I was especially so, while you—only so-so, but you were not in need of anything. So our purity, to some extent, can be related to our spiritual serenity about the future.... But Polzikov was poor; his father was a modest civil servant in the district office—could the father give him any money? He barely had enough for the ticket, and he didn't even have any warm clothes.... Yet with what fiery optimism did he look into the future! As opposed to you and me! And then later, when he became a writer-warrior wasn't it he who made wicked fun of our helpless state at that time, our self-flagellation, our fruitless searching for a path? 'Hey, you, sons of gentry!' he would shout, 'you wander all around the forest in search of a path, hoping that the path would be smooth and well worn.... Move forward without a path, regardless of obstacles, make your own way, and we'll thank you for it.' That's what he used to say then, and we were ashamed, at least I was and, perhaps, I'm obligated to his righteous mockery for my spiritual equanimity.... And now ... What's all this about?"

"There were many reasons, Dmitry Petrovich," replied Baklanov. "The main one was the capital. If it hadn't been for the capital

9. The correct Latin phrase from Terence is: *homo sum humani a me nihil alienum puto* ("I am a human being; nothing human is strange to me").

with its nerve-wracking atmosphere, pervaded with burning hot, venomous, and alluring pleasures and comfort, perhaps, even Zoya Fyodorovna. . . . You know about her? (Racheev nodded his head.) Perhaps even she, would have become much more thoughtful about her foolish action. After all, it began with her. You know, when a person feels personally unhappy, he forgives himself a great deal. And then he had bad luck with his literary endeavors. . . . And support for his income didn't exist, as it did for you and me. . . . The search for comfort plagued him. . . . In a word, everything became confused, mixed up. . . . Let's leave this topic, Dmitry Petrovich. . . . I'm simply afraid of it. . . . It will lead me to outpourings, which will completely upset me. Let's put them aside until later. . . ."

"Let's do that, if that's what you want!" Racheev muttered almost with annoyance.

He didn't like his friend's fear of difficult topics, and as though it was a conscious avoidance of something. And he himself was beginning to feel deep in his soul some sadness from all these scenes and conversations. Recalling everything that he saw and heard this day, he was becoming convinced that the women had made the most salubrious impression on him. Before him arose the image of a young woman with golden reddish hair, modest, self-controlled, probably narrow-minded, but not stupid; she was rational and congenial. But this image faded somehow unnoticeably and gently, when he heard in his imagination Katerina Sergeevna's resonant, unguarded laughter and her lively, uninterrupted cascade of words—flirtatious and witty; he remembered her animated, lovely face, her cheeks, flushed with agitation, and her eyes, sparkling with intelligence.

"Why did Polzikov call her a lunatic?" he wondered.

On the other hand, Racheev, in the happy mood in which he found her, thought her a completely normal, healthy woman.

"Listen, Dmitry Petrovich," said Baklanov after a prolonged silence. "I've come to see you for a reason. . . ."

"I'm at your service!" Racheev said automatically, still engrossed in his own thoughts.

"Do you recall that I was telling you about a certain interesting, remarkable, if you wish, woman, Evgeniya Konstantinovna Vysotskaya?"

"Ah, yes, yes! Yes, she must be something really amazing, if so many people are talking about her. I've been in Petersburg only a few hours, and already I've managed to hear wonders about her: from you, from Katerina Sergeevna, and from Polzikov. . . ."

"What? Polzikov mentioned her, too?" Baklanov asked in surprise.

"Yes, and in very lofty terms. . . ."

"Hmm. Yes. When he's sober he abuses her and regards her distrustfully, but I've always suspected that in the depths of his heart he's prepared to kiss her feet. . . . So here's what I wanted to say. You should know that yesterday, as soon as I received your telegram, I informed her about your arrival. She's very, very interested in you as a true 'worker in the field.'"

"Well, as usual you've already created a whole fable!"

"Not really. I told the whole truth. . . . And I just received a note from her. Read it, since it concerns you. . . ."

He gave Racheev the open envelope of thick uneven paper, with an address written on it in firm, fine, and unusually energetic handwriting: "To Nikolai Alekseevich Baklanov."

On Friday evening I am hosting a gathering of good and not-so-good friends, our common acquaintances. It would be nice to see you, Nikolai Alekseevich. Please, bring Racheev, your friend who recently reappeared, about whom you've told me so many wondrous things. I await you not otherwise than with him.

E. Vysotskaya.

"This means that we'll begin to examine each other, as a wonder!" Baklanov burst out laughing.

"That's your own business!" he said. So, shall we go? On Friday?"

"Why not? In general, I'll be glad to go wherever there are a lot of people!"

Baklanov accompanied him to the Severnaya Hotel, but didn't go in because the dinner hour was nearing and in no way did he want to spoil Katerina Sergeevna's happy mood. Racheev had declined to dine with them, because, at last, he'd begun to feel tired. After parting from his friend, he went up to his room, got undressed, and lay down in bed. For a long time Polzikov prevented him from falling asleep, but at last his exhaustion won out. He dozed off, but not with that deep, dreamless sleep that he was used to at home after a day well-spent; rather it was a nervous, disturbed sleep, filling his head with extraordinary scenes and providing him with more torment than rest.

Racheev jumped up from bed and grabbed his head with his two hands.

"No," he thought, "it must be that the air here really is poisoned!"

He lit a candle; it was after midnight. He opened the small window-vent, washed his face with cold water, and, having calmed down considerably, lay down again.

He lay there with his eyes open and this time a different picture presented itself to his awakened imagination. A young woman, with a face brimming with that healthy, clear, open beauty, which could arouse in one's bosom only healthy feelings, was looking trustingly into his eyes and saying to him in a joking and loving manner:

"Be careful, Mityusha, don't start drinking there; and don't forget your wife and child!"[10] WHY??

The forest looks blue in the distance; the trees' last autumn leaves rustle softly. The stream rushes noisily down the slope. The air is clean, clear, and healthful. . . . And he is unnoticeably overcome by that feeling of spiritual equilibrium that he had somehow lost during the course of that day.

Racheev dozed off and this time slept soundly until morning.

IX

On Friday morning Racheev planned out his day in the following manner: "Before dinner I'll sit in the reading room and peruse all the

---

10.   Mityusha is an affectionate diminutive form of Dmitry.

newspapers and journals there; I'll have dinner with the Baklanovs, and from there we'll go to the newly brought-to-light wonder—Miss Vysotskaya. In all likelihood, this will exhaust me so much that with this last visit I'll have to end my day."

He left the hotel to fulfill this program because it was his intention since his arrival in Petersburg to become thoroughly acquainted with the social life of "the principle town of the Russian empire," with its prevailing intellectual and moral tendencies, in equal degree devoting his attention to the good and the bad.

When he returned to the hotel, they handed him a letter in a small envelope without a stamp. The address was precise: "Dmitry Petrovich Racheev, Severnaya Hotel." The handwriting was completely unfamiliar, drawn-out, and uneven, apparently belonging to a woman. He put the letter in his pocket and, without hurrying, went upstairs; only after he'd entered his room, taken off and hung up his coat on a hook, did he unseal the envelope and begin to read the letter. There he found the following in the same drawn-out uneven handwriting:

> Dmitry Petrovich! A certain lady, to whom you showed your respect some seven years ago, very much wishes to see you and speak about a certain important subject. Do not try to guess; it won't matter—you won't be able to; rather you should simply come today around three o'clock. Don't think about dining beforehand, if you don't wish to offend a person who truly respects you.
>
> Peski, 7th Line, House 14, Apartment 8.

"What sort of mystery is this?" wondered Racheev, pacing his room, "a certain lady, to whom I showed respect some seven years ago?" Hmm. There were plenty of people to whom I showed respect seven years ago! Perhaps, I'll not show her any respect this time? But this is almost how it is. She didn't sign the letter and by this, she gave herself away. I won't go see this mysterious person."

But this decision, which occurred to him immediately upon reading the letter, was soon replaced by another. That's how he would have behaved if he'd been in the ordinary surroundings of his domestic life, where everything took place according to an established norm and proceeded according to a set path. There he lived his own life, arranged in his own way, but here he was no more than an observer without a set program.

"In essence there won't be any difference between my visit to Vysotskaya and to this woman!" Racheev thought now. "What's Vysotskaya to me if not 'a certain lady' of her own sort? And if I go see her, that is, a certain lady, then why shouldn't I go to see this one, that is, the other lady?"

It was almost three o'clock. Racheev wrote to Baklanov that he wouldn't be having dinner with them today, but would drop by around eight o'clock, to leave for Vysotskaya's apartment together; he dispatched the letter with the messenger.

Racheev proceeded according to the directions. After he reached the third floor taking note of the number 8 above the door, he rang the bell. He could hear hurried steps; the key turned in the lock, the door opened, and Racheev saw something that he'd least thought about and that had never occurred to him before.

A woman about thirty years old, tall, with a thin, expressive face with large, sharp features, an unpleasant aspect, but interesting, noteworthy, at once calling attention to itself and making an impression, stood in front of him and was laughing loudly, displaying her large, even teeth. She was wearing a simple gray skirt and a pink cotton blouse, but her elegant figure conveyed a sort of special flirtatiousness to her modest apparel.

"Well, confess, that you didn't expect it would be me? Even in your imagination? Everything's possible, but not this? And you look so confused. . . . Ha, ha, ha, ha! You're dumbfounded. . . . Ah, kind Dmitry Petrovich! I'm very, very glad to see you! Take off your coat; come over here. Excuse the mess: I moved in only yesterday. . . . Please forgive me! Have a seat. . . . Say something! Ha, ha, ha, ha! Is it really so awful—to find yourself in my apartment?"

"There's nothing awful at all, but I'm still very surprised that it turned out to be you, Zoya Fyodorovna! And I confess, I'm even embarrassed. . . . And if I say foolish things at first, don't pay them any attention!" said Racheev, shaking her hand and blushing deeply.

"But why. Why so? Sit in the armchair. . . . The back of the sofa is unreliable; it will fall apart at any moment. Why are you so surprised?"

"Why? I'll gather my thoughts in a moment and tell you why."

He really was thinking and passing his hand over his forehead, as if trying to collect his thoughts. Then he started laughing and said in a simple, serene tone of voice:

"I confess—there's no reason! There really is no reason to consider this surprising. And do you know what? I should thank the occasion that brought me here. . . ."

"Not the occasion, but me. . . . I'm the one who lured you here!"

She started laughing again.

"Why does she laugh so often? I didn't notice that before!" thought Racheev.

"Thank the occasion for what?" she asked.

"Wait a minute, Zoya Fyodorovna: let me first have a good look at you and your surroundings, and come to terms with all the changes that have taken place. . . ."

"Splendid. Take a good look, and come to terms, but only on one condition: out loud and absolutely candidly! Agreed? Ha, ha, ha!"

"She's laughing again! No, that's not good!" thought Dmitry Petrovich.

"Why? I agree!" he said out loud. "Don't expect any compliments from me; you and I have nothing to share with each other, and that means—you won't get angry with me. Besides, it's so nice to tell you the truth directly and it happens so rarely, but here you yourself want it. So here we go. In the first place, you laugh a great deal, something you didn't do before. I managed to observe that, in spite of the fact that I haven't been here for more than three minutes, and it's not in vain. . . . Your manner's changed, and that means your way of life has changed. . . . And now, let me take a good look at you. . . ."

He squinted slightly and examined her with a lighthearted smile, while she slowly turned her face in various directions and laughed merrily.

"Your appearance has improved, Zoya Fyodorovna. You've matured, and haven't aged at all. Previously your features were softer, and therefore more agreeable; now they've become coarser and sharper, but on the other hand, very expressive. . . . You've endured a great deal, that's apparent. . . ."

"Splendid! So far there's nothing offensive!" she said cheerfully.

"You've developed; your movements are broader, rounder; your voice more resonant, more assured. You regard God's world directly, even boldly. . . . It seems to me that you're a true-blooded egotist; you love life passionately and don't like anything else. . . . You have strange eyes: deep and shining, but cold. . . ."

"Oh, I'm afraid that I'll turn out to be capable of committing a crime: ha, ha, ha, ha!"

"No, enough of that. . . . I don't like your surroundings. . . . They don't suit you. It's barren and uncomfortable. . . ."

"I'll add, Dmitry Petrovich," she interrupted him, "that this woman who loves life passionately, this true-blooded egotist—is engaged with. . . . What would you think? I swear on my word of honor that you'll never guess. . . ."

"No, I even know: dental art, and judging by your surroundings, not too successfully!"

"You do know! How do you know? Who told you? Whom have you seen? Tell me, tell me straightaway!"

Now she wasn't laughing. Unrestrained curiosity shone in her eyes; her cheeks flushed from her strong agitation.

"I've seen Anton Makarych. . . . What's so surprising?" said Racheev.

"Yes. . . . You've seen him. . . . Well then, of course. . . . That's a different matter. . . . Now I understand your confusion. . . . He set you up. You've formed a preconceived opinion. . . . That's clear! When you saw me, it seemed you were in some sort of den, isn't that right?"

She was saying this as she paced the room nervously. Malice could be heard in her voice and offense, and even, as it seemed to Racheev, some sort of hostility toward him. He tried to calm her.

"Enough of that! What sort of foolishness are you saying, Zoya Fyodorovna? You don't know how hard it is to 'set me up' against anyone. . . . All the more so for Anton Makarych, who made a very unpleasant impression on me. . . ."

"Yes? Really?" she cried, standing in front of him; wicked joy appeared on her face. "Is that how you found him? Isn't it true that he produces a squalid impression, like a mangy dog that one doesn't want to get close to? Well then, that means you can understand my situation!"

"But wait, Zoya Fyodorovna, as far as I know, he became that way after . . . after you separated. . . . Perhaps, even as a result!"

"Ah, that's precisely what no one can understand!" she said, suddenly hitching up her shoulders and starting to pace the room again. "They say: here was a good man, but a misfortune occurred to him; his wife left him, and he became a scoundrel as a result of this *misfortune.* . . . How stupid it is to say that! If a man's good, no sort of misfortune can make him a scoundrel! Haven't you ever seen people who are completely defeated by life, who have lost all joy, but nevertheless remain honest? And those, of a kind like Anton, have inside them some baseness long ready, and they merely wait and wait until someone treads on their corn. . . . Then they shout: I've been offended and therefore I'll become a scoundrel! Schopenhauer says. . . . Just don't think I've studied his works and want to show off by quoting him. . . . No, I just happened to read a sentence in *Secret Word*, and I liked it very much. He says: naive people think a man changes under the influence of circumstances. No, he always remains essentially the same. Anton was always like that, but hadn't appeared as such. . . . No one had seen this, but I did because I was his wife and interacted with him closely. I saw that he was always like that and at any moment ready to become what he finally became. . . . Ah, but why talk about this? It doesn't make any difference, no one will believe me, and you don't either, I can see from your eyes that you don't. . . . Well, you don't have to! Let's talk about something else. . . . About you, for instance. . . ."

"Please, Zoya Fyodorovna, you wished to speak with me about some important matter?"

"Oh, ha, ha, ha, ha! So I'll begin to lay it out for you! After I found out you'd met him? Well, no, now I have to find out first who you really are. No, as a matter of fact, let's leave that. . . . Let's talk about you. You know how I learned your address? From Liza Baklanova. Yes, we're acquainted and meet occasionally. . . . But first I saw you on the street. . . . You were sitting in a horse-drawn tram. . . . Tell me something about yourself. . . ."

She sat down again opposite and laughed cheerfully again, as she had before. But suddenly her face assumed an anxious expression, when in the hallway a shrill, confident bell sounded.

"Why have you frowned?" asked Racheev.

"I wanted us not to be disturbed. . . . I wanted to have a chat with you! Ah, do you know who this might be? Your friend. . . . Yes, previously he was your friend. . . ."

"Who's that?"

"Mamurin! Semyon Ivanovich Mamurin! Yes, of course—it's him. No one else knows where my new apartment is! Nevertheless," she added in a tone of regret: "I could tell him to go to hell. . . ."

"Yes, do so! Although I'd be very curious to meet Semyon Ivanovich, I'll find another opportunity to do so. Send him away, please. I also wanted to have a chat with you. There's something I need to clarify. . . ."

"I can't!"

"Why not? Say that you're busy. . . ."

"No, I can't, I really can't. . . . I can't, Dmitry Petrovich. . . . I must receive him!"

The bell sounded again.

"You hear how impatient he is? Ha, ha, ha, ha! He's one of my most fervent admirers. . . ."

"It seems he was your husband's close friend?"

"Yes, he was; well, what follows from that?" she said, vigorously emphasizing her words; then she went into the hallway to open the door.

Left alone for a minute, Racheev was about to examine the surrounding room with greater freedom and attention; he fleetingly glanced into another room, and was convinced once more that Zoya Fyodorovna lived rather sparsely. Everything was unrefined, bought at the market, inexpensive; and there was nothing superfluous. At this time the sound of lively conversation could be heard in the hallway.

"No, you can't imagine whom I will show you next!" Zoya Fyodorovna said in an intriguing voice. "You haven't even dreamed it!"

"So help me God, I haven't dreamed of anything and I never do!" replied Mamurin, in his previous rude and abrupt bass voice.

"Well, in a word, it would never, ever occur to you! And you'll be very pleased!"

"Well, I'm never opposed to being pleased! Show me, show me."

Mamurin entered the room; catching sight of Racheev, he suddenly stopped on the threshold, and froze in astonishment.

X

"Dmitry Petrovich! Is it you?" he asked at last, opening his arms for an embrace.

"It is me, Semyon Ivanovich, it's me!" said Racheev in an unassuming, serene tone of voice, without a trace of enthusiasm.

There was no embrace. They settled for exchanging kisses.

"Well, gentlemen, keep yourselves occupied with each other!" the hostess said to them. "I have a new cook and I'm still not familiar with her skills. Yes, I think you have enough to say to one another!"

She left the room.

The friends sat down and for a minute looked at each other. Then Mamurin noticed that Racheev had grown a full beard and was very surprised that he, in spite of this, had recognized his friend at once. Racheev declared that Semyon Ivanovich hadn't grown a centimeter taller but, on the other hand, he had grown noticeably heavier.

"Well, Anton Makarych, one's become thin as a rail, but you've put on all this weight!"

"Hmm.... That all depends on your tendency, Dmitry Petrovich.... Yes, yes, it depends on your tendency!" said Mamurin, trying to get his short body with his small round belly more comfortably settled in the armchair.

"How's that?" Racheev asked in surprise.

"From one's tendency; Anton Makarych, as you know, contributes to the newspaper *Secret Word* cheerfully practicing a barking tendency, adhering to which, a man enters into a struggle with his own conscience. Such a struggle desiccates a person. So, as a result, he's all dried up. I'm an active contributor to the newspaper *Our Century*, which upholds a moderate-liberal tendency. You can't imagine how this tendency promotes support of a vibrant, jubilant frame of mind! And keep in mind that everyone who maintains this moderate-liberal tendency, without fail becomes fatter and acquires a healthy, pink blush to his cheeks. It's almost obligatory. Take, for example, an obscurantist: he preaches—go backward, backward, backward! Serfdom, birch rods, old courts, centralization to *nec plus ultra*![11] But he knows that this is impossible, because a historical law exists, which says: 'What's done is done.' And the obscurantist suffers from the awareness that he has to shout himself hoarse for no reason. As a result, genuine obscurantists are always worn out, with pale-green and yellow faces, with sunken eyes, long, thin, bony fingers; they're always yakking about something and they have saliva on their lips; one can even say, the foam sparkles there. Now, take a radical: he shouts—forward, forward, forward! To hell with everything old, rotten, worthless! Give us everything new! And once again he knows that the old was never inclined to consider itself bad, that nations get the mange for dozens of centuries to hang around on the rotten foundation and that our worthless goods are often taken for masterpieces of art, and that therefore moving forward, no matter what—is absolutely impossible; and they're also shouting this slogan in vain. As a result they fall into despair and grow thin. But the moderate-liberal tendency is quite a different thing! It's simply

11. "Nothing more beyond" (Lat.).

a delight! We say: a little backward and a little forward! Quietly, graciously, without shocks, without destroying social orderliness or decorum. We don't say: everything's going well, but we also don't say, everything's going badly. We say: everything is so-so, neither unsteady nor shaky; that's how things are, and that's how they'll always be! The world was always *so-so*, people were *so-so*, and history was *so-so*. And that's our inherent motto: 'So-so!' We're always peaceful and balanced, we know that the policeman will never look in upon us, because he has nothing to do with us since we do not threaten the social orderliness or decorum. . . ."

"For me this comes as an entire revelation!" said Racheev. "Keep talking, please, do! I'm simply spellbound listening."

"Yes, you see, I could go on talking without stopping for one hundred days and nights, but I wouldn't say anything new, simply modify it more or less. I've told you our entire program, my *profession de foi*. . . .[12] As for your comparison of me with Anton Makarych, the difference in our constitution is explained by one other private circumstance, namely: he lost Zoya Fyodorovna, while I'm acquiring her!"

"How are you acquiring her?" asked Racheev, more and more astonished by Mamurin's words.

"I'm courting her and beginning to notice her favor. She finds only one fault with me—that I'm short and fat, but I have given her my word of honor that I'll lose weight and grow taller, if she demands it."

"Gentlemen, things are going well; dinner will be ready soon, and it seems I will feed you properly!" said the hostess, who had appeared in the room. "You're not spoiled, Dmitry Petrovich, are you?"

"If you like, I *am* spoiled: I'm used to wholesome food!"

"Oh, don't worry on that account! I go to the market myself!" declared Zoya Fyodorovna, taking a seat closer to them.

"Yes, just imagine, Dmitry Petrovich! Such an interesting, clever woman as Zoya Fyodorovna, and she goes to the market herself!" said Mamurin. "Isn't that foolish? Isn't it shameful?"

12. "Profession of faith" (Fr.).

"Hmm. Perhaps it is shameful, but it seems there's nothing foolish about it," replied Racheev. "But here's what I'm surprised about: you're courting Zoya Fyodorovna—why don't you lighten her work and accompany her to the market, if in fact you find it so shameful?"

"Ha, ha, ha! That would be very nice! Ha, ha, ha!" Zoya Fyodorovna said, bursting into laughter. "The moderate-liberal Semyon Ivanych goes to market with a basket! Ha, ha, ha!"

"No, why? I'm . . . I'm ready to go!" declared Mamurin. "If I'd known that this would improve my suit with Zoya Fyodorovna even a little bit, I'd pick up that basket at once!"

"You see? That means a special reward!" observed Racheev.

"But, of course. There's no other way! A royalty for each line, a royalty! I don't submit a single line for nothing to my moderate-liberal editor-publisher. Here's a line for you, give me fifteen kopecks! It's not possible any other way. That's even included in the program of our moderate-liberal tendency."

After these words Racheev suddenly stood up and paced the room several times.

"But listen, Semyon Ivanych. There's no way I can tell whether you're joking or this is seriously how you relate to your tendency," he said with some fervor.

"How's that?" asked Mamurin, and in surprise raised his large, handsome eyes to look at him.

"That's just it—I can't understand!" Racheev continued in the same tone of voice. "All of you here are speaking in some sort of humorous manner, to which I'm not accustomed and which I can't understand. You just now stated in detail your *profession de foi* to me, but it was something that could be attributed to a joker or to a man who despised himself.... Is this really what your moderate-liberal tendency consists of?"

"Precisely in that, precisely, Dmitry Petrovich! I'm telling you this with a clear conscience! If you like, I'll even swear to it: well, so help me God! Seriously!"

"And you really believe in this tendency?"

"Believe? Ha, ha, ha! What a word! We don't even have that word in circulation! Is it possible to believe in such foolishness?"

"But why do you declare yourself to be an adherent of this tendency?" Why do you espouse it in print? Explain it to me, please!"

"Explain? Allow me. It's very simple and it would be best if I clarify this by an example from real life. We had a certain newspaper not long ago by the name of *Hope*; you remember it, of course. The newspaper was enjoyable and independent, and even, perhaps, influential. All of us worked on it—Anton Makarych and I, and many others; we worked, one may say, with feeling because it was an enjoyable job. But then, as you know, one fine day *Hope* dispersed like smoke; it no longer existed. We remained empty-handed. We felt sorry for *Hope*, so to speak, essentially, but we all had to face the problem of earning a living. We began thinking about what to do. A certain Chumenko, a specialist on technical matters, solved that question at once so simply, that we were astonished. No later than the third day after *Hope* disappeared, he appeared at *Secret Word*. Just imagine: all its life *Hope* was at odds with *Secret Word*, and he didn't even blink! I, he says, work on technical matters, and that doesn't relate to the tendency.... And now he flourishes there working on technical matters. I look around and see that in *Our Time* they were lacking a journalist in my field. I went there. Besides we had a critic Mirnyi, who, without much thought, went to work on a camera obscura....[13] Well, at first it was out of necessity, and then we gradually got used to it and everyone feels as if they had been born at their various newspapers.... So as not to go too far: take Matryoshkin, a well-known enfant terrible at *Secret Word*, a fulminator and lampoonist, in prose and verse.... By the way, you'll get to see him today.... Forgive me, Zoya Fyodorovna, but I invited him here.... Yes, he used to be a radical before, and what a radical he was! He was, my friend, dissatisfied with Nekrasov....[14] This, he says, is weak, but just you wait, I'll write some verse, and I'll expose all the people's sorrow

---

13. A camera consisting of a dark chamber with a lens through which an image is projected onto an opposite surface.

14. Nikolai Nekrasov (1821–1878), a poet, writer, and editor, was considered the outstanding representative of the "realist school" in Russian poetry.

on the palm of my hand, and the entire world will weep! But once, for some nasty reason they drove him out of a radical journal, and kicked him in the ass; and what do you think? He didn't hesitate for a minute, he went to *Secret Word* and there had himself put on a long chain and did this voluntarily in order to get enraged. Well, he did get enraged and now he barks like a rabid dog at the whole world.... That's what a tendency is, my dear Dmitry Petrovich."

"In other words, according to you there are no honest people sincerely devoted to their jobs, working not only to earn a living, as you say, but for some idea? Do you insist on this view?" asked Racheev and in his voice one could discern a hostile note.

"Well, why so? There are some. Who says, there aren't any? There are such people. But I don't envy them. They don't live; they all struggle against obstacles.... And for what? It's not clear. All the same their voices are lost in a friendly chorus of cheerfully barking, gloomily roaring, and moderately lamenting people! No, their time has not yet arrived.... There is no ground for them, none at all...."

"And you're preparing that ground? Right?" asked Racheev, and this time he looked Mamurin right in the eye with blatant hostility.

"We are preparing it.... Ha, ha, ha, ha! Yes, we are...."

Dmitry Petrovich began to button his jacket abruptly. His hands trembled; his eyes gazed angrily from under his frowning eyebrows.

"Do you know what? He asked shrilly and loudly: "Do you know what, Semyon Ivanych? I never thought that after a separation of some seven years, I would find it so difficult and repulsive to spend half an hour with you.... Forgive me, Zoya Fyodorovna, I won't be staying to dine with you today."

He hurriedly shook her hand, which she had extended to him mechanically, completely distraught and taken aback, and he went out into the hallway. Zoya Fyodorovna caught up with him.

"What's all this about, Dmitry Petrovich? I'm offended, I really am! Why are you doing this? He always talks such nonsense—he has that habit!" she said sadly, not really understanding what he could find so offensive in Mamurin's words.

"No, it's not nonsense: it's vile! It's impossible to forgive such words, such laughter, such cynicism, Zoya Fyodorovna!" said Racheev, hastening to put his coat on.

"Enough! What are you doing? He used to be your friend, even a close friend.... Can you break it off so suddenly?"

"The worse it is, the more offensive! Good-bye, Zoya Fyodorovna! We'll talk another time about the matter you wrote about...."

"Yes, please, come by sometime ... eleven o'clock tomorrow morning.... Then no one will interfere. You should definitely come! Ah, what a pity it turned out like this!"

Just as Racheev was heading for the door, the bell rang. Zoya Fyodorovna went ahead of Racheev and opened it. A good-looking gentleman entered, smiling; he was very elegantly dressed, well-built, with a face that was carefully and completely clean-shaven.

"You're not acquainted? This is Racheev, my good old friend; and this is Matryoshkin!" Zoya Fyodorovna hurriedly introduced them.

Matryoshkin extended his hand and politely, gently, as if he was even a little embarrassed, said:

"It's very nice to meet you!" The expression of his clever, somewhat cold eyes was entirely good-natured.

"My compliments!" Racheev replied tersely, briefly shook the hand of this new, unexpected acquaintance, and ducking behind the door, almost ran down the staircase.

"What's all this about?" he wondered, with considerable agitation, as he strode along the sidewalk. "Are they making fun of themselves or of me? I don't have time to draw up the list of transformations. I've met Polzikov—corruption, dishonesty; I encountered this one blunt cynicism. What else will fate send me? What kind of surprises? And this fellow's worse than Polzikov. That one, apparently, suffers in part because he drinks and is disfigured; he's heading for destruction and, he must know this. But Mamurin takes life easily, he's self-satisfied; he's growing fatter and despises himself so thoroughly! But Mamurin was also in our circle; he also burned with tender passion for the truth, for the good; he also got excited, was upset, and spoke out.... Can it be that all of this was false, put on? But for what purpose? Who were they trying to fool? To what end? What advantage? Ah, all this is so difficult!"

Without thinking he approached the Severnaya Hotel and went up the stairs to his room. It was almost five o'clock. It was still possible to go to dinner at the Baklanovs and to share with them his impressions of today's visit.

He left the hotel again and took a cab to the Baklanovs. When he rang the bell, it took a long time for them to respond. Finally he was admitted to the apartment where everything was unusually quiet. From the entrance hall he saw that Liza was hurriedly tiptoeing from the study through the hall into the dining room. "Are they asleep or what?" Racheev asked himself.

"Is the master at home?" he inquired of the maid.

"Yes, sir. He's in his study...."

"And the mistress?"

"She's also home.... But she's ... not feeling well."

"Is she ill?"

He walked quickly to the study and saw Nikolai Alekseevich, who was nervously pacing the room in his soft slippers.

"Ah, it's you," he said, and it seemed to Racheev that Baklanov wasn't particularly glad to see him.

"What? Perhaps I've disturbed you?" he asked cautiously.

"Oh, no, no.... I asked because you wrote me a note.... You said that you wouldn't be coming to dinner.... Excuse me, my dear, I'm very glad to see you, but ... I ... I'm a bit out of sorts...."

"What's wrong with Katerina Sergeevna? Is it something serious?"

"Ah ... They told you.... What did they say?"

"That she was unwell ... What's wrong with her? Tell me, please? You really do seem troubled.... Perhaps I should go fetch a doctor, do you think?"

"No, no, it's simply a case of nerves! Ah, nerves, nerves, nerves!"

Nikolai Alekseevich was whispering the whole time, as if afraid to disturb someone, and he uttered his last exclamation even softer, but simultaneously with an undisguised cry of despair, grabbing hold of his head with both hands. His face was pale; his lips twitched nervously. Racheev had never seen him like that.

"Tell me, Dmitry Petrovich, for what purpose do nerves exist?"

he asked, pausing in front of Racheev and staring directly at him with such a look as though he was waiting for an answer to this most important question.

Racheev smiled. He understood that some sort of typical spousal scene had occurred between the Baklanovs; he tried to calm his friend, taking hold of his arm, and seating him on the sofa next to him.

"Where we live in the country, nerves exist to perceive impressions and do other things, prescribed in physiology; but here in Petersburg, Nikolai Alekseevich, they exist to spoil the lives of very nice, decent people!" he said in a soft voice, with a friendly smile.

"Yes, that's true, it is!" cried Baklanov with his eyes closed.

"But it seems to me that if people promise themselves to regard trifles as trifles, that would improve their lot."

"There are too many trifles! All of life consists of trifles! All of it!" Baklanov cried in his previous tone of voice. "However," he added, turning his face to Dmitry Petrovich and trying to smile, "don't pay any attention to me. I think that you don't even understand such a situation.... It comes and goes without reason.... Now we'll have dinner, Dmitry Petrovich!"

"Will Katerina Sergeevna be joining us ... Is she all right?" asked Racheev with a slight grin.

"That's as God wills it!

"I will treat her!"

The maid appeared on the threshold and announced that "the mistress invites them to dine."

Baklanov stood up and was about to head for the door, but suddenly he turned around, took off his slippers, put on his boots, and then they both proceeded into the dining room.

Katerina Sergeevna met Racheev with an apathetic look, shook hands with him formally, and made no reply to his greeting. Liza bowed back to him in silence and dropped her eyes at once. Tanya sat discreetly between her and her mother and didn't object at all when the nanny tied a napkin around her neck. Baklanov poured two glasses of vodka and placed one in front of Racheev.

"It's true that they can all sit silently during dinner, as if they were all deaf and dumb," thought Racheev, and he stubbornly resolved to pretend and behave as if he didn't notice the general mood.

"Today I was the hero of a certain adventure!" he said. "An adventure of an almost romantic sort!"

"Ah!" replied Baklanov, and all the others answered him with deep silence.

But Racheev decided to plow ahead as if nothing was amiss. He continued:

"And I'm willing to wager that you will never guess where I was! Go on, guess, Katerina Sergeevna!"

This was too risky an opening. Baklanov anxiously raised his eyes to look at him, while Liza, blushing slightly, stealthily peeked at Katerina Sergeevna.

"I'm not very good at guessing!" Katerina Sergeevna replied in an even tone, obviously trying to restrain her anger and not waver.

"In that case I'll tell you. Just imagine, today I received a note with such intriguing content. . . ."

Racheev related everything in detail, without hurrying, and at the same time continued to eat. He reached the moment when the unknown woman turned out to be Zoya Fyodorovna. Baklanov said, "Ah!" Katerina Sergeevna made a scornful face. Liza simply remained silent. Racheev begins to relay Mamurin's words. Nikolai Alekseevich says: "Yes, he was always a joker!" Katerina Sergeevna's face expresses doubled disdain; Liza listens conscientiously, but still remains silent. Coffee is served to him and Baklanov (or was it more vodka?). He finishes his story, taking it up to the point where Matryoshkin enters. Katerina Sergeevna stands up and says in the same even tone, holding her left temple:

"Excuse me. . . . I have a headache. . . ."

And she leaves. He looks around: Liza and Tanya are no longer in the dining room: they slipped away unnoticed. Then he begins to understand that his cure proved to be ineffective, and it seems to him that his story, which took all of dinnertime, during which he alone was speaking while all the others were silent, was a very stupid undertaking. He vigorously stirs his coffee with a spoon and now he himself falls silent, leaving it up to his host to entertain him.

Their conversation was lethargic and disconnected. They couldn't stay on any topic for very long. Baklanov was distracted; he often didn't hear the question or replied irrelevantly. He had the look of a man whose hands and feet were bound.

When the clock struck seven, Racheev said:

"Isn't it time to go? You told me that people gathered at Vysotskaya's very early."

"Yes, yes.... Right away.... Wait a moment!" Baklanov said with a quivering voice and for some reason entered the bedroom on tiptoes.

He didn't return for a long time. About twenty minutes later he came out in his black frock coat and wearing a fresh collar, but his face was distraught and pale.

"Let's go, I'm ready!" he said, hurriedly donning his coat, which the maid handed him, and swiftly heading for the door, as if he was afraid that someone might stop him or call him back.

Racheev barely managed to grab his coat and hat and ran after him to catch up.

XI

But they had scarcely set foot on the street and hired a cab, when Nikolai Alekseevich suddenly seemed to be reinvigorated. Racheev looked at him in surprise. Obviously, the man who had been so constrained formerly, felt as if he had grown wings.

"Yes, he was always a clown, that Mamurin! I never could learn to take him seriously. Today, my friend, a great number of these types have multiplied here, who could have drawn a hand with a pen dipped in ink on the entrance door to their apartment and written under it: 'Master of these matters,' with the addition of 'according to the suitable price and depending on the circumstances. . . .' Especially these gentlemen publishers of new organs of the press! It's not that a person harbors in his soul a cherished idea and creates a new organ to turn this idea to life; no, he simply opens a shop and then looks around to see what kind of bait the fish are attracted by: bread, worms, or flies. . . ."

In such a tone was Baklanov confidently developing his idea until they reached the large house on Nikolaevsky Street, where the cab stopped.

The doorman met Baklanov with a cheerful smile, as he did someone who would give him a good tip. In reply to his question: "Is anyone here yet?" he replied politely:

"Of course, sir! Innokenty Mikhailovich is here, Fyodor Grigorich has been here since dinnertime, while Semyon Ivanych arrived just a minute before you."

"Who's Semyon Ivanych?" Racheev asked Baklanov as they were climbing the stairs. "Might that by any chance be Mamurin?"

"Yes, indeed!"

"But is that the flowering of the intelligentsia? What sort of society has gathered here at her place?"

"You'll see for yourself in a minute. You'll see, my friend, that both Mamurin and Polzikov, and many similar people become completely respectable in her drawing room."

"Yes, but after today's scene at Zoya Fyodorovna's, I confess that it would be nicer not to encounter him here. . . ."

"I tell you that here you'll meet an entirely different Mamurin!"

After ringing the bell, a door opened before them and they entered a brightly illuminated hallway.

"Welcome!" the footman said in a pleasant baritone, and without announcing them, opened the door to a large, long room in which it would have been completely dark except, for the light coming in from the hallway.

They continued on and suddenly the soft, slightly pink light from a tall lamp on a round table to the right fell upon them. Racheev took in the room with a glance, trying first of all to make out his surroundings, but just then the mistress of the house rose from the sofa and began approaching him; he fixed his gaze on her.

She went up to Baklanov, who was walking ahead. From the first glance, her face seemed to him too plain and unremarkable. "Pretty, no doubt, but I've seen many faces like hers," flashed through his mind. But as for her graceful figure, which was highlighted by a simple silk dress the color of a ripe plum, as if lending her some modesty or restraint, he acknowledged it at once, without hesitation, as astonishingly elegant, and involuntarily began to admire her slender pale neck, so tenderly shaded by a wide, turned-down lace collar.

When she began chatting with Baklanov, Racheev hastened to alter his opinion of her face. It came to life both with its smile and the slight flush on her cheeks, and the bright light and play of her eyes, suddenly lit up by something like secret laughter, or by cunning: her face became distinctive and interesting. She was saying to Baklanov, as she shook his hand:

"You're never the first to arrive.... That's what fame means! You know, I like it when people come early, so that it makes the evening longer! Thank you for the kindness; and you, Monsieur Racheev, for the attention you pay to my small drawing room! I'm very, very glad to make your acquaintance!"

And she took her hand from Baklanov's hand, and extended it to Racheev.

" Let's go in here, gentlemen! Get acquainted, please! Racheev. ... I'm sorry.... Dmitry Petrovich? You see, I do remember.... Innokenty Mikhailovich Zebrov, Fyodor Grigorevich Dvoinikov, Semyon Ivanovich.... Are you acquainted?

Racheev shook hands with Zebrov and Dvoinikov; turning to Mamurin, he said only:

"We've seen each other today!"

"Gentlemen," the hostess said, turning to the earlier guests with whom Baklanov had joined, "amuse yourselves; I won't pay you any attention.... I'm terribly fed up with you. I shall occupy myself with my new acquaintance.... Dmitry Petrovich, let's sit here; let them do what they want. They're all tame!"

Everyone started laughing and, as a matter of fact, in a small circle sitting at a round table, a conversation arose.

"You can't imagine what Nikolai Alekseevich told me about you! Genuine marvels!" the hostess said in a slightly shrill, sonorous voice; turning to him with her full body, she looked right at him, as if studying his face. He responded with an observant, serene glance.

"Then, after he left, I sat in the carriage and all the way to the Shopping Arcade I thought about you, trying to imagine your face and figure. . . . Women are all like that; we can't be any different. We like it when everything is depicted on people's faces. And here's what's surprising: I imagined you just as you are, even with your beard. . . . Only it seemed to me that you had to have large, powerful hands, but yours are quite small."

She started laughing again and, as it seemed to Racheev, not exactly for him, but partly for the others who were sitting at the round table.

"But why powerful?" he asked.

"Really, I don't know why. Nikolai Alekseevich didn't tell me anything about you, but just imagine! But tell me, is it true that you live permanently in the country?"

"Yes. . . . But is that really such a rarity? There are quite a few landowners who live permanently in the countryside. . . ."

"And I've known three sorts of such landowners; first—those who havecompletely devoted themselves to estate management, giving their body and soul to this vocation, yielding profit. They travel around to village fairs, sell, buy, trade horses and livestock, they learn the price of grain and wool. These are the 'industrialists.' The second group works in the springtime, summer, and autumn, to spend the winter abroad; and the third lives all year in the country because they lack the means; they complain of hard times and curse their fate. You, of course, don't belong to any of these three groups. . . ."

"You've described them well, but you've forgotten about one sort, the most recent," said Racheev. "It's those who philosophize deviously and who bare their souls!"

"Do you belong to that group?" Evgeniya Konstantinovna asked in horror.

"Oh, no, under no circumstances!" Dmitry Petrovich replied definitively. "Under no circumstances! I belong to the group of those who live in this world, and who don't philosophize deviously. I don't hold to any teaching, except that of my own conscience. . . . But I think that you, Evgeniya Konstantinovna, also live the same way?"

She shook her head slowly in the negative.

"That's an open question, Dmitry Petrovich!" she said pensively. "But please don't think that I'll immediately make you proclaim the teaching of your conscience for me. . . . I only hope that this won't disappear after we become better acquainted, if you would like that. . . ."

"Oh, yes, I do want that! I find you very interesting. . . ."

"Really? Why? Tell me. I like how you said that so simply and seriously, without a smirk and without the look that usually accompanies such words. . . . I think that it's not a compliment. . . ."

"No, as a matter of fact, it's the truth: you interest me greatly, and do you know why? It's a trifle, a small point, one trait, not more, and perhaps, it will seem amusing. . . ."

"Oh, come on, come on! I'm sure it won't."

"You just reacted to my words: it's still a question, Dmitry Petrovich! And you said this in such a tone. . . . It seems to me that at this moment something like a whirlwind of scenes from your life is flying in front of you. . . . And, at this moment you were astonishingly truthful. . . . And that's what aroused my interest."

"Ah, how right you are, a thousand times right! It's so rare that one has a chance to be truthful—for the most part, it happens when one is not thinking about it, it's just like at this moment which you caught. . . . Forgive me, I must leave you for a minute. . . ."

The figure of a tall, older woman in a white lace cap appeared in the depths of the doorway leading into an adjacent room; she was something like a housekeeper. The hostess went up to her and disappeared immediately behind a curtain.

Racheev began to survey the room. It was rather spacious, but seemed crowded, thanks to the large amount of furniture and the multitude of magnificent, though for the most part, totally useless objects. The furniture was heavy, deliberately angular, but soft and comfortable. On these sofas, armchairs, hassocks, and simple benches placed along the walls, one felt somehow surprisingly free and easy, probably because there were no indications whatsoever of the formal furnishings of a drawing room.

Taking advantage of the fact that a lively conversation was in progress at the round table, and that everyone had forgotten all about him, Racheev began from his distant corner to scrutinize his new acquaintances. The surnames—Zebrov and Dvoinikov—were known to him, especially Zebrov, whose speeches for the defense had always astonished him with their brilliance, wit, and eloquence. He had recently heard something or other about Dvoinikov. It was a new name, which, however, promised rapid prominence. His paintings at two recent exhibitions had gathered crowds.

Both of them at first glance made a not very favorable impression on him. It seemed to him that Zebrov, that handsome, elegant fair-haired man with the tasteful style of his thick, light brown hair, a carefully clipped beard, with clever, quick eyes, was too concerned about the form of his speech. Everything about him was too good-looking—his bearing, gestures, the shape of his lips, the cast of his eyes, and the intonation of his speech—and for some reason it seemed to Racheev that Zebrov was aware of all this, because he was doing everything constantly and carefully. Dvoinikov represented the complete opposite. He was a stocky, strong fellow with broad shoulders and short legs, a flat face, too simple, even crude, with an unusually high forehead. He spoke with hesitation, wheezed between his words, expressed himself indistinctly and incomprehensibly; in spite of all this, he looked powerful and resolute, apparently, in his soul, considering all the objections to him superfluous. He was fortuitously discovered by one old well-known artist, who invited him to the capital and had begun to teach him real art. Dvoinikov vindicated his hopes. It was noteworthy that however modest his opinion was of his own capabilities, when he was painting icons, he began acknowledging himself as the greatest talent in all of Russia and he would state that directly, in his sincere simplicity, not even suspecting that this was immodest. This made being in his company uncomfortable and at times demanding, because he talked exclusively about himself. As soon as someone began speaking in his presence about a new painting by Repin, Shishkin, or Makovsky, Dvoinkov's shrill voice would ring out: "Hey. . . . I conceived of a painting . . ." or "Hey . . . if I had more free time, I would be painting that. . . ." And it seemed to him that by such a declaration, he was, so to speak, completely outdoing Repin, Shishkov, and Makovsky, and all other artists.[15]

Now the conversation continued about the picture of a certain artist, which was still being painted in his workshop, but there was already a lot of talk about it in town, and those who had seen it were enthusiastic. Mamurin announced that he was planning to write about it in *Our Time*, and therefore studied it in detail; Zebrov was eloquently and passionately trying to prove to him that this task shouldn't be undertaken "because," he said, "a picture is like a poem and only becomes a social property from the moment when it's presented to the public. This means that it's when the artist himself recognizes the completion of his work and says 'Come and admire it!' While it's still in the workshop, it's a holy of holies, a secret, wrong to divulge!"

"Hey . . . yes. . . . And it often happens," cried Dvoinikov, "that people make a lot of noise about a painting, and lo and behold, it turns out to be pure rubbish!"

Baklanov and Mamurin took the side of the artist about whom they were speaking, trying to prove that his painting couldn't be bad.

"Hey . . . this spring, after I finish work for the exhibition, I'll take on a new subject. . . ."

He was about to describe this new subject, but just then the mistress of the house entered and everyone, as if forgetting about the artist, turned toward her.

15. Ilya Repin (1844–1930) was the most renowned Russian artist of the nineteenth century; Ivan Shishkin (1832–1898) was a landscape painter closely associated with the Peredvizhniki (Wanderers) movement; and Konstantin Makovsky (1839–1915) was another influential Russian painter, also affiliated with the Peredvizhniki.

Racheev found it timely to join the others. He went up to Baklanov and took a seat next to him. Baklanov immediately began to introduce him to his interlocutors.

"Beware of him, gentlemen. He spent seven uninterrupted years in the country, and now has come to Petersburg to do research: to see how things stand in the city. He doesn't miss a thing; he delves into every detail. He's a government inspector from the country. . . ."[16]

Racheev cast a questioning glance at him: "Why, pray tell, are you spouting this nonsense?" But Baklanov's remark occasioned a lively conversation about the countryside. Zebrov defined a seven-year uninterrupted stay in the country as voluntary confinement in a stone tower. Baklanov passionately interceded on behalf of the country, and even expressed the thought that if he weren't encumbered by family, he would have abandoned Petersburg a long time ago. Mamurin said, "Gentlemen, I choose a middle path: the countryside is a wonderful thing, that's indisputable, but I will live in the capital!" Dvoinikov for some reason began to enumerate the country churches that contained icons he'd painted, and concluded, "Hey. . . . No, the countryside is a great thing! I was born and grew up there!"

"Yes, and that is the only circumstance that can justify its existence!" remarked Zebrov, not without malice.

Everyone smiled, but Dvoinikov didn't get the sarcasm and said very seriously:

"Precisely!"

The conversation on the theme of the country continued during tea, which was served, but during the whole discussion only two people remained silent—the hostess and Racheev.

"Why won't you share your opinion, Dmitry Petrovich?" asked Evgeniya Konstantinova at last. "You're the most qualified person on this matter!"

"What can I say?" replied Racheev. "I live in the country, live there by my own desire, and I experience great enjoyment! It seems that's enough to convey my opinion!"

---

16. Another reference to Nikolai Gogol's comedy, *The Government Inspector.*

"Oh, yes! That's true!" agreed Vysotskaya.

Having asked her guests to arrive earlier, Evgeniya Konstanti-novna didn't like it when they stayed too long. Therefore Baklanov, and soon after, Racheev, began to bid her farewell at eleven o'clock.

"So, I hope, Dmitry Petrovich, that we'll get to know each other better!" she said bidding him good-bye. "The next time, I hope, there'll be more people here. Today it turned out that I had only a few friends."

"In general there are very few true friends!" Baklanov offered with a smile.

Vysotskaya nodded her head, but went on, addressing Racheev:

"I'll also be glad to see you here some morning. . . . I'm at home on Sunday around twelve o'clock, noon."

"I'll definitely come to see you!" replied Racheev, shaking her hand.

"By the way, I must confer with you about one particular matter. . . . Will you allow me?"

"If I can prove useful to you!"

"Oh, I know what matter! Evgeniya Konstantinovna is publishing books for the masses. . . . She doesn't just sit at home doing nothing. . . . And she's even honored one of my small works. . . ."

"Books for the masses? Hmm," thought Racheev and then felt sorry that this information almost seemed to spoil the absolutely fine impression that Vysotskaya had made on him. . . ."

Baklanov kissed her hand; Racheev refrained from doing so. They left her apartment.

XII

"Well, then? What do you think?" asked Baklanov, as they were walking along the pavement. "Isn't it true that she's a marvelous woman?"

"In what sense or manner do you mean that?"

"In all senses and manners!" Baklanov declared enthusiastically. "In the first place, she's beautiful and kind!"

"Indeed!"

"In the second place, she's smart!"

"Perhaps!"

"What do you mean 'perhaps'? If you spoke with her for quarter of an hour, then you'd have to admit it to be true. And then, there's nothing trite, ordinary, or vulgar about her!"

"Ah, my friend, she's very rich. Your wife justifiably says that this gives her the possibility of showing herself in splendid form!"

"Well, in that case my wife and you are mistaken about her! Are there really so few wealthy women on the earth? But are there many like her? No, for this you require both intelligence and an original character!"

"What for? I just can't understand what it is that you value in her!"

"What do I value? I can tell you in a few words: she stands head and shoulders above all other women. . . ."

"But that's still not so difficult. . . ." *Based*

"How's that? Today an educated woman, with whom one can discuss anything, just like with an educated man, is by no means a rarity. At least in Petersburg there are enough of them. But, it's worth noting: as soon as a woman begins to make an effort to truly surpass the average level of a so-called educated woman, she gradually begins to lose some of those marvelous qualities that make a woman attractive to a man. But this is not the case here. Evgeniya Konstantinovna has demonstrated that this is not true! See what an active interest she takes in all outstanding aspects of social life, how clever her opinions are about everything, how much and how judiciously she reads!

In a word, she's an educated woman in the sense in which one uses it to describe a man by saying 'he's a well-educated man.' It's not a matter of a so-called female intellectual. Oh, no, so-called 'intellectuality' comes from spending three years in a gymnasium. Yes, and at the same time, just see how charming she is, enchanting, how charming! She leads a social life and at the same time she gives herself up to pursuits that have nothing in common with her social life, such as the publication of books for the masses! She's a splendid woman! Listen," added Baklanov, "Shall we drop in somewhere to have supper? Well, what about to Palkin's Restaurant?[17] We'll recall old times. . . ."

"Have supper? But, my friend, I've grown unaccustomed to having supper in the local manner. That means—to get sozzled," Racheev said.

"What do you mean? You forget that I have a wife. Would I really allow myself to arrive home intoxicated? No, just to have supper. . . ."

"Why don't you have supper with your wife?"

"We never eat supper. We don't have that habit."

"Then why are you inviting me to an inn?"

"Ah, but that's an entirely different matter. Just imagine, I've been married for five years and lead, so to speak, a modest domestic life. It seems that it's time to break completely from such habits. But it's an astonishing thing! At times I feel an unbearable longing to visit an inn. That's what a background with inns produces! So, shall we go, Dmitry Petrovich?"

"Why not, let's!"

They crossed Vladimirsky Prospect and turned toward Palkin's. Racheev entered a brightly lit hall, turned left, walked over to the fourth table, and took a seat. Baklanov, who followed right after him, laughed softly.

"Why did you choose to sit at this table?" he asked his friend.

Racheev looked around and started laughing in turn.

"Damn it all!" he said, shrugging his shoulders. "I unconsciously sat down at 'our table,' so-called. Here's where we held our 'little drinking-bouts,' and our bigger ones in a separate room. Yes, you're right, Nikolai Alekseevich! These tavern habits are very much alive. . . . Well, you've been living in the capital, and from time to time have revived them, isn't that correct? While I, swearing by my word of honor, haven't been in a tavern for some seven years, and now, just imagine, it's as if I left here only yesterday!"

---

17. An exclusive restaurant on Nevsky Prospect in St. Petersburg.

"Yes, Dmitry Petrovich, yes, indeed!" Baklanov agreed. "But it must be said—you recall all this for a reason. Why, it was here, at this table, we spent so many joyous hours! Precisely here, my friend, we worked out those lofty ideals, which now brighten our life at least from afar!"

"Yes," Racheev uttered with a sarcastic smile. "Brighten! Both Polzikov, and Mamurin also brighten our life!"

"Hmm. . . . Well, what of it? Polzikov has gone astray, while Mamurin was always a nonentity! But have you noticed how properly he behaves at Vysotskaya's? Thank God, there's such a place where people like Mamurin feel they need to maintain their silence. . . . Hmm. . . . Look!!"

Mamurin entered the hall and, not noticing them, walked on past and sat down to their right, but then he saw them, quickly stood up, and with an extremely affable look on his face, began to draw near them.

"I didn't notice you, my friends!" he said in an absolutely simple, amicable tone of voice, and extended his hand to Baklanov, who took it; then he stretched out his hand to Racheev and added, "What sort of trick did you play today at Zoya Fyodorovna's?"

Racheev leaned back in his chair and put his hands on his knees.

"You won't shake my hand?" Mamurin asked, blushing slightly, while Racheev frowned and turned pale.

"No, I won't!" he replied abruptly and harshly.

"However, this is foolish!" Mamurin replied, concealing his annoyance and pretending that he didn't attach any major significance to this circumstance. He slipped his hand into his jacket pocket and took out his cigar case. "I stated my views; you're not in agreement with them, and that's all there is to it! It's impossible for everyone to have the same views!"

"It would be better, Semyon Ivanych, if you left me in peace!" said Racheev, looking down sullenly.

"But why? Isn't it better to have it out?" Mamurin continued insistently.

"You absolutely wish to have it out? By all means!" Racheev replied with a clear effort to restrain his agitation. "There are views with which one may disagree and even argue against; but there are also views that one can despise, just as one despises those people who profess them. Those are the same views that you stated today. . . . That's all I have to say."

Mamurin's eyes flashed with rage.

"But this is . . . this is too much, Mr. Racheev!" he cried, breathing heavily: "For such things one must pay dearly!"

An alarmed Baklanov regarded both of them.

"Pay with what?" Racheev asked with a contemptuous grin. "Are you challenging me to a duel?"

"And what if I did?"

"I won't accept it!"

"In other words, you're a coward!"

"You may think that. I won't risk my life because of someone I don't respect. . . ."

"That's enough. In other words, you're denying me satisfaction?"

"You demanded that we have it out; I told you the truth about yourself. Tell me the truth about myself, however bitter it might be, and that will be your satisfaction. . . ."

"That's the old excuse of cowards. . . . You're making it necessary for me to seek satisfaction in another way. . . ."

"That's your own business! But if you intend to slap my face or something similar, I warn you that I shall strangle you with my own two hands."

And Racheev placed his two tight fists on the table.

"We'll see about that!" Mamurin said and immediately left the hall, his short, broad body wobbling awkwardly.

The two friends remained silent for a minute or more. Baklanov wanted to give Racheev time to calm down.

"You'll excuse me, Nikolai Alekseevich, for this scene!" said Dmitry Petrovich, regarding him with his still distressed, flashing eyes. "But basically I'm very glad that I said that to him. You know, if all decent people agreed among themselves not to shake hands with such gentlemen, they wouldn't appear to be so self-confident and there would be fewer of them. . . . It's necessary that they see themselves as outcasts, pariahs. . . . Whereas here they feel themselves to be almost heroes of the present time! People despise them and amicably shake their hands. . . . And all they need is for people to fulfill this formality. They don't care at all about your opinion of them!"

They were served vodka and something hot.

"Nevertheless I'm very glad that I said that to him!" he repeated, already completely calmed down. "Let him embark on whatever he likes!"

"You can be sure that he won't embark on anything. Why, he's a coward, I know him!" said Baklanov. "He didn't seriously propose a duel to you; and if you'd accepted his challenge, he would have run away. . . ."

After they paid the bill and got up to go home, Racheev observed that Baklanov's face was suddenly looking somehow overcast. He recalled that strained atmosphere that he'd found today in his friend's house, and he thought that a turbulent scene would certainly await poor Nikolai Alekseevich at home. On the street Baklanov silently shook his hand, took a cab, and left with an absolutely morose face.

Racheev went along Nevsky Prospect and thought about Nikolai Alekseevich's morose expression and about the impressions of this day.

At home he found an envelope on the table and hurriedly began to unseal it when he noticed the handwriting of the address. This was the first letter he had received from home since his arrival in Petersburg. The letter contained the following:

Dear Mityusha! First of all, rest assured: I am well, and Masha is, too, and everything is fine, except that you're not here, and we miss you very much. Masha has cut two new teeth, and that went smoothly; she wasn't ill. There haven't been any special events. The peasants came and requested permission to cast their nets in the pond. As you told me not to interfere in any way, I didn't. They caught a whole mass of carp! Vlas says: it was because Dmitry Petrovich was thinking about us on his journey, that's why we had such good luck! It would be impossible, detrimental to catch more with their nets this autumn. So I said that they couldn't fish anymore. The winter crops are already standing: both ours and in the village. Old man Fedotik says that this year will certainly yield a very good harvest. He saw how the ravens were flying in a particular way and that means there'll be a good harvest. Tatyana's oldest daughter has fallen ill with typhus. We took her to the hospital. The medical assistant, Ivan Ivanovich, says that it's not serious, that she'll recover, but Doctor Korobkov still hasn't arrived; he was taken away somewhere in the district; he'll return only on Friday and will come to see us right away. Mikita's widow came to ask for rye, and I gave her some; you see, I do everything you ordered. Yesterday the teacher's baby was christened. Marya Grigorevna gave birth to a daughter—such a healthy little girl, simply a delight. While Fyodor Petrovich rejoices and jokes: it's fine, he says, that it's a daughter and not a son. A son would undoubtedly become a village teacher: what would we get out of it? Whereas a daughter can marry anyone she likes, even the king of Serbia. We celebrated at their place: we sang songs and danced. I recalled old times and danced a Russian folk dance with Fyodor Petrovich; after all, he's our relative now—a godfather. The priest was there, Father Semyon; he watched us and said: "You, Aleksandra Matveevna, dance so well that, so help me God, it isn't even sinful." And how are you faring in Petersburg, Mityusha? Do you think about us? You do, you do, I know you do. You wrote that you encountered much that was sad and little that was good. I always used to say that it was so much better where we are! Write about what else you've seen. The threshing machine is finishing its work and for some reason is rattling. The workman in charge of our machinery says that it should be taken into town for repairs this winter. I kiss you a million times and Masha does, too. Don't forget to look for a turquoise ring for me and a little cross for Masha. Yours, Sasha.

Racheev sat reading the letter for an entire hour, without stirring from his chair. A series of quiet, serene, simple country scenes flooded his imagination, and when he came to himself and recalled all the impressions of the past few days, he was horrified at the thought of the striking distance that existed between that life and this one.

"It's an entire abyss!" he thought to himself: "Everything's so simple there, healthy, and natural; here everything's confused, sickly, and turned inside out! Why do people live in such torment, when it's possible to live so peacefully?"

XIII

During his student days Racheev's friends assigned him the humorous nickname of "the ladies' confessor." In their circle, as in every circle, there were people who played the role of romantic heroes and, on the pretext of working toward their self-perfection, they quietly carried on affairs with persons of the female sex, who, having delved into some profound socioeconomic treatise or having devoted themselves to some passionate argument on a lofty subject, all of a sudden unexpectedly for themselves, turned out to be head over heels in love. Then doubts would arise, mix-ups, minor episodes, unexplained scenes, and misunderstandings; as a result it happened that someone would be insulted, disappointed, or feel her life was ruined. And it almost always occurred that the heroine of this sort of romantic event, feeling herself helpless, would turn to Racheev and open her soul to him. Apparently there was something in him that inspired trust and a desire to speak freely. Perhaps responsible for this situation was the particular simplicity with which he treated everyone, men as well as women.

Racheev had to listen to confessions of the most diverse content, which, however, all came down to one and the same thing—misunderstanding.

And when he posed the question to himself why Zoya Fyodorovna chose precisely him for the declaration of a particular "matter," him, the one who'd just arrived in town after a seven-year absence, when she had so many acquaintances and, apparently, quite a few admirers, then he recalled unconsciously that former time, and wondered whether the strange trait that had at one time earned him the nickname "confessor" had in this case played a role.

He considered it inappropriate to put off his visit.

"I knew that you'd come!" Zoya Fyodorovna said cheerfully, opening the door for him.

"How did you know? I certainly might not have come today!"

"No, I felt that you would. . . . And I'm grateful to you, very grateful!"

"Tell me, Zoya Fyodorovna, perhaps you have calling hours? I just saw your sign. . . ."

Zoya Fyodorovna's face assumed an expression of displeasure and annoyance.

"Ah, don't talk to me about that, just don't!" she cried even with some trembling in her voice. "What sort of calling hours? If two people show up during the entire day, thank God! And who comes to Peski, tell me, please, somewhere in the courtyard, up a narrow staircase, the devil knows where, when there are such splendid signs on Nevsky Prospect, all sorts of clinics with marble staircases, velvet-covered furniture, and stucco ceilings? What sort of calling hours? Have a seat, please! You see, I'm settling in. . . . Here are my instruments of torture, here's an armchair, unfortunately, it's still unoccupied, and here's a small workshop. . . . I also know how to make false teeth. . . . Ha, ha, ha!"

"Well, Zoya Fyodorovna," he said, taking the armchair. "I'm at your service, ready to hear your business matter!"

"Matter! Hmm. What a strange person you are, Dmitry Petrovich! So strange. You haven't seen me in seven years; you've met me in a setting that should seem surprising to you, and you don't even ask how all of this occurred? You heard the fairy tale told you by Anton Makarovich, and that was enough for you. . . . Well, ask me, at last, how did it happen that I became a dentist. Well?"

"I didn't consider it my right to ask about that!" replied Racheev.

"That's strange! It seems that you and I were friends. . . . You were even my relative."

"Hey, Zoya Fyodorovna, we were friends! What follows from

that? Everything changes so much. . . . It's hard to believe that in seven years people are capable of changing so much. Was Anton Makarovich like that seven years ago, or Mamurin? And you, too: seven years ago you looked at things in a certain way; and now, how do I know how you see them?"

"Ha, ha, ha, ha! Ah, Dmitry Petrovich. How I looked at things? How could I regard them when I didn't understand a thing? Yes, indeed, I looked at them as if they were curiosities displayed in some museum, and I thought only what I was prompted to think about them. . . . I turned up in your circle where people thought a certain way; I listened, listened, and heard enough, and I began to think in the same way! That always happens to us, women, until life wears us down or grinds us up into flour. . . ."

"Well, and if it does wear you down and grind you up, then what?"

"Then? Then, as a matter of fact, we learn to look at things! Then our own views are formed, but they're so firm and solid that by then you can't beat them out of you! Yes, and I now have my own views, really, I do!"

"Well, apprise me of your views!"

"I have only one view, and everything else derives from it. . . . All people are swine, every single one! That means it's not worth living for others; one should live only for oneself!"

"Oh!"

"Yes, yes! I've come to this conclusion! And no one can disabuse me of it, no one!"

"In order to maintain this, you had to study a lot of people!" retorted Racheev.

"Two were enough! Ha, ha, ha! I studied two thoroughly, and the others, only so-so! Yes, yes, note this: if Anton Makarych slandered me to you, as if I went with everyone and with the first one that came along, that's foul slander!"

"He didn't say anything of the kind to me!"

"He didn't, but he will. . . . One can expect anything from him! You can't imagine what sort of disreputable fellow he is!" she said with an expression of deep hatred.

"But what did he do to you?" asked Racheev, sincerely interested in her explanation.

"But you know that story! He was telling you. . . . But, I can imagine how he told it. I imagine how much slander he heaped on me, on everyone, on the whole world! No, I should tell you how it was. . . . You know how this is said in Latin? How does it go? Anton Makarych often used to repeat it. . . . *Altera, altera.* . . ."

"*Audiatur et altera pars!*"[18] Racheev prompted her.

"Well, that's it, precisely! So, won't you be so kind as to *audiatur*? Don't pay any attention to the fact that I'm pacing around the room. You recall how well we were living. . . . Of course, I didn't harbor any enthusiastic feeling for Anton Makarych, and it was impossible to demand that. As you well know, he was never distinguished by his good looks, and a woman, say what you will, always remains a woman! A woman is an aesthete by nature: a need for beauty always lives in her soul. . . . But I respected him and nurtured some feeling for him. . . . How can I explain it? A feeling of attachment, habit, call it what you like, in a word, a serene and kind feeling. But then Pavel Petrovich Kirgizov appeared! Things stood as follows: our little Antosha fell ill with diphtheria. We invited Kirgizov and he began to treat the lad. He took care of him as if he were his own. At that time Anton Makarych was writing some sort of work that was urgent; he would hardly get up from the desk; meanwhile Pavel Petrovich and I sat at the patient's bed day and night without a break. . . . You understand how this works! As I said, he was very handsome and I . . . I'm a woman. . . . Well, it's understandable that he lit a spark in my soul. . . . We became close. But don't think we became intimate at the time. Nothing of the sort. We didn't even say a word to each other, and perhaps we didn't even know anything about our feelings. Antosha died, the poor lad. . . . Ah, those were terrible days! I was grieving and couldn't find consolation in

---

18. A Latin phrase meaning "listen to the other side," or "let the other side be heard as well." It is the principle that no person should be judged without a fair hearing in which each party is given the opportunity to respond to the evidence against them.

anything. . . . Just think, to lose one's only son! My God, it's even horrible to recall it now. . . ."

She stopped in front of the window and regarded it for a minute. Her face grew dark with the painful recollection; her eyes became moist. She continued speaking, all the while looking at the window:

"Pavel Petrovich continued to visit us and we spent many hours together, while Anton Makarych hardly emerged from his study during these days. Just imagine, our son, our only son died, while he could sit at his desk and write some kind of articles. "Can you really write now when the misfortune's so fresh?' I asked him once. And what do you think he answered me? He regarded me as an enemy and cried, 'And you, if I may ask, you, while the grief is so fresh, have you forgotten to have breakfast, lunch, and dinner? Have you refrained from ordering your coquettishly sad mourning dress that cost forty-five rubles, which I am obligated to pay for?' Just imagine! At such a moment the man reproaches me for buying a mourning dress! After all, I couldn't bury my son wearing a pink dress. . . . And it was not so much what he said, but his look, full of malice, that pushed me away from him. . . . The only thing left for me was to seek solace and caresses from Pavel Petrovich. . . . And here there occurred another story. Once my husband came into the living room, just as we were sitting next to each other on the sofa. . . . Well, perhaps we were sitting a bit closer than we should have. . . . My goodness, what a to-do! He turned deep red, then dark green, trembling, and raised his fists to Pavel Petrovich, called him a quack and some other strange words, which I had never heard. . . . 'Get out,' he said, 'immediately! Otherwise I'll call the caretaker and have you thrown down the stairs!' That's the sort of man he was! Well, tell me, could a reasonable fellow, and a progressive one, as he thought himself, behave so rudely? Pavel Petrovich, naturally, had to leave. Then he gnashed his teeth at me and almost hit me. . . . 'And you,' he says. And do you know what word he used? The most offensive word for a decent woman. . . .[19] A terrible word! Vulgar! And right

---

19. Probably "whore!"

to my face! 'And you,' he says, and then he used that word. You and he murdered my child.... Do you understand?' 'Murdered'? I sat up nights without a break with terrible pain in my heart, while he took it easy in his study, but I 'destroyed' him.... I'm his mother, and I 'destroyed' him! 'You,' he says, 'you and he, that ignoramus-quack, you weren't thinking about my son, but only about the satisfaction of your own base desire at his bedside.... What sort of mother are you? You, you're a ...' and he used that word again, 'and you're not a mother!' And now I shall lock you up and you can sit there all alone in your foul-hypocritical mourning dress, which you ordered not for your son's sake, but to please that quack!' Just imagine: 'lock me up!' Just like one of Ostrovsky's heroes.[20] Well, after this, you understand, what was left for me to do? I was consumed by indignation.... I didn't faint and didn't have hysterics; no, neither is to my taste.... I simply said plainly and definitively to him: 'After this I'm no longer your wife!' And I began to gather my belongings.... I remember how, just like now, I took a long time to collect my things. I kept hoping that he would come to his senses, fall at my feet, and say: 'Zoya, forgive me; it was an outburst! I can't live without you! Don't leave; stay....' Something of that sort.... But he didn't even think.... He said, 'Good riddance!' and locked himself up in his study and didn't emerge! Well, tell me now, what sort of love was that from this man? Why, he was a man and a smart person, experienced; he should have understood that this was just an infatuation; and he should have gently, carefully brought me to my senses, stopped me.... Then nothing of the sort would have occurred. But he said: 'Good riddance!' Well, if that's the case, there was nothing to talk about. I gathered my clothes and moved in with Pavel Petrovich! Are you bored?" she asked suddenly, turning her face toward him and pausing.

"On the contrary.... Go on, please! I'm listening with great attention!" replied Racheev.

"Hear me out until the end.... I'm in good form; we got into the spirit of things!"

---

20. Alexander Ostrovksy (1823–1886) was a leading nineteenth-century playwright.

And once again, crossing her arms on her chest, she began pacing the room.

"Pavel Petrovich took me in as a friend. I'm sincerely saying that in him I found true consolation. Yes, I'm saying this sincerely, in spite of the fact that he treated me like that afterward.... He behaved like a swine to me. We lived together well.... He didn't have abundant means, but it was enough for everything. He had a capital of about seven thousand rubles, and that was enough for a year. We lived like husband and wife. That was how he presented me in society: 'My wife.' We didn't have any children.... That is, there could have been a child, but ... I, of course, wouldn't allow it and took appropriate measures in time. What for? What would his fate be? After all, Anton Makarych wouldn't have acknowledged him.... By this time he became a scoundrel and sold himself out to *Secret Word*, which he had previously despised.... But then the seven thousand came to an end. Pavel Petrovich accepted a position and departed for the provinces leaving me empty-handed.... That's when I realized that all men are swine, and also that all people are swine. Anton Makarych knew that Pavel Petrovich had abandoned me and that I was left with nothing, but do you think he thought of asking me to rejoin him? Of course, I myself wouldn't ever broach that subject first, but he.... He's a man, it seems he could have.... I could have still become a good wife.... But, no! He abused and reviled me from all the rooftops.... What could I do? Can you believe, I worked as a copy clerk, that's what I came to. At last I decided to enroll in dental courses. Well, I completed the program, received my diploma, and opened an office..... What was the use of that? I had hardly any clients! I needed furnishings and advertisements: where would I get the money? I had already changed my apartment: I was living on Voznesensky Street and then moved to the Petersburg district, then to Kolomna, to Vasilievsky Island, and now here in Peski....[21] No one ever comes here. My practice is pitiful; I don't even have enough money for dinner; you see how honest I am being with you. I do

---

21. A list of lesser and lesser desirable neighborhoods in St. Petersburg.

have sufficient suitors. There's Matryoshkin, have you seen him? He brings me sweets, and thinks. . . . Hmm, yes. . . . Not a chance! And Mamurin, the swine, proposes outright: 'I,' he says, 'am ready to give you, Zoya Fyodorovna, one hundred and fifty rubles a month! Well? How do you like that? Yes, you told the truth then: he's a cynic, that Mamurin! But I still haven't sunk that low! To put it so frankly and simply—what a swine!"

"However, you say this and continue to receive him; you even, as I observed, prefer him to the others!" said Racheev.

"But they're all the same, all swine, and he, at least, is well-disposed toward me, and renders services. . . . But that's not the point— here's what: I have a request to make of you, Dmitry Petrovich. . . . Only you can do this."

She stopped pacing, moved closer to his armchair, and sat down. Her voice, up to now sounding shrill, became softer and quieter.

"Perhaps from your point of view this will seem strange, but in my position, I can't worry about points of view. . . ."

It seemed to Racheev that she was embarrassed and was feeling awkward about the request that she was planning to make.

"What is it, Zoya Fydorovna? I'll try to see it from your point of view!" he said.

"Well then . . . you see my situation. . . . How pitiful it is. . . . You see that I struggle against all odds to remain an honest woman, and how difficult I find it. . . . Of course, I made a false step, but I was compelled to do so. . . . And then, I was punished! While Anton Makarych earns seven thousand rubles a year and is all alone. . . . What does he need it for? You could influence him if you wanted, so that he gave me, if not half, then even two thousand a year. . . . That would be enough for me. . . ."

"You? From him? Would you take it?" Racheev almost cried out with great astonishment. "You, Zoya Fyodorovna?"

"Why not?" she replied in a tone of serene surprise, as if not understanding what could astonish him so much. "Why not? After all, he's still my husband!"

"Your husband? Zoya Fyodorovna? What sort of husband is he?"

"What do you mean? Legally. He's my legal husband!"

"Yes, but . . . everything was done so that this would lose its meaning. . . ."

"Lose it how?" Zoya Fyodorovna objected heatedly. What did you say—'lose its meaning'? This can never lose its meaning. I'm still his wife. I bear his surname, which doesn't afford me any pleasure. . . . I'm Polzikova, no matter what you say, I'm still Polzikova. . . . I can't marry anyone else. And that, I hope, is very important! Just imagine. . . . Take Mamurin, for example. He's certainly courting me. . . . Perhaps I'd force him to marry me, but I can't do that now because I'm still Polzikova. What shall I do? Shall I become his kept woman? Why, the matter is clear: if I'm married to him, then I'm his wife; but if it's impossible, then I'm his kept woman."

"Why does it have to be so? There's a third option: when decent people come together in mutual love and respect," replied Racheev.

"Ha, ha, ha, ha! Decent people! Is Mamurin a decent fellow or Matryoshkin? Ha, ha, ha, ha! You're so amusing, Dmitry Petrovich! No, what are you saying? In my opinion, Anton Makarych is obligated to provide me with proper support. He's obligated!"

"But, Zoya Fyodorovna, what can you give him? After all, one must maintain some sort of balance. . . ."

"What can I give him? Whatever he wants. Ha, ha, ha! That which every woman can provide!"

"That is, you're prepared to. . . ."

"I'm ready to take up with him, if he should desire!"

"You? After everything that's happened? After what you've said about him?"

"Ah, you know it really doesn't make any difference to me now. . . . It's really all the same! All men are alike, they're all swine! No, you know, Dmitry Petrovich, take this on! Would you really refuse my request?"

Racheev made no reply. He looked at her and thought, not about whether he would fulfill her request or whether he could succeed, but about Zoya Fyodorovna herself, who was sitting in front of him—this living embodiment of the confusion of moral concepts, complete lack of principles, and her willingness to do anything for the sake of her comfort.

Racheev stood up with the look of a man who considers the question settled.

"I can tell you one thing, Zoya Fyodorovna," he said in a somewhat stern tone of voice: "that I don't like any of this at all, but, naturally, you don't care about that one bit and you can't; as far as your request is concerned, I don't believe it can be fulfilled. . . . As far as I understand Anton Makarovich, he's dead set against you and considers himself deeply offended. But . . . I also can't consider myself a judge in this matter allowing no appeal, and therefore I shall pass on your request to Anton Makarych. . . ."

"You've agreed? You'll try to influence him?" she exclaimed with an expression of sincere joy. "Ah, I thought you wouldn't dare refuse me. . . ." She extended her hand to him. "Thank you, Dmitry Petrovich! You know, if this succeeds, I . . . I . . . I really don't know. Perhaps I could even become a proper wife!"

This hope seemed to Racheev completely unexpected and not at all proceeding from all that had transpired previously. It further confirmed to Racheev that Zoya Fyodorovna's moral principles were so mixed up that she herself couldn't ever make sense of them.

He bid her a restrained farewell and left.

XIV

Sunday morning, while Dmitry Petrovich was still in bed, there came a knock on his door.

"The door isn't locked, come in!" he cried from behind the curtain separating his bed.

"My goodness, Petersburg has spoiled you so soon!" Baklanov's voice announced. "It's ten o'clock and you're still in bed!"

"I had no reason to get up earlier!" said Racheev, hastening to get up and get dressed quickly. "In the country our entire life begins with sunrise and ends with sunset. The sun governs everything and rules our lives. Here no one pays any attention to it and everyone treats it as if it were a stearin candle."

"Well, it doesn't especially bestow its favors on us. That means: an eye for an eye! Just look at today: it's gray and wretched! However, get up, get up, Dmitry Petrovich, you have to pay a visit. . . ."

"What sort of visit? I'm not in the mood to pay any visits. . . ."

"What? That's impossible! You don't have the right! You're invited to Vysotskaya's today."

Racheev recalled that it was Sunday and, in fact, today he was supposed to be at Evgeniya Konstantinovna's. But, for some reason, at the thought of this quite short trip, he felt some sort of incomprehensible opposition in his chest.

At last Racheev emerged to meet him. Greeting him, Baklanov repeated his argument.

"But you've been invited, Dmitry Petrovich! You must agree that it's a special honor when a lady asks a man whom she barely knows: please come pay me a visit, and she names the day. . . ."

"Yes, yes, of course. . . . But I would be very happy if this honor passed me by!" said Racheev, sitting down to tea.

"I'm surprised at you, Dmitry Petrovich!" cried Baklanov, shaking his head. "You're simply beginning to be fickle. . . ."

Racheev pushed his glass of tea away and regarded his guest not without a certain astonishment.

"Well, let's suppose that I go, and I really will! But please tell me why are you pleading so insistently."

"Oh, for the most mercenary reasons!" Baklanov replied half-jokingly. "If you like, I'll tell you. For a long time I've been interested in this woman as a sociopsychological type. And I've studied her thoroughly. I still need only one thing: for her to fall in love with someone. I've seen this sea in all conditions of light—on a bright sunny day, at twilight, during a light rain, on a starry night, and in the frost, but I've never seen it in a storm, when thunder roars and lightning flashes, and the waves rise up as if they were mountain ridges. . . . I imagine what splendid beauty it must be! And for some reason I think that she will definitely fall in love with you. . . ."

Racheev burst out laughing.

"I really don't know whether to be angry with you or to laugh! That means you're preparing to use her for some sort of composition?"

"Why, of course? The central figure in a large sociopsychological novel! It's hard to conceive of anything better!"

"But you forget, that I won't fall in love with her under any circumstances!"

"That's not necessary! All I need is a hint, and the rest is a matter of my imagination. But you know what, Dmitry Petrovich, I'm willing to bet that you'll pay for this! I'm not saying that you'll definitely fall in love, but . . . so to speak, your heart will beat faster, and perhaps, you might even fall in love, so help me God, even fall in love! Well, wouldn't this suit a work by Shakespeare? Someone's borrowed my book and forgotten to return it; I must buy another copy."

"It would! Although I have a copy of Shakespeare, it seems that it's incomplete. It would, it would! Naturally, you're relying on my honesty!"

"Naturally! The fateful hour draws near; get dressed."

On the corner of Nevsky and Nikolaevsky Street they were parting, when Racheev inquired about the state of Katerina Sergeevna's nerves.

"Well, on that count I can never vouch for more than half an hour ahead!" said Baklanov. "Here, Dmitry Petrovich, come up with a treatment for this malady and you'll receive a diploma and become the savior of humanity!"

Racheev went to Vysotskaya's.

Pausing for a moment on the threshold, Racheev surveyed the room and saw that the lady of the house, sitting on the sofa, was not alone. On her left, next to the sofa, sat a tall, lean gentleman on a chair; he had a long, thin neck, and with a pale, emaciated face, very expressive; his large, dark eyes, big straight nose, and his long, full mustache without a beard or side whiskers, were his outstanding traits. His hair was thin; a small, round bald spot was clearly visible on the middle of his head, which he didn't try to hide from the world, not even trying to disguise it in any way. He was dressed all in black; all the buttons of his frock coat were tightly fastened. Another man sat farther away on a small rocking chair, almost made for children, in which he sprawled in great comfort. He was a short old man, with closely cropped, rather thick gray hair; he was thin, agile, with a clean-shaven face—lively and genial in a childlike manner. He held onto the armrests of the rocker with both hands and was rocking back and forth, clearly not in a condition to sit still.

Racheev went up to the lady of the house and extended his hand.

She said Racheev's name and then introduced him both to the tall gentleman and to the little old man. The tall fellow stood up decorously and slowly, shook hands with him reluctantly, and said not a word. His name was Aleksandr Ivanovich Muromsky, but Racheev forgot his name at once. The old man, whom Vysotskaya referred to somehow as "Your Excellency," jumped up from his place, rushed to Racheev, began shaking his hand, and said that he was very glad to meet him, although he really felt as indifferent as Muromsky. But he had this way of behaving.

"Well, sir, aren't you fed up with Petersburg yet, Dmitry Petrovich?" asked Vysotskaya,

Racheev replied that he'd no time to think about that.

"That means you must be having a good time?" she said, turning to him again, but not waiting for his answer, she began chatting at once with the old man. "So, you, Your Excellency, are advocating taking strong measures? It's surprising how little that matches your good-naturedness."

"Yes, what's to be done? It's been my conviction from time immemorial! In all other respects I'm good-natured, but as for school . . . oh, there I'm a Spartan!"

And the old man started rocking along with his chair.

"Hmm! That means you'll cast your vote for severe measures. . . . It's decided! Well, and if," she added with a coquettish smile, "and if a certain person whom you respect said to you, 'Your Excellency, do me the honor of voting for gentle measures. . . .'"

The old man burst out laughing.

"If this person turned out to be you, I'd do it without hesitation!" he said, placing his hand on his heart.

"That's real chivalry! You wouldn't do that, Aleksandr Ivanovich!" she turned to Muromsky, casting him a sideways glance.

"Me? I'd simply send in my resignation!" he said in a dry, bass voice, and smiled with a dry, wooden smile.

"Oh? Well, that's already heroism!"

Conversation in the same vein continued for about ten minutes. Racheev didn't take part in it, as an outsider, and the lady of the house didn't address him at all. He had begun to feel out of place, and was annoyed at himself for coming.

Having nothing to do, Racheev took to examining the lady of the house, who today seemed to him very little like the person he had taken her for on Friday. She was wearing a heavy gray dress. On her belt she wore a thin chain with a miniature open watch; two small diamonds sparkled in her ears, and over her shoulders was draped some sort of colorful wrap with fur trim at the collar. This wrap and her tall hairstyle gave her a look of ample solidity and some sort of coldness, and the very expression of her face today was cold and forced. At that moment Muromsky stood up and began to bid farewell, and the old man soon followed his example. They respectfully kissed the lady's hand and withdrew together.

When their steps had quieted down, all of a sudden Vysotskaya turned unexpectedly to Racheev and extended her hand to him.

"Forgive me, for heaven's sake, that I didn't entertain you, Dmitry Petrovich!" she said in a simple voice, filled with warmth, not at all like the voice she'd used with the two guests who had just left. "I knew you'd stay. The main thing is that I don't feel like entertaining you; I want to speak with you, simply to speak!"

"That's much better!" said Racheev, whose face suddenly brightened when he heard the sincere tone in Vysotskaya's voice.

"I thought so! Let's go in there! I can't stand this room; here I receive only those who plan to stay no longer than twenty minutes. . . . It's uncomfortable. Let's go into my room!"

She opened a door and Racheev found himself in a familiar room.

"I said, 'to my room,' because here I feel myself at home! Sit down, Dmitry Petrovich, feel free to smoke, and forget these two gentlemen!"

She rang the bell. The footman entered.

"Say that I'm not at home. Absolutely!" she said to him.

The footman bowed and left. She explained to Racheev:

"This is essential or else I'd have to receive some twenty people! I have too large a circle of acquaintances, Dmitry Petrovich, too large," she added in a tone of regret.

"Why do you complain about that?" asked Racheev, unconsciously occupying a place on the same sofa where he'd sat on Friday.

"I'm not complaining, but I'm repenting," she replied with a smile. "Although perhaps I really should be complaining about it. . . ."

"In my opinion, you shouldn't complain or repent," said Racheev. "I even think you could be envied. . . ."

"Me? Oh, Lord! I don't know how to escape from all of this. . . . Just think how much time I have to waste to keep up such a wide circle of acquaintances. . . . I'm so glad that I was able to form my small circle, which I receive here. It's my relaxation. Here, in the course of three or four hours, I feel completely free. I don't have to worry that the thin thread of conversation might somehow break. My guests worry about this, and I can do what I want: I listen if they're talking about something clever; I think my own thoughts if they're talking nonsense, which happens often; and I object, if I have the desire. And this merely demands sacrifice and provides nothing in return."

"Forgive me, but I don't believe that!" objected Racheev. "You're a completely free person and you wouldn't begin to offer sacrifices, if it didn't afford you pleasure."

"That's true! But that's exactly what I repent. . . ."

"It's been noted that Russians repent too often. As soon as they begin to feel the least bit of disconnect between their aspirations and reality, they begin to repent. We devote a great deal of time and energy to repentance, and the matter stays put and doesn't move forward a single step. . . ."

"And don't you ever repent?" she asked with deep interest, after listening to his words.

"Unfortunately, I've spent too much time and energy on repentance. But I did it so well, that now I don't repent any longer...."

"And instead, you take action?"

"I simply live the way I consider: comfortable, reasonable, and just. And action happens by itself.... But tell me," he added, having noticed that the conversation was beginning to concentrate on himself, "Who are these gentlemen to whom you introduced me?"

"They could hardly interest you! Let's continue our conversation, Dmitry Petrovich!" replied Vysotskaya.

"Oh, everything interests me. After all, I visit Petersburg once in seven years...."

"If you like, I'll introduce you. The old man is called Migultsev, a well-known figure in people's education...."

"Migultsev? The terror of schools and pupils? That cheerful, genial old man? I never would have thought so...."

"But this happens by chance. When he began his career this tendency was the law. If he had upheld some other one, he would not have had a career. And now, let's assume, times are different, but he has a known history. Everyone is accustomed to connecting his name with strictness in school; he can never renounce it. But you can't possibly imagine how he willingly pleads for indulgences when you ask him about this matter.... And I pile dozens of requests on him...."

"That means, he's a good man in a cruel job!"

"That's so, if you like. Well, and here's the opposite: Muromsky. He's making a career in philanthropy. But you saw how withered and stuffy he is.... I don't know what sort of philanthropy he does. ... Here's an example of a cruel person in a good job! Now you're acquainted with them.... Let's return to our conversation...."

"Here's what, Evgeniya Konstantinovna," he said in the same somewhat strident tone in which people suddenly change the conversation.

She shuddered slightly and looked at him in surprise.

"I don't like misunderstandings and innuendos, and in particular, I wouldn't want any of them with you. As far as I can judge, you're very interested in me, even though I'm probably not worth it. It seems to you that you'll encounter something new in me, something unlike what you know too well; that in my life you may find the answer to some of the questions that keep you awake at night. I won't conceal the fact that I have something to tell you, that is, I understand that my life must seem agonizing to you. And I tell you directly, that I even want to tell you how it was that I lived, how I live, what I thought and what I'm thinking. . . . But I want to know the same things about you, that is, how you lived and how you live now, what you thought and what you think now. . . . You seem to me to be unlike other women, and of course, you won't refuse telling me this tale. But tell me, if I turned to you now with this request: tell me about your life, your thoughts and feelings! What would you say in reply?"

She thought in silence, and he answered for her:

"You would say: I know you too little for this! Isn't that so?"

"In all probability, yes!" she replied, blushing noticeably.

"Well then, you see. And this is completely understandable, and I would say the same," continued Racheev, "and you, forgive me, Evgeniya Konstantinovna, you want to know my story little by little, in the meantime. . . ."

"Enough, enough, enough, Dmitry Petrovich!" she interrupted him forcefully. "You've embarrassed me, but told the truth. . . . Thank you. . . . Thanks precisely for saying it so plainly. I understand: you don't want your life and your thoughts to become simple food for a woman's curiosity. . . . That's true. First we have to get to know each other. But you know, that's happened because I've taken too active an interest in you. . . . It's my impatience, Dmitry Petrovich. Let's go and have lunch together! We'll talk about Baklanov, Zebrov, Dvoinikov, Migultsev, about the whole world, but not about each other. That's the best way to get to know each other better. Isn't that true?"

"It seems so!" replied Racheev with a smile.

Around two o'clock Racheev exited using the door onto Nikolaevskaya Street. He was disturbed, but that disturbance was pleasant, light, having nothing in common with the feeling that had oppressed him after his meeting with Polzikov, Zoya Fyodorovna, or Mamurin. He thought: "Yes, this woman must conquer everyone whom fate brings to meet her. Yes, I understand that the broad circle of her acquaintances soon turns into a broad circle of her admirers. But that's her strength! It's a vital strength that is capable of moving mountains. Could it be that she doesn't know this?"

But thinking in this manner, he saw himself standing on the side of this broad circle as an observer, who chanced upon an interesting spectacle. "No," he added in his thoughts, "Baklanov won't manage to acquire Shakespeare at my expense."

PART II

I

Natives of Petersburg love to brag about those few weeks in the beginning of autumn, when the sun shines lovingly in the clear, pale-blue sky; the days are still rather long, and the nights haven't yet begun to lengthen.

Racheev awaited the arrival of such days in Petersburg. For several days in a row he hadn't left his room, spending his time in a most joyless mood. He wasn't ill, and he wasn't longing for his family; nothing had occurred that had deeply affected him personally. During the course of his three weeks' stay in Petersburg, he hadn't once departed from his role as outside observer. No, only the weather was to blame for his mood—that light rain, which pitter-patters against his window frames with such stupid and insolent consistency, which has been tapping for the past three days, as if insistently trying to obtain something from him; this lead-gray color of the air, from which one's eyes hurt; this stubborn absence of the sun; and this entire condition of late autumn, which came on so suddenly after the magnificent sunny days.

He visited Vysotskaya three more times, but the visits were all unsuccessful. Some acquaintance or other was always hanging around—a new person for him to meet. At that time she'd assume a look of that cold cordiality, which he didn't like at all.

He hadn't been to the Baklanovs in several days. As of late a disconsolate mood prevailed there. Katerina Sergeevna hardly ever appeared, while Nikolai Alekseevich always made excuses that he was occupied. In fact, he took to writing earnestly, and was writing so much that he became pale and thin. Only Liza preserved her constantly serene appearance. Once he happened to have lunch with her alone. Nikolai Alekseevich had gone to see some publisher to conduct urgent negotiations about something very important. Racheev guessed that the negotiations concerned money. "In order to keep this apartment and to live, denying oneself nothing, one needs to have money, a great deal of it," he thought, and seeing Baklanov's gloomy agitation during the past few days, he decided that he must have needed money for some extraordinary expense. Katerina Sergeevna declared she had a headache.

"Lizaveta Alekseevna, tell me the truth," he said addressing Liza, "perhaps my presence is not altogether convenient? If so, I can leave...."

"Oh, no; that would offend Katya!" replied Lizaveta Alekseevna. "If it was someone else, then perhaps.... But she excludes you from her general rule."

"Really? Why?"

"She says you're not like all of Nikolai's other acquaintances.... You always say what you think...."

"That's not quite so! Racheev objected. "Often I keep my thoughts to myself...."

"Yes, perhaps.... But you don't ever say what you don't think! I've always been meaning to ask you, Dmitry Petrovich," she said suddenly, raising her voice a bit and blushing deeply. "I've been wanting to ask about your wife.... I knew her as a girl, and it seemed to me...."

"It seemed to you that there could be nothing in common between her and me!" he finished her thought for her. "This would probably occur to anyone else. But you see, there was something...."

"That's very interesting!"

"Of course, it wasn't exactly like what you think! You remember Sasha, my steward's daughter. She was a lovely girl. . . ."

"Very beautiful! I remember how graceful she was, with extremely regular facial features, with wonderful golden-brown curls, exuding good health. . . ."

"Well, then, you see this is the first part of the solution. I fell in love with her beauty—it seemed only natural!" Racheev said with a laugh.

"Yes, but . . . Was that one thing really enough? As I recall, she was completely uneducated, which, of course, didn't prevent her from being a splendid person!" she continued, blushing even deeper. It was apparent that she didn't raise this ticklish theme without a struggle. But Racheev heard her out and replied simply; apparently, he was not at all surprised by the fact she'd brought up the subject. . . .

"No, it didn't prevent her, that's true. . . . Besides, she was an excellent singer; she also played the guitar and danced very gracefully!" he said, laughing as before.

"You're not talking very seriously with me, Dmitry Petrovich," she said, frowning slightly. "I understand that this isn't really any of my business!"

"Oh, what nonsense!" he said in a completely affable tone of voice. "If this interests you, then it's your business. But why do you think that I'm not being serious? The ability to sing well at the right time, to play the guitar, and even, perhaps, to dance—all this is a great distinction. Our life in general isn't boring; we hardly ever feel bored because we have too many small daily cares. My wife is always healthy and cheerful! She's not well educated, of course, but she understands me and she does that splendidly because she loves me. Well, and little by little, she's catching up with me."

"So in your opinion educated men should marry simple girls?"

"Not at all. How did you come up with that? A person should marry the one he or she falls in love with. I was simply very lucky. Given my way of life, my wife suits me very well. We live a life of simple, small everyday interests. . . . But my friend Nikolai Alekseevich needs the sort of wife like Katerina Sergeevna. . . . Yes, yes, this is my sincere conviction. Katerina Sergeevna has a nervous nature of the latest type. In the course of a minute she's capable of experiencing a thousand different moods. Well, this is just what Nikolai Alekseevich really needs. In Katerina Sergeevna he can find as many heroines as he wants for his works. . . ."

As he was saying good-bye, Liza said to him:

"You must live well, Dmitry Petrovich. . . . You must be a very happy man. Many people ought to learn from you!"

"Yes, I'd like everyone to learn this. . . . In fact, I feel very sad to see that good and clever people don't know how to be happy!"

Both Liza and Racheev understood that each of them, without naming names, was referring to Nikolai Alekseevich and Katerina Sergeevna.

Racheev impatiently awaited a letter from his wife, convinced that it would set his thoughts on the correct path and dispel this "strange mood," as he thought about his melancholy. Someone knocked at the door.

Dmitry Petrovich's face expressed extreme surprise when the tall figure of Polzikov appeared on his threshold.

"It's you, Anton Makarych? I confess, I wasn't expecting you!" he said unwittingly.

He couldn't account to himself why he hadn't expected this, when it was only natural that Polzikov, his old friend, would pay him a visit.

"Hee, hee! That's too bad!" replied Polzikov with his usual tone of exaggerated irony, shaking his hand. "In our places, my friend, one should expect some sort of unpleasantness at any time. . . ."

"No, why do you say that? I'm glad to see you!" said Racheev.

"Glad? Me? Well, excuse me, but I just don't understand what's so pleasant about it! A plastered mug that spouts only nasty things. . . . I don't understand! And if I didn't know for certain that you didn't like to say things just for effect, then I wouldn't even believe you!"

He sat down and placed both his arms heavily on the table.

"And tell me, please, Dmitry, why do you do me such honor? Ah?

Really and truly I, using high style, am no more than a drenched piece of trash, an old, soiled frock coat of a department civil servant, turned inside out and given away to the department doorman. . . . Nothing more. Meanwhile, you, for example, didn't shake hands with Mamurin, while to me you said you were very glad to see me. How to explain this, ah?"

"And you've really heard about it?" asked Racheev in surprise.

"Well, of course. Our literature is like a gossipy old woman: by the next day it whatever happened becomes known, whether it's within four walls or in a married couple's bedroom, locked with a key. Naturally, it's all known. But that's not the point. So, I ask, why do me this honor? Ah?"

"And here's why, Anton Makarych, if you want to know the truth!" replied Racheev. "It seems to me that your conscience is bothering you, but Mamurin's—not at all. And that's still a valuable thing, and you must cherish it when your conscience can still bother you. From there a person can still see a piece of blue sky. . . ."

"Hmm. . . . Yes . . . Perhaps that's so!" Polzikov said pensively. "Conscience. . . . Well, Mamurin, let's suppose, never had one. . . . Ha, ha, ha! So he delivered his *profession de foi* to you. A moderate liberal! Ha, ha, ha, ha! And here, as a matter of fact—how well these words are chosen: moderate liberalism! What is liberalism? An aspiration for reasonable freedom, for the rationally free development of a nation's strengths—intellectual, moral, and material. . . . Isn't that right? After all, it seems as if it's an immeasurably splendid thing, a singular thing, toward which it's fitting to strive mightily. But they put a semicolon after it, too: strive, they say, for development, but not too much! Do you understand? You can drink vodka without restraint, but to strive for the development of a nation's strengths—only moderately. . . . Ah, hell! But don't think that I came to see you to discuss the theory of moderate liberalism. I merely mention that in passing. . . . Why not use the opportunity to curse? But I came. . . . No, I'll tell you later. Tell me, how are you? How is Petersburg affecting you?"

"Not very well. Here you see: something like melancholy has come over me."

"Aha! Well, I'll say! What a cherub—because your views of life are cherubic—and all of a sudden you've fallen into the local hustle and bustle! But tell me this, Dmitry, what did you talk about with Madame Polzikova, Kirgizova also, and so on and so forth."

"With Zoya Fyodorovna? Can it be that you already know about it? How can that be?" Racheev asked, definitely astonished.

"Ah, you cherub, cherub! You're a real cherub!" cried Polzikov, shaking his head. "I tell you that here we know everything, word for word, to the smallest detail. But this is still nothing, thank God, but that man of letters Matryoshkin in *Secret Word*, in the feuilleton, will describe all the details about you: how you're getting along with your wife, how often and under what circumstances you cheated on her, and in addition, for a finer style, he'll attach a list of all the vile deeds you've committed. . . . And so, what did you talk about with the aforementioned lady?"

"The conversation was interesting, and I've been planning to speak with you, Anton Makarych. . . ."

"With me? What's this? Some commission? A claim?" asked Polzikov, twisting his mouth into a contemptuous smile.

"I'll explain it to you immediately. I confess, it's not easy. She was nonetheless all confused."

"Everything is confused there, my friend! Well, tell me, do, I'm curious!"

"I don't plan to tell you everything she said to me. . . ."

"Well, I should think not. . . . I'm a scoundrel, a rogue, a robber; I destroyed her life; while she's an angel, oppressed innocence, and so on. I should be hanged for refusing to support her together with Mr. Doctor Kirgizov. . . . That's not even worth stating. . . ."

"Not exactly, but something like that!" Racheev continued where he left off. "But, you see, I must tell you that she's in a very bleak situation. . . ."

"In what sense?"

"Of course, in the material sense!"

"Hmm. That means her tooth extractions didn't save her! Splendid! Well, what else?"

"Furthermore—something that in my view is very strange. She considers that you're obliged to provide her with support, and even substantial support. . . ."

"Ha, ha, ha! Delightful! But I don't see anything strange about it. Similar subjects always find that someone's obliged to provide support, and of course, it should be substantial! That's in the order of things. . . . But it's curious, extremely curious. So, that means, she declared it plainly: I'm obliged to provide it? Well, and was there a reason? Just as substantial as the desired support? Ah?"

Polzikov somehow unexpectedly leaned back so that the back of the armchair emitted a crack. His face nervously came to life; his eyes began to wander. The usual sarcasm in his tone could now be heard as shriller and thicker.

"Tell me, tell me, Dmitry! It's very interesting!" he added, adjusting his glasses with an abrupt gesture.

"There was a reason: for all that, she's still Madame Polzikova; she bears your name. . . ."

"Damn it all!" Polzikov cried furiously, and jumped up from his place with rage, raised his head high, and seemed to draw himself up to his full height. "My name! Yes, she bears it and defiles it, that's for sure. Let's assume, I don't give a damn, but I'm upset that she dares say so! Furious! No, judge for yourself, Dmitry, what sort of thing is that? That woman deceived me, disgraced me, insulted me, destroyed my life, turned me into a drunkard and a scoundrel, and the main thing, the main thing—she stole my name. . . . Well, yes, she stole it, because I wouldn't have given permission for my name to enter the bedroom of that Doctor Kirgizov. . . . And she reproaches me with that, and that's not all, she demands payment for using my stolen name in a disgraceful manner. No, what's all this? What's happening here?"

Panting for breath, he lowered himself with difficulty into his previous place. His head was shaking and his eyes blinked constantly. Racheev waited a minute, giving him a chance to calm down.

"I don't know, Anton Makarych, are you in a condition to hear more?" Racheev uttered in a restrained voice.

"In a condition. . . . There is no such dirty trick that I'm not in a condition to hear!" replied Polzikov, caustically emphasizing his words.

"But it will be even worse later. . . ."

"So much the better. . . . At least it will be consistent."

"I asked her what she could offer you in return. She replied that. . . ."

"Aha! I'm curious. . . ."

"She answered: I'm ready to take up with him, if he wishes it!"

Racheev attentively and not without misgivings regarded his friend. After these words he expected some sort of unusually violent outburst, but, to his surprise, Polzikov didn't budge from his place and didn't utter even one word. Only his face   twitched several times, as if under the influence of an uninterrupted series of painful injections, and finally, it assumed a strange expression, in which pity was mixed with contempt. He sat there in silence, sunk into deep thought, his eyes no longer wandering, but staring fixedly at an indefinite point.

"What do you have to say to this, Anton Makarych?"

"He looked at Racheev absentmindedly, stood up silently, and began to pace the room. After rather prolonged thoughtful pacing, he paused and, without turning to face Racheev, asked:

"Well, then, were you commissioned to convey a reply?"

"There was no such commission, but I can do so, if you like!" replied Racheev, knowing full well that there could be no reply other than an abusive one.

Polzikov started pacing again, and after a few more turns, he stopped once more, then went to the coat rack, and took his hat and coat.

"This is what you can tell her, Dmitry. . . . This is what," he said too firmly and abruptly. "Tell her that I agree . . . I accept her proposal. . . . Yes, yes, yes! I accept it!"

"You? You accept this proposal?" cried Racheev, struck unexpectedly by these words.

Racheev looked at his face, hoping to find there some trace of a joke, because it had to be so. Or else everything here was mixed up and turned upside down, or else his views of the simple things of life departed to such an extent from the views of these people, that they couldn't understand each other at all.

But Anton Makarych's expression was very far from a joke. It was decisive and gloomy. He continued:

"Don't be astonished, there's nothing to be astonished about. . . . Here's how you should convey this message to her! Only not now, but. . . . Well, in a week's time. . . . Yes. . . . Well, yes, in one week precisely, on Tuesday of that week, I shall prepare everything and will expect her. . . . Only you come, too, please. . . . Otherwise, you know, it will be awkward to see her for the first time. . . . Do you understand? Around twelve noon. . . . Well, farewell, friend. . . ."

He quickly shook Racheev's hand and departed with the same gloomy expression.

After this scene Racheev didn't feel like staying in the cramped room. He had to go and visit a publisher and have a talk with him about sending some books to the local school.

II

It was Baklanov who had recommended Pavel Melentevich Kalymov to him. This surname was indicated on the cover of all Nikolai Alekseevich's works because Kalymov was his publisher. But, besides Baklanov, that name was also well-known to Racheev, since without fail Kalymov's many diverse publications occupied a tenth of the space in the windows of bookshops. His publishing career began some twenty years ago and grew with each passing year. In the past few years he issued book after book, and what was most noteworthy was that among these books there had been not one vacuous, useless, unnecessary book; and if one were to consider that not one line in his editions ever appeared in the world without Pavel Melentevich's personal attentive control, then in fact one could marvel at the indefatigability of this man.

The Fifth Line on Vasilievsky Island was reached not without great difficulty. In spite of the defense provided by an umbrella,

Racheev turned out to be soaked through and, before ringing the doorbell, where Kalymov's calling card was displayed, he had to stand for a few minutes under the entryway, to shake the water off himself. At last he decided to pull the bell handle. The maid opened the door.

"Is Pavel Melentevich receiving?" Racheev asked.

"This way please!" was the reply.

He entered the hall where it was dark and began to take off his wet coat and galoshes. The maid closed the door and disappeared, without paying him the least bit of attention.

"Please come in!" said a deep, but not too loud voice.

Racheev opened the door and saw a small room with two windows, all the furniture of which consisted of two glass bookcases, as wide as the whole wall, chock-full of books; a large table, also covered with books, pamphlets, proof sheets, and drawings; several chairs, and a small writing desk. At his appearance on the threshold, a tall, lean, stiff man stood up from the desk; he had closely cropped gray hair and a clean-shaven face. He was wearing a short jacket made of simple gray cloth, from which the patterns of a Ukrainian shirt showed at the collar and the cuffs. The sallow color of his face and a certain slight swelling of his cheeks in the lower part of his face confirmed the fact that Kalymov, almost never went out, was seated at his desk working.

The host stretched forward a bit, placed both palms on his desk, and asked officially in a polite tone of voice with a dry formal smile:

"How can I help you?"

"Forgive me, please, for taking up your time," said Racheev after a bow. "My name is Racheev. . . . Nikolai Alekseich sent me to see you. . . ."

"Ah, I know; he told me!" said Kalymov, and this time he smiled, as it seemed to Racheev, more sincerely. "I'm very glad you've come! Have a seat, please!" he added, extending a hand to his guest.

At this time Racheev was studying his writing desk, on which proof sheets in various formats and typefaces were arranged in exemplary order.

"Do you really read through all of this personally?" Racheev inquired.

"Absolutely! Of course, I have proofreaders; they read the rough draft, but the final word belongs to me. Not one of my publications goes to print without my signature, and I never sign off without having read the manuscript carefully. . . ."

"But how do you have the time?"

"I find time because that's all I do. It's my only job to which I've devoted my entire life. I've always held the opinion that every task can be done in an exemplary fashion if only one gives oneself over to it entirely. Besides, this is nothing new and it applies in every case with the exception of the book business. In our country the book business is run chiefly by businessmen, who understand nothing about the books they publish and who are interested only in profit. . . . Would you like some tea?" he asked, when the maid brought in two glasses and placed them on the desk.

Racheev moved one glass over to himself.

"Your publications enjoy great respect among the public," he said, wishing to draw his host into providing further explanation.

"Yes, I value this respect highly and will never allow myself to forfeit it knowingly!" replied Kalymov. "But isn't this strange? Doesn't it seem strange to you? All it has to say on the cover is 'Published by Kalymov,' and the public willingly buys it. . . . But what is this Kalymov? What sort of name is it? No one's ever heard of this name in literature, in science, or in art. . . . It's the name of a publisher, specifically a publisher. And why do people respect it? Only because I work conscientiously, with knowledge of the business and with love for it. Only because of this. We have publishing houses that have existed for some fifty years and have issued masses of books. Whole shops are filled with their books and they publish everything: literature, science, and children's books, and scabrous books—whatever you want. They spend huge sums; their book covers cost more than the books themselves, but they're lacking in one thing: soul, because no one there loves his job, and everyone who works there is interested in only one thing—that there be a profit. Well, and I—excuse me, would never provide my readers with a scabrous book. Why do it? We already have enough of those depraved books as it is. I want not only to market books, but to increase the desire for books, to multiply the number of readers. And thank God, our business is clearly thriving. Not too long ago I published a serious book, scientific, but written in an accessible style, and I published some ten thousand copies of it and am absolutely convinced that it will soon be sold out; but ten years ago I wouldn't have dared to publish even two thousand copies of it.... Yes, our business is expanding! The business of healthy, reasonable, useful, decent books."

He uttered those last words with genuine enthusiasm: his large eyes, surrounded by wrinkles, came to life and sparkled. Only a man who loves his work and gives his whole soul over to it could speak like that.

"Nikolai Alekseevich told me," Kalymov continued after some silence, "that you wished to acquire a constant correspondent on the subject of books for your school...."

"Yes, I would like it if the person were not just a publisher, but a man who understood things, and that's why I've turned to you," replied Racheev. "An ordinary publisher will send me, without any sense, everything that comes off his printing press. All he worries about is his sales."

"Do you need children's books?"

"Yes, especially intended for the masses of simple folk. This has to be strictly adhered to. They've sent us some children's books. Well, you open one of them and read a story about how *papa* and *mama*,[1] going off to the opera, left the children with their governess, and how the children were mischievous and didn't obey her, and how as a result of this a lamp fell down onto the rug and the whole house would have burned down had their horse-guardsman cousin Serge not arrived at that very moment and by his prudent intervention prevented a misfortune. Well, tell me, what will peasant children understand from all this? *Papa, mama,* opera, governess,

1. These words are in French.

horse-guardsman, and cousin—all these are empty words for them, and the moral that emerges doesn't apply to them at all.... I chose, perhaps, too glaring an example. There are other kinds of books where the moral permeates everything, from beginning to end, even the print itself, in such a way that it conveys a moral. I don't know about urban children, but rural children can't stand morals and don't learn anything from these books...."

"Have you studied this matter closely?" asked Kalymov, with particular curiosity, as it seemed to Racheev.

"Oh, yes! I direct a school myself. Our teacher is a practical person and we try to run the school as intelligently as possible. We think that the main point isn't to maintain some sort of strict program or system, but instead to meet the lively inquiry of the children's minds."

"Precisely!" cried Kalymov with joy: "You ... excuse me, Dmitry Petrovich, is it? You, Dmitry Petrovich, are a genuine treasure for me! Really! You know, it's as if fate intentionally, after long years of work, were sending me just such a man as I need! You're surprised, of course, and you don't understand what I'm talking about. I should explain to you a thing or two about my intentions...."

Racheev really didn't understand how he could make Kalymov so happy, and began listening to his words with spirited curiosity.

"You see," began Kalymov, leaning back against his hard oak chair, "you must know that when I began this business, I had only the vaguest understanding of it. I was much younger, even though I was no longer a young man—I was thirty-five at the time. Up until then I had been working in an office, but I was a bad civil servant. I was hindered by one weakness—the literary urge. I was constantly tempted by writing; I wanted to create something and definitely publish it. I tested myself in all genres. I wrote verse, prose tales, tragedies, and comedies, and I even tried to write a philosophical treatise.... But nothing came of it. I was very strict with myself, and as rarely happens, I was very fair. I evaluated my own works and in good conscience found them lacking. But I didn't stop; it was the urge, you understand, the literary urge. It happened that I received an extremely handsome inheritance. Naturally, I immediately ceased working, which for some time had been a burden to me, and I began to rush around like a madman. All of my intentions, without doubt, focused on literature; I kept wanting to undertake something—a journal, an anthology, or some kind of almanac. And it goes without saying, to have the chance to publish something. . . . The urge, you see, hadn't yet passed. I don't know how it happened, but fate brought me together with a very respected writer-translator—at that time he just happened to be finishing a translation into Russian of a very solid treatise on natural science. This subject was fashionable at the time. He turned to me to publish his work. He said that I had money and he had this treatise and that we should get together. Well, so, it was a good match, why shouldn't I take it on? I did so. But as soon as I began work, I felt immediately that it interested me very much, that it was a vital matter, and not at all boring as it might seem from outside. The more deeply I got into the work, the more I became committed to it; the book became close to me, dear to me, just as if it were my own work. I felt as if it would provide satisfaction of my constant need to scribble in vain attempts to create something easy to read. My literary urge vanished as if it had never existed. In a word, I had found my calling; I became a 'born publisher,' as a certain man of letters and a good friend loved to call me. The book, needless to say, sold sluggishly because it was issued without any regard for the demands of the market. It turned out that a similar book by another author was already on sale. . . . In a word, I suffered a loss, but that didn't stop me. I had found an enterprise that attracted me, so why worry about losses? I began to publish book after book. I proceeded blindly, without any definite program, without specialized knowledge or any understanding of publishing and. . . . Well, it's sufficient to say that in the course of six years I squandered three-fourths of my substantial wealth. . . . Forgive me for telling you all this. But it's necessary for you to understand what follows. . . ."

"On the contrary, on the contrary!" Racheev objected energetically. "This is all very, very instructive!"

"Yes, but on the other hand, I had acquired experience!" continued Kalymov. "Or, better to say, I learned how to conduct my business expediently. During the course of the fifteen years that I've been working, beyond those first six, I was already standing on firm ground. Now, of course, I've achieved excellence in my business. I know such fine points that would seem unbelievable to you. I've thoroughly studied my public; I know its demands, tastes, even its whims; I know what book to offer it at any given moment, or, better to say, to foist upon it. Yes, it's necessary to foist it because the taste in serious books is still not well developed among us. . . . I know what kind of book a certain class of readers will purchase, and accordingly, I publish fewer or more copies and set the price higher or lower. . . . Would you believe that a certain book won't sell if it's priced too low. . . . And another one must be sold at a loss, cheaper than it costs to print. . . . Oh, the emergence of each book into the world is accompanied by thousands of the smallest factors. The paper, the type, the format, the color of the cover, all play their role and I get involved in all these details. Books are my children: I take care of them as if they were children; I want them to go out into the world well brought up. . . ."

He stopped once more, ordered more tea, and then continued:

"Now you see how I became a publisher whose name enjoys a certain respect in the market. You see that the reason for this respect resides solely in my love for the enterprise. That same love did not permit any other relationship to the enterprise but a conscientious one, and it compelled me to devote myself to it with my entire soul. For example—my wealth. I treat the business in such a way that I have no capital of my own. That's the wealth of my books, my publications. Each book published and sold nourishes the next book, one or two, or one and a half, depending on the price, the success, and other factors. As a result the quantity of my publications grows so quickly. I have no right to leave my capital without movement: as soon as I notice that it's increasing, I rapidly strive to invest it in flesh and blood, that is, to turn it into a book. I myself am merely the steward of my publications; I receive a salary from them, exactly the amount I need for a relatively modest life."

"However," he added, after a little thought, "this isn't the point. I'm telling you all this not to brag, but for the sake of the following, although I think that it isn't a sin to brag. . . . So, you see what the point is. You started talking about books for the masses. I confess, I've dreamed about this for a long time, but. . . ."

"Dreamed about it?" said Dmitry Petrovich. "I've seen your publications for the masses!"

"Yes, there are some. Nevertheless, I'm still only dreaming. What I've published has been done at random, and in all likelihood, with large gaps. You see, in the past twenty years, I've come up with the profound conviction that before publishing a book, you have to know the public for which you're publishing it very well. But I don't know the rural public at all and that's always frightened me and given me pause. After all, that public is not at all like the urban one; its demands, tastes, and questions are entirely different; a book, like a bomb, mustn't be fired into thin air; it must hit its target. Yes, that's a large deficiency in my publications, a large deficiency. I've produced hardly anything for the peasant reader; meanwhile, the demand for books is rising there and one must take advantage of that in order to satisfy this demand, by selling one book, make the reader imperceptibly want to buy two others, and so on and so forth. You can't imagine how I thirst for this activity and how I fear my own inexperience. Yes, inexperience, in spite of my twenty years. I'm not familiar with the countryside and its mills. That's why I've said that you're a real treasure for me. You will help me in this enterprise. I won't ask for advice or ideas from you. No, that won't lead to anything. I'll keep to my system here, too, a system of errors. I'll publish books as I see it, and send them to you; you'll carefully watch there to see how they fit and, if necessary, you'll reject them mercilessly and write to me in detail—what and how. By such means I'll gradually learn all the details, and the time will come when I won't make any more mistakes. Can I count on your assistance?"

"Do you know what?" Racheev replied with warmth and suddenly extended his hand to him, which Kalymov shook firmly. "You'll forgive me, it's the first time we've spoken. But I simply admire you!"

It's my dream that every job should be done with love. I think that then everything will run smoothly, and we'll really move forward. No, it's not talent, not inspiration that instills soul into the enterprise, but love, and love alone; it's even capable of giving birth to talent. We have many talents, but the enterprise doesn't advance, because our talents don't love the enterprise; they love only themselves. I'm entirely at your service, Pavel Melentich."

"I hope that we'll see each other and chat more often before your departure for the country!" said Kalymov.

"Oh, I'll pester you to death! You've reconciled me with Petersburg!" cried Racheev. "Up until now I've encountered only negative phenomena here, which have distressed me and even occasioned my melancholy. But this conversation with you, you can't possibly imagine, how it's raised my spirit. . . ."

Racheev said good-bye and left.

Night was falling. The electric streetlights were already lit on Nevsky, and lights were on in the shops. In spite of the continuing rain and the damp, saturated air, Nevsky had its usual appearance— cheerful, colorful, with a crowd of idlers, at every step overtaken by professional people.

After arriving home, Racheev found two letters on his table. One was delivered by a messenger and turned out to be from Polzikov. Anton Makarych wrote:

"I understand that my decision might have seemed like a wicked joke to you. But I've thought about it a lot and haven't altered it at all. I beg you to do as I asked. Convey that I have agreed and will await her on Tuesday of next week at twelve noon. Yours, A. Polzikov."

The other letter said:

"Why have you, Dmitry Petrovich, forgotten Nikolaevskaya Street? That's not nice. You still remain an enigma to me. I'm very curious. Besides, that's not it. It will simply be pleasant to see you more often. Are you well? E. Vysotskaya."

Dmitry Petrovich read over this second letter twice; after slowly folding it into quarters, he placed it into the side pocket of his jacket. He thought with a smile: "I'll show all the letters I receive from women to Sasha; I must save them." And he decided to pay a visit to Vysotskaya's that very evening.

III

"Have a seat, Dmitry Petrovich; no one else will be here today; I can lay my head on the line to vouch for that! You're very kind to come. But it's clear that my musicians inspired your considerable melancholy, causing you to avoid me for several days!"

Evgeniya Konstantinovna was saying this in a polite, friendly tone of voice, and as she was speaking, her somewhat pale face lit up with a nice, open smile.

"No, it wasn't the musicians. . . . Your musicians, Evgeniya Konstantinovna, may be the most peaceful people in Petersburg!" replied Racheev. "No, I'm simply experiencing the feeling that occurs when you have yourself vaccinated against some disease, like smallpox, for example. . . . The disease takes hold, the organism protests, and the person feels that he's become a battlefield. . . . A feeling of passivity, I don't know how to explain it to you. . . . I'm having no luck in terms of impressions. All of them are joyless and upsetting. Here's one for you: not more than five hours ago I saw and heard something striking. Imagine: Polzikov's wife, Zoya Fyodorovna, has proposed to rejoin Anton Makarovich. . . ."

"What? Can that be? However, I don't know her at all; I merely know their history. . . ."

"Yes, but God help her! But he, Anton Makarovich, has agreed. . . ."

"But that can't possibly be so! It can't be!" Vysotskaya declared definitively. I know him well; I know that he never forgives anything!"

"But it is so. He authorized me to convey that message to her!"

"No, no, there's something wrong here. . . . You'll see that this will lead to something unexpected. . . . However, God help them! God help them! All the more so, since this so upsets you. . . . I want you to have a rest here. . . . Ah, I want everyone who feels distressed to rest here. . . . And clearly you feel very distressed. . . ."

"Yes, indeed! For pity's sake! Why, all these people once comprised a whole, with one soul, one aim, with similar aspirations, and I was one of them. . . . And now see how they've all gone in their different ways and in various directions! Polzikov, Mamurin, Baklanov, Zoya Fyodorovna. . . . Are they really the same people? No, they're completely different, totally, totally different. . . ."

Racheev was saying this with sincere sadness and he saw on his hostess's face empathy that was just as genuine.

Racheev looked into her bright eyes, this time open, childlike eyes, and for some reason felt like complaining to her about all these offenses. Those eyes knew how to inspire trust. He said:

"It's awful to think that no one can vouch for himself! Why, if someone escapes, it's only thanks to happenstance. Take me, for instance, I'm capable of being filled with genuine indignation at all this, but it's only happenstance! I didn't remain in Petersburg, and they did. If I had stayed here, I might have turned into some sort of monster. . . . Why, if a skinflint like Anton Makarych could succumb, then no one can vouch for himself. . . ."

"Why did you leave Petersburg?" she asked softly and blushed slightly.

"Why did I leave?" repeated Dmitry Petrovich, addressing this question more to himself. "Several weeks ago I wouldn't have been able to answer this question correctly, but now—I know why I left. Then I did so out of a feeling of self-preservation, which, apart from my own will and consciousness, drove me away. And my feeling wasn't mistaken; it seized the right moment when I could still amount to something. Had this happened a year later, perhaps nothing would have come of it. But now I can say frankly that I have indeed amounted to something. You wanted to know, Evgeniya Konstantinovna, what that consists of, that is, speaking in simpler terms, what I amount to, what it is that I'm doing, what affords me the possibility to feel right before my conscience. To this question, I've already replied: I live simply, without philosophizing cleverly; I live what I consider to be a proper and an honest life. You see, it's my profound conviction that every man who possesses any moral sense cannot live on earth peacefully only because he's provided for, healthy, well-fed, well-clothed, clever, and educated, if he sees that around him there are people who don't enjoy any of this. I can affirm that people who enjoy all the blessings of life, who allow scenes of hunger, cold, and ignorance to pass calmly in front of their eyes—are lacking in moral feeling; they are monsters, morally diseased. I wish to explain to you, Evgeniya Konstantinovna, the theory of my life, so to speak, so that afterward my life will be more comprehensible to you. It's a little boring, but what's to be done?"

She nodded to him with a weak smile, as if asking him to continue, and indicating that she didn't find it boring. He went on:

"And so, the striving to do something useful for one's neighbor is the normal characteristic of a healthy soul. But there are people who devote themselves passionately to this task, bringing to it all their resources and strengths, and who, for its sake, renounce personal happiness and all earthly blessings. These are the zealots. It's appropriate to step aside and cede the path to them, but it's not obligatory for anyone to follow them. I'm an average man, Evgeniya Konstantinovna. It's good fortune that I realized this in time and realized it conscientiously and sincerely. There was a moment in my life, when I nearly perished merely because I hadn't realized this. We have a great many people who perish in such a manner. During certain years (I'm talking about youth), we're pressured by the need to perform some feat, some great deed, a great sacrifice that would benefit the entire world. At that time we're still too inexperienced, and we don't know that—'one's blood is boiling and there's an excess of strength,' and that's all;[2] after our entrance into practical life, the boiling blood, thanks to various cooling influences, gradually sinks to a moderate temperature; the excess of strengths, by practical life, is simply and unnoticeably divided up among various inevitable trifles. I said to myself: no, I'm not capable of a heroic feat; I'll live according to my conscience, and that's also good. And when I definitely said this to myself, all of my despair, stemming from my fruitless searching for a path, passed and complete harmony was

---

2. A quotation from a lyric by M. Yu. Lermontov titled "Don't Believe Yourself" (1839).

established in my soul. My life is very simple, Evgeniya Konstanti-novna! There's nothing noble in it, nothing majestic. If you won't be bored by the details, I'll tell you that I live in a stone house that has eight rooms. There are three of us: myself, my wife, and a child; of course, we could fit very well into three rooms and some moralist might insist on that. But we live in eight, and that's our weakness. The furnishings aren't God knows what, but they're also not austere. I spent some two and a half thousand rubles. Once again, a moralist would be horrified, because one could purchase all the necessary items for three hundred rubles. What's to be done? It's a weakness. The habits of one's upbringing. I can't stand seeing a shabby sofa in the market and no matter how long it would stand in my room, I won't sit on it, and it would inconspicuously, but constantly irritate me. Why should I make a problem out of this? I'm listing all my sins for you, but, it goes without saying, I also have some virtues. But my virtues are just as ordinary and simple as my sins. During a time of restless impulses, I imagined how I would make the entire Russian people happy, if not the whole world. But once I had acquired a practical base, I modestly limited the area of my activities to the small neighborhood where my estate is located. The little village bordering on my estate is called Racheevka. Previously it belonged to the Racheevs, but now, naturally, it belongs to no one. Never-theless it retains this name and doesn't object to it at all. This fact alone makes the person who bears the name Racheev responsible for certain things. And if you are going to ask me now about my program or my system, I won't be able to give you any answer. I don't have any kind of program. I'm trying to get to the bottom of all the details of life in my small region, and try to relieve and improve its existence. . . . If it doesn't have enough grain, I help as best I can, given my means; if it's lacking in intelligence, knowledge, I provide it with advice; health—I help it to get better; it's used to regarding me as a good man, who will help it in all regards in case of need, and therefore it comes straight to me with an open heart. I myself lead a rather simple life; this gives me the chance to make some good savings, which in one way or another go to improve the life of the inhabitants of Racheevka. All these cares take up so much time that I never sit at home without something to do; consequently, I'm never bored. And so, you see, Evgeniya Konstantinovna, that I'm by no means a hero; on the contrary, I'm a person who appreciates all human weaknesses. I love myself, I love my wife and child, I love life and comfort, and I don't deny myself anything. But I have a healthy nature that demands harmony in all things. This harmony wouldn't exist if I lived exclusively for my own pleasure. This is the source of all of my activity, which I can summarize like this: I do good without any effort and constantly experience spiritual balance."

He fell silent and looked her in the eyes, which, it seemed, were waiting for more. But then she sighed softly and said:

"I envy you, Dmitry Petrovich!"

"You? I don't understand! You mustn't envy me!" he objected.

"No, I do!" she repeated insistently. "Why do you say I mustn't? Do you consider me happy just because I'm rich, fuss about my clothes, and receive hundreds of people? You can't assume that I'm happy thanks to all *this* and that *this* affords me spiritual balance! However . . . you don't know me. . . . And I can't demand from you that you think of me correctly; I owe you that. . . . I owe you my own story. . . . I think that only the beginning will be difficult, and then it will get easier . . ." she added, blushing slightly.

"Yes, like an examination. By the way, you look like a board-ing-school girl today!" observed Racheev with a laugh, examining her dress. "And a lesson will be very suitable for you!"

IV

She smiled.

"Well, fine! First of all—a preface, Dmitry Petrovich," she began not with that same self-assured, somewhat weary voice with which she usually spoke. "We certainly know how to talk all sorts of non-sense. Then our speech flows smoothly, without hesitation; we're even inventive and witty, at least that's what other people tell us. But when it comes to saying something important, our eloquence deserts us; we stumble and have to search for words. So don't be too strict with my style. . . . That's the first thing; and here's the second. My life has turned out this way, and not differently, who knows why, as if by its own volition. So I will tell you without any theory. The first thing that you will hear is the most striking. I am a Russian, that is, my father was a Russian landowner and of Russian nationality, from Penza. . . . And my mother was, too. I'm now thirty-two years old, yet it was only four years ago that I saw Russia for the first time. . . . Doesn't that surprise you, Dmitry Petrovich? That means I lived as a foreigner for twenty-eight years, only not knowing what nationality I was . . . international, or what? I can't explain very well why this happened. My father was a marvelous man—a good-natured fellow, very well educated, clever, and he loved me a great deal. My mother suffered from a nervous disorder and was sometimes unjust, but that was understandable; in general, however, she was a splendid woman. . . . But I lost her very early, when I was only nine years old. My father never told me why we didn't live in Russia; since we were living well, that question didn't interest me. In our house people spoke all possible languages, because the servants were of various nationalities. I even heard Greek being spoken: for a time our cook was Greek; but no one spoke Russian, and I never heard that language spoken. We would spend our winters in Paris or in Rome; summers we would retreat somewhere into the mountains, in Switzerland or in the Tyrol; twice we traveled to the north—to Sweden. Just think how close I was to Russia! When my mother died, my father invited his cousin from Russia, Marya Antipovna, with whom we had tea. . . . She had already been widowed and had no children; and she loved my father very much. How surprised she was when she came to see us in Rome! She began speaking in Russian with me, and I didn't understand a word! I remember that she confronted my father: that's a crime! No one dares do that! What if she grew up and wanted to love her motherland, then what? My father dismissed her concern. But Marya Antipovna also disregarded him and took me in hand. She spoke Russian scrupulously with me and only Russian, and therefore it's thanks to her that I know my native language.

Thanks to her I learned about many other things. Marya Antipovna was a woman with little education, but she was a marvelous person. She used to say to me: 'Do you know why, my dear girl, your father doesn't live at home and took you away from Russia? It's because he has a hard heart and because he's an egotist.' I gawked at her and asked, 'My father is an egotist?' This good-natured fellow, who's willing to give away everything in his wallet to the first pauper he meets? 'Oh, my dear, such good-natured fellows carry no more than two francs in their wallet at any time; besides, it's not their kindness, but their vanity. . . . Besides, I'm not saying that your father isn't a kind man, but he's an egotist, an egotist. . . .' 'You see,' she would explain to me later, 'you live here and see only free people. There are rich people and poor people, but each one is master of his fate. Your father's servants, if they're dissatisfied with something, can leave at any time. . . . But in Russia it wasn't like that. There land-owners owned servants and treated them like livestock. I'm not talking about your father: he was never cruel. . . . But others, ah, if only you knew what transpired, how they tormented those poor people! But our good sovereign thought about these unfortunate people and ordered them to be set free. Just think what a fine act that was! But your father, like many other people, didn't understand this and didn't want to understand. He was offended or . . . I don't know how he explained it to himself. . . . He picked up and left Russia. 'I don't wish to live under such circumstances,' he said. . . . Pride, do you see, what pride! Here he uses polite forms of address and says 'Monsieur' to some Greek who's his cook, but there it was no longer allowed to strike the peasant Pakhom across the face; and he found that offensive. . . . No, he wasn't right, your father, not right at all! You see, Dmitry Petrovich, what sort of woman my cousin Marya Antipovna was! She was the first to impart some understanding of my motherland. . . . It's surprising how circumstances could change for the Russians, and perhaps still can! There are many foreigners in Russia, more than there are Russians living abroad. But all of them live here only to acquire wealth; as soon as they acquire some, they leave for home right away. Have you seen an Englishman, a Frenchman, an Italian, or a German who would come to Russia to spend money? But my father, and not only he, left his homeland to spend his available means abroad. Many Russians do the same thing, but no one else on earth. Yes, so Marya Antipovna taught me to know my homeland and to consider myself a Russian.... She succeeded so well in this task that I promised myself and her that I wouldn't marry anyone but a Russian. Well, that's exactly what happened. My husband lived constantly in Rome, but not for the same reasons as my father. He was forbidden to live in Petersburg because he had weak lungs. But he loved Russia passionately and longed for it. He was a fine, positive person. He was nervous, responsive, always kind, easily carried away, capable of all good things, but ... and in spite of all this—he was good for nothing! It's strange, but that was the case. Previously there were many people like him, and he was one of them: I became his wife when he was forty years old and I was only twenty-two.... He had indefinite aspirations—simply for the good, as every kind man has, and an inborn hostility to evil.... But he lacked character and convictions. It must have been because he was, in essence, a very sick man. He loved everything tender, elegant, beautiful, and noble; he himself embodied all of those qualities. He was a man whom it was impossible not to love, but from whom it was absurd to expect some definite, significant action. I admired him for four years as an infinitely sympathetic being, but then I grew bored, simply bored, because our life was completely vacuous. Those last years were over-shadowed by my husband's illness. He caught a cold and his sickly chest could not withstand it. He suffered for eighteen months, and I suffered next to him. We traveled to the south, spent five months in Cairo, but that didn't help: he died in Rome in terrible agonies. Then something strange occurred. Although I had never seen Russia, I suddenly felt a passionate desire to do so. It was such a tormenting feeling that after my husband's death, I could stay on in Rome only three weeks to arrange matters; then I hurried here, literally rushed. And what an astonishing thing! Here, in a completely alien city, with strange customs, with a climate that should have seemed disgusting, I felt as if I'd come home. What does that mean? How do you explain it? It means that a homeland is the sort of thing with which sooner or later you have to settle your accounts. . . . Let's posit that I now had contacts here and that in a month I had established a wide circle of acquaintances. You know, it's as if I wound up in a different world or on another planet. It's astonishing! A whole year I'd spent in some sort of intoxication and only in the summer, when the noise abated and I was living in a dacha almost alone, I began to think; all of a sudden I posed a question to myself: what have I learned from them about Russia? And what is Russian about them? Nothing! Meanwhile, I felt exactly like learning something about Russia, just as someone living in remote absence wants to find out more about his relatives. The first person from whom I heard serious words was Zebrov. He surprised me, having informed me that in Russia there was a very rich literature! From this you can conclude what sort of upbringing I had. You can imagine how I hastened to read this literature! Zebrov organized a special circle of acquaintances for me, which is my consolation. Now—the most important thing, Dmitry Petrovich. I don't know from where this came. Was it the books that had such influence, or was it my conscience that started speaking, but the fact is it's been three years since I've been experiencing an uneasy spiritual condition. I feel that my life has been spent futilely and I feel like doing something for those in greatest need. I want to be useful to my homeland, which I've only recently come to know. . . . Don't think that these are only words. . . . No, not only words; this is how I feel! I know what you'll say in response to this. Here's what: how can you, you, who have wealth consisting of half a million, not know how to make yourself useful? Give your wealth away to those in need. In a word, it's the Gospel's reply to the rich man. . . ."

Racheev shook his head no.

"I won't ever say that, because that wouldn't be an answer!" he said. "If I understand you, you want to be useful—yourself, your personality, and only that can satisfy you!"

"Yes, yes, yes!" she affirmed passionately. "Precisely with my personality! But that's also not all. I can't give away my wealth, because I can't live in any other way than this! Of course, it's a weakness, but.

... But I'm not ascribing heroism to myself. My entire life has accustomed me to ample surroundings. Take this: I have a huge apartment, offensively huge, I occupy a whole floor all alone. I recognize that the society surrounding me is vacuous and insignificant, but it's necessary for me, because it fulfills my bad, old-fashioned habits. People tell me thousands of trifles; I recognize that it's all trifles, and I listen to them with enjoyment; hundreds of petty people pay court to me and cringe before me; I know they're petty, and yet it still gives me pleasure. I'd spend the saddest evening of my life if in the course of a day no one had paid me even one compliment. . . . But what's to be done, Dmitry Petrovich, with such a person as I am? I can't refrain from my weaknesses, I can't. . . . I can't live one day without them. . . . And at the same time I feel such a tormenting desire to bring some sort of use to those who need it most, those whom you serve! I know that I should renounce everything, go to my country estate, and live there the way you do in yours. . . . But I wouldn't endure that life; I'd perish from melancholy and wouldn't do anything. . . . The one thing that still consoles me is a small matter that I sometimes spend time on—it's books for the people. I've already published five books, but I hope in the future to broaden this enterprise. . . ."

Racheev stood up and began to pace the rug past her with slow, serene, small steps.

"I'll tell you the truth, Evgeniya Konstantinovna!" he said, without stopping, "when I was here the first time and learned about your book publishing, I thought, 'What a shame! It would be better if she didn't publish any books.'"

"That's what you thought? Why on earth? Don't you consider it a useful occupation?"

"No, I don't" he replied as before.

Without any words, with her glance alone, she expressed her extreme astonishment.

"Have you heard of the book publisher Kalymov, Pavel Melentich Kalymov?" asked Racheev.

"Yes, of course I've heard of him and I've even been promised that I would meet him!" she replied.

"Today I visited him. For the past twenty years he's been publishing books, devoting all his efforts and all his means to it. He's learned the business to the last detail and he knows his public as well as you and I know our acquaintances. But up until now he's published books almost exclusively for the so-called educated public. Now he wishes to publish books for the people. And what do you think? This respected man, having wasted half of his life on book publishing, trembles before this new enterprise like a little boy. . . . He's afraid that not knowing this public, that is, the people, the countryside, its tastes and needs, he'd provide the wrong sort of book, unnecessary books, and he's searching for people who could help him, teach him. . . . He respects this public as much as he respects any other. . . . And you, Evgeniya Konstantinovna, having no idea whatsoever about book publishing, and all the more, no knowledge of country people, lightheartedly publish books for this public: here, you say, go on and read it, what the masters are giving you! And that's the way everything is done for the masses!"

He sat down opposite her and became thoughtful, lowering his head; she regarded him with an attentive glance, but seemed distressed. At last he lifted his head and began speaking again:

"Yes, that's how things are done in our country! Up to now in Russia the people are no more than a target for noble impulses of well-intentioned people. A man lives for his own enjoyment, but his conscience is beginning to speak. In fact, the people are ignorant, uninformed, poor, and helpless! It's a shame for a good man not to do something for them. So a good man builds a hospital, without knowing if really that's what's most needed in that place; or he establishes a school, without any idea about what sort of school is needed by the people; or he publishes books, without inquiring in the countryside if anyone will read them. No, it's not good and I was pained to learn that you, with your sensitive soul, haven't escaped this fate. . . ."

"So, it's also not good!" said Evgeniya Konstantinovna, as if thinking to herself.

"No, it's not good, because it's derived from the error that the people will accept anything, will say thank you, just as if you were to give a pauper anything—a kopeck, a rusk, or an old boot. . . . But the people are not beggars. They're poor, but they're not beggars. They have their dignity, their character, and their worldview to which one must adapt."

"Does that mean that people like me should reject the idea of bringing some good to the people? What a sad truth!" she said with sadness. "Well, you see. And you envied me."

"I still envy you, Evgeniya Konstantinovna!"

"Listen, Dmitry Petrovich, that's like a wicked joke!" she said with a bitter smile.

"Never on earth! Never!" Racheev passionately objected to her suggestion. "Why it's the same story as book publishing. To do something for the people definitely means to thrust a roll into its hands. Ah, it's time, finally, to be done with this delusion! There is no area on earth where it's impossible to do some good for the people. You regard the matter as if everything in Rus was splendid,[3] except for one thing—the people are ignorant, they must be raised up, and then we will have an earthly paradise. What a blunder! Well, those who fill your drawing room, those who dance at high society balls, who attend races and ballets constantly, who waste their nights in endless drinking bouts, etc., etc.—aren't they just as ignorant and uneducated? Are they really less in need of enlightenment than the people, that is, the masses of people? Isn't it as difficult, or even more difficult to compel them to read a good, clever, decent book, as it is for the dumb peasant? If all this weren't so, then what would we have to wish for? It's true that it's still not clear which task is more necessary or urgent—to enlighten the peasants or the upper class, the so-called intelligentsia, which also needs enlightenment, just as the ignorant masses do. . . . After all, it's not the peasant who holds in his hands the springs controlling the world, but they do. . . . The more enlightened the upper classes, the better it is for the people—that's as clear as day! And there's no need for everyone who desires to do good for the people, to rush out into the countryside, which they do

3. Rus is the old name for Russia.

not know, where they don't know how to live, and where, even with all sincerity, will only be ridiculous.

Work can be found everywhere; enlightenment is needed in every corner. If you're a merchant and if a sacred spark is burning in your chest—then enlighten the merchants; you know them; you know how to approach them; here you're a master of your business; if you're a civil servant—then bring light to the ranks of civil servants; if you're an aristocrat—then enlighten people like you, because such ignorance reigns there just as it does below them. The crux of the matter is to increase the number of truly enlightened and genuinely honorable people. The more of them there are—in whatever spheres—the better it will be for the people. And you, Evgeniya Konstantinovna, possess all the means so that your life will not be spent in vain. You could triple or increase tenfold your broad circle of acquaintances. You have intelligence, beauty, wealth—all of these things are great helpers! Let them court you, let them grovel to you, splendid! But you do your business; you influence them, enlighten them, unnoticeably, by degrees, you will force them to become better: demand this from them! Oh, if I were a woman, and a beauty, and in such circumstances as you, I would make of my beauty a tool of propaganda! How much of this divine gift is wasted without a trace! That's why I envy you, Evgeniya Konstantinovna! Don't you agree with me?"

She raised her head, as if waking from a trance.

"No, that's not it, not it. . . . I don't agree, but . . . all this is so new for me . . . and never occurred to me before!" she said in an agitated voice, and as she said this her eyes seemed very animated.

"Well, so what?" he asked, following the expression of her face.

"And I'm so taken with these ideas. . . . You can see this yourself. . . . They seem like a revelation to me. . . . You know. . . . Yes, yes, that could fulfill my life! But one would need great intelligence . . . a very great deal of it. . . ."

"You have it! You're made for this role, Evgeniya Konstantinovna!"

She was silent, her head lowered, but it was apparent from her face that she was excited. He stood up and paced the rug several times.

"You see how we've come to an understanding today!" he said.

"When are you leaving, Dmitry Petrovich?" she asked, as if not hearing his last remark.

"Sooner than I thought! I long for home!" he replied.

"But we'll see each other more than once. . . . And then you'll . . . write to me? Won't you?"

"Yes, it would be very pleasant to receive your letters. . . ."

He began to say good-bye.

You've filled my head with a million ideas! I won't sleep all night!" she said, shaking his hand.

"Never mind. That's sometimes very useful!"

When he came out onto the street, it was almost half past one in the morning.

V

Dmitry Petrovich found it more convenient to inform Zoya Fyodorovna in writing. He wrote to her that he had conveyed her request to Anton Makarovich, and that on his side he agreed that she should move in with him; he reminded her that he would expect to see her on Tuesday. His letter was short and dry. It laid out the essence of the matter and was limited to that.

But Zoya Fyodorovna was not satisfied by such laconic communication. That very day, around four o'clock, with a flushed face she went to see him in his hotel room; and, without removing her coat, without extending her hand, she asked him directly:

"Tell me, my dear, what happened. He agreed just like that?"

Racheev opened his eyes wide, seeing an unexpected guest in his room, who hadn't even knocked on his door. She added:

"Excuse me for bursting in on you like this! I'm very curious. And he didn't even protest? Ah! And he didn't laugh?"

"Does this surprise you? Me, too, just imagine!" said Racheev.

"Yes, it was difficult to know what to expect. . . . Difficult! But how did it happen? Tell me, my dear man! Did he accept it in all seriousness? Ah?"

"Even too seriously. He fell silent, became thoughtful, paced the room, right here, in my room, and finally he said: 'I agree.'"

"How very strange! I expected that he would start swearing, at least. . . . You know, it's unpleasant. . . ."

"What is? Isn't this what you wanted?" Racheev cried in astonishment.

"Yes, as a last resort, of course. . . . But, naturally, I'd have preferred if he'd just paid me . . . even a small sum. . . . Why, it'll be hard to get along with him. . . . He drinks now. . . ."

Racheev didn't know what to say to this, and kept silent. She also fell silent and began to examine the room carefully.

"Well, when this is all over, I'll stop practicing my dentistry!" she declared. "Ah! Isn't it surprising how some circumstances force one to rejoice? It would seem, what could be pleasant about uniting one's fate once again with such a gentleman as Anton Markarych; but I am glad about it. You can't believe how sick and tired I am of trying to make ends meet from day to day! But, I'll say good-bye. . . . So, Tuesday? Right? Fine, then let it be Tuesday. I thank you for carrying out my commission. You see how good it is that you came to Petersburg. You've reconciled spouses. . . . Ha, ha, ha, ha!"

"Ugh, how nastily she laughs today!" thought Dmitry Petrovich after she left. "However, this entire episode is nasty, and I don't know why I got involved in it!"

During the course of the week he met Polzikov twice. Once Polzikov was strolling along Nevsky Prospect, pausing at shop windows.

"What are you doing here, Anton Makarych?" Racheev asked him.

"Ah, so it's you, Dmitry Petrovich?" Polzikov cried cheerily. "What do you mean? I'm looking at this, that, and the other thing. . . . I t's impossible, my friend, a family matter. . . . I'm thinking, should I buy a double bed from San Galli. . . ."[4]

He winked his left eye in an unusually devil-may-care manner, and then suddenly burst out in unrestrained loud laughter, and he added, "What do you think?"

---

4. One of the best shops in St. Petersburg.

Dmitry Petrovich only realized then that Polzikov was drunk.

"So, perhaps we could drop in somewhere and have a bite of lunch?" Polzikov proposed. "You see, I've had plenty to drink, but still haven't eaten. . . . Would you like to go to Yaroslavets or to Palkin's?"[5]

Racheev refused and tried to get rid of him expeditiously.

"So, remember; come to see me on Tuesday!" Anton Makarych said to him in farewell. "Absolutely, do you hear? Come at eleven o'clock! It's impossible without you, because this is the work of your peacemaking hands!"

Racheev promised. The second time he met Polzikov somewhere in a lane. This time he was completely sober, extremely gloomy, and absolutely taciturn. He was going somewhere on business, greeted Racheev briefly, and reminded him once again about Tuesday.

"You must absolutely be there, I beg of you! Yes, and have you given her my answer?" he suddenly asked with a worried look.

"I did. I wrote to her and then she came to see me."

"Well, that's splendid. She accepted it then?"

"Of course, she did."

"Aha. . . . Well, that's excellent!"

He was terribly pale and his face was continually distorted.

"Listen, my friend, I have no time. . . . Invite Baklasha, you hear?[6] Will you do so? He'll come; he's curious. . . . He has to see all this for his book. . . ."

Racheev promised to invite Nikolai Alekseevich.

On Tuesday morning he dropped in on Baklanov and told him what was happening. Baklanov said:

"Let's assume I'm not surprised at anything; nevertheless, never-theless. . . . This is really outrageous! And he invited me for a book? Ah? Is he perhaps preparing some sort of mad scene? Well, so, let's go. . . . It's true that everything may prove useful to me. . . ."

They set out. Polzikov lived on Sergievskaya Street, in a neat courtyard on the second floor. He had a servant who had a dis-

5. Two fine restaurants in St. Petersburg.
6. An affectionate diminutive for Baklanov.

tinctly drunken appearance. The whole apartment, consisting of four rooms, was provided with Turkish furniture and hung with carpets; there were sofas, couches, and little tables for smoking. The bookshelf was derelict; two panes were dislodged and the books stood in disarray, some with their spines facing in, and some without spines altogether. In all the rooms there were piles of neglected issues of *Secret Word*.

At Anton Makarovich's apartment they found a certain gentleman, portly and wearing blue eyeglasses, who turned out to be a foreign correspondent from *Secret Word*. Baklanov greeted him as an acquaintance. He was sitting in the third room, where a small round table was covered with a white tablecloth, and on it stood a decanter with vodka, several goblets, bread, a metal can of Tallinn sprats, a piece of sausage, and a piece of cheese.

At that moment when the sound of a bell rang in the entrance, Polzikov was with his guests. In an instant and, it seems, involuntarily, he lowered himself onto a sofa and covered his face with his hands. The servant, meanwhile, was opening the door and loudly announcing, "This way, please, sir!" Footsteps could already be heard in the study as well as someone fussing with bundles. Polzikov lowered his hands, and his face seemed strange to everyone present. It resembled the face of someone in a fever. He began to pick at his scanty hair and to adjust his glasses, but he didn't get up from the sofa and clearly tried not to look in the direction of the study. The steps drew closer. Zoya Fyodorovna—wearing a long plush blouse and a dark-green hat with a huge luxurious feather, carrying boxes in her arms, her face flushed, agitated, and smiling—was making her way toward them with decisive steps. Now she was standing on the threshold; she was a little surprised to meet so many strangers here and she regarded everyone with slight confusion.

All of a sudden Polzikov stood to his full height and straightened up. He was trembling and his head was nervously swinging from side to side.

"Is it you?" he asked in a hoarse, muffled voice: "You deigned to come to have my financial support? Ah? Ha, ha? And what about Mr.

Kir ... Kirgizov? Ah? You should have brought him along, too. ...
Ah? At once. ... And all your. ... Ha, ha, ha, ha, ha! Get out! Get out,
you vile ... base creature ... Get out of my house, you filthy thing!"

And he, shaking his fists, rushed forward, as if wanting to hurl
himself at her.

All this happened so unexpectedly for everyone and so quickly
that no one had time to take any measures; it was only when Anton
Makarovich took a step forward that Baklanov grabbed him by the
shoulders and dragged him to one side. Zoya Fyodorovna cried out,
dropped her boxes, and tottered. Racheev ran up to her, literally
took her in his arms, and escorted her into the next room, slamming
the door behind him. He and everyone else had only one choice:
to accept what had happened as fact. Through the closed door one
could hear Anton Makarovich's guffaws and a whole stream of the
most abusive words that exist in human language. Anton Makarovich
hastened to revel in his ferocious revenge while Zoya Fyodorovna
was present; he wanted her to hear all his offensive words. They
tried to dissuade him, to appeal to his conscience, but that didn't
help the situation.

Zoya Fyodorovna came to her senses and, like a cat, jumped up
from the sofa on which she was lying. She instinctively rushed toward the door, but Racheev stopped her.

"Enough! He's insane. ... Can't you see? It was not a good idea
to conceive of this plan, Zoya Fyodorovna. ... It's impossible to joke
about such things. ..."

"No, I'll pay him back! I'll definitely pay him back!" she cried,
gasping, trying to tear herself away from his arms.

"But he'll kill you. ... He's capable of it!"

She seemed to shrivel and fell silent.

"Take me home, Dmitry Petrovich!" she said, in a crying voice,
and her eyes were full of tears. "And I'll get these boxes later!" she
pointed to her bundles and boxes.

"Let's go!"

All the way home she kept repeating, "Oh, what a villain! What
a villain! There's never been such a villain in the whole world. ...

But I won't forgive him! He'll find out what it means to disgrace a woman.... Oh, what a villain!"

Racheev didn't argue with her, giving her free reign to vent her rage. He delivered her to 7th Street in Peski, helped her out of the horse-drawn cab, and said farewell.

VI

Baklanov was nowhere to be seen. For a whole week Dmitry Petrovich didn't drop by to see him. Various commissions from his village interfered, some of which he had put off until the final days of his stay in Petersburg.

"Listen," Vysotskaya said to him one time. "I'm worried that something might have happened to Nikolai Alekseevich.... You should be ashamed for not going to see him; you're friends!"

"I keep planning to do so. I confess that I'm also concerned!" replied Racheev. "But why don't you go see him? It would make him happy...."

"In all likelihood. But, unfortunately, that's risky. Katerina Sergeevna and I aren't very fond of each other...."

"And you, also, don't like her?"

"How can I put it? I reciprocate her feelings unintentionally. We usually like those who like us; but to love one's enemies—that's already a heroic feat...."

"Enemies? Come on! She's such a nice, clever woman!"

"Well, of course, we're not enemies.... But, in a word, she can't stand me.... I'd go for his sake, but I'm afraid.... I've been to visit them a few times, and each time she's received me with such coolness that I felt uncomfortable. The last time she simply didn't come out to greet me at all, although I knew she was well.... I bumped into her in the Shopping Arcade half an hour later. You'll agree, it's risky."

Racheev found a free hour and set off for the Baklanovs half an hour before dinner. The maid let him in—a young woman with a cheerful face; in reply to his questions, she said they were all home and all well."

"That means nothing untoward has occurred. We were alarmed for no reason," Racheev concluded.

In the entrance Liza was playing with Tanya. He greeted them.

"Is that you, Dmitry Petrovich?" Katerina Sergeevna's voice came from the dining room; from behind a half-opened door her lively face peeked out, while her whole body was still hidden behind the door. "I was already angry with you. I thought that you'd completely forgotten your old friends because of your new friends. . . ."

"What new friends?" asked Racheev, bowing to her from a distance.

"New friends just met recently!"

"Ah! No, there's room enough in my heart for both new and old friends. . . ."

Katerina Sergeevna started laughing.

"I can't come out to see you right now. I'll be ready soon. Will you stay for dinner?"

"If you invite me!"

"I do."

Her face disappeared and she closed the door.

"That means you have splendid weather today," Racheev said to Liza in a joking manner. She smiled and nodded her head.

Racheev went into the study; a small change had taken place there. The doors had been taken down and replaced by a curtain. Baklanov was sitting at the table; he was wearing a soft, colorful shirt, over which he wore a very short gray jacket. At first he didn't notice his friend who'd stopped behind him and was examining a piece of paper with writing on it.

"Are you working, my friend?" said Racheev.

Baklanov roused himself.

"Ah! Dmitry Petrovich! How glad I am to see you! This is splendid! I haven't seen a male face in over ten days. I've been sitting at home the whole time . . . writing!"

"Don't you even go out?" Racheev asked in surprise.

"Not once. I write, my friend, in a particular way. In the morning I sit down and stay seated until breakfast; I have breakfast, then I sit working until dinner; I have dinner, and I sit working until teatime; I have my tea, and then I sit working until . . . I fall asleep. . . ."

"What are you saying, Nikolai Alekseevich? Can you really write that way? Does anything really come of your work in that manner?"

"Yes, *something* comes of it, *something* always comes of it; but whether what's necessary or what I want comes of it, that's another question. But the point is, I urgently need some additional funds. . . ."

"Ah, so that's it!"

"And a considerable sum. . . . I've been writing a novel for some time, but I write that differently—decisively, carefully, without hurrying. . . . But Mr. Opukholev came to see me, the publisher of *Light and Darkness*, you know, the illustrated journal, and he asks, implores me to give him something by December. . . . He proposes to pay me good money, and, as it turns out, I need some good money right now. Well, I yielded to temptation. I put my novel aside and am writing this. . . . And how I'm working! Posthaste!"

"Well, and tell me, please, if, for example, it turns out badly, how will you manage?" asked Racheev, having become interested in this "literary" question, about which he understood nothing.

"But it can't be good! I'm telling you how I am writing it!"

"But then the publisher won't accept it!"

"What do you mean? Why wouldn't he? He won't read it; and if he does, he won't understand anything; and if he does understand it and sees that it's bad, he'll publish it anyway, because it's under my name. . . . Are you outraged? I am too. It's not literature, only literary technique. . . . I know, I know. . . ."

"But, in the end, what will the critics say?"

"The critics will abuse it, of course. . . . But the point is, my dear friend, that the critics will abuse it anyway, whether it's good or bad. That's what they do. . . . The public will read a thing speedily and you'll hear the praise: 'Ah! How fine it is! Ah, how profound! Ah, how artistic!' And you yourself will feel how hard you worked on it, thought about it, suffered through it, and at last it turned out well. And the critic says: 'I don't like it, and that's that! It's not profound, not artistic, not real, and that's the end of it!' Well, my friend, we've

gotten a long way past journal criticism. You won't learn anything
from them, and it'll only spoil your liver! However, I'm really very
glad to see you. I've been working fanatically. Another three days,
and I'll be able to put down my pen. . . . Only I don't know if I'll last.
There's such confusion in my brain. All these characters with whom,
strictly speaking, I'm not even well acquainted, boss me around in
my head in such a brazen fashion, as if they were at home. What's
new with you?"

"You've become thinner and turned pale, Nikolai Alekseevich!"

"That's nothing. What's new? Well, so, will I receive my Shakespeare?" he started laughing.

"I will, but you won't! Evgeniya Konstantinovna is an interesting
woman, but I see no need to fall in love with her. I visit her often. . . ."

"Fine, visit her more often and don't be in a hurry to avoid talking
about her. . . . I might still be the one who'll end up getting Shakespeare. Wait a moment, let me finish writing one more phrase, or
I'll forget what I was going to say. . . ."

He finished his phrase and began changing clothes. He could
never appear for dinner in his careless attire. Katerina Sergeevna
found the look of his cotton shirt, short jacket, and soft slippers unbearable, and that could spoil the entire day.

They were summoned to dinner. Katerina Sergeevna was lively,
cheerful, and talkative.

"You're in an extremely good mood today. . . . I'm very glad," said
Racheev.

"Oh, yes, splendid!" she replied. We're going abroad in a week. . . ."

"What? Where to? What for?"

"My goodness, he's so surprised and upset! You're going abroad?
With your limited means? Oh, you hard-hearted wife! She's the one
dragging her hardworking husband; she forces him to sit day and
night at his work, to satisfy her whims! Well, that's the way it is. It's
my whims. . . ."

"Based on something, of course. . . ."

"I think so! We've stayed here too long! We've both become
touchy. Nikolai Alekseevich repeats himself in his novels. He has

to refresh his observations, broaden his horizons. . . . We'll be more amicable abroad, and will love each other more. . . . Family life's essentially an artificial thing; it has to be supported by artificial means. If you come back to Petersburg, you'll see what nice model spouses we've become. . . ."

Now Racheev understood why the Baklanovs needed lots of money. He also understood Katerina Sergeevna's liveliness. She was entirely absorbed by her latest project, which promised her tempting perspectives. She herself was extremely dissatisfied by her own nervousness, which lately had reached dangerous proportions, and she definitely felt like remedying her condition. What pleasure was there in being a grouch, always poisoning the good mood of others and seeing around her people engrossed in gloomy thoughts? They were planning to go to Italy, and if there was enough money, to spend some more time in Greece.

"And you, Lizaveta Alekseevna, are you also going abroad?" asked Dmitry Petrovich.

Liza started to blush for some reason.

"No, I'll stay here," she replied.

"She doesn't want to go under any circumstances, no matter how much I try to persuade her!" remarked Baklanov.

"Liza? "Oh, what are you saying? She's not going on principle!" said Katerina Sergeevna with a good-natured, sly grin. She continued in a comically imposing tone of voice: "How can she travel in Europe, when she hasn't studied her poor motherland? How can she spend money for pleasant strolls in Italy, or Greece, when right here, in distant villages, peasants are in need of enlightenment? They can hardly wait until she, Liza, comes to enlighten them at long last. . . ."

"Liza, don't get angry, I'm joking!"

"No, she really has very serious intentions. . . ."

"I have no intentions at all!" Liza said, blushing even more deeply than before.

"Well, how's that, tell us! That's her modesty speaking! Ah, yes! We forgot to tell you the most important thing: Liza and Nikolai's aunt died. . . ."

"Your aunt? Irina Matveevna?" cried Racheev in astonishment.

"Yes," replied Nikolai Alekseevich. A few days ago we received a telegram. She died, and, of course, she's left everything to Liza."

A brief silence ensued. Racheev compared this news with Katerina Sergeevna's communication about Liza's serious intentions, and in his head he began to formulate surmises about these intentions. But he didn't say anything on this score. The conversation took a different direction. Dmitry Petrovich started talking about the latest episode between Polzikov and Zoya Fyodorovna. Coffee was served. Nikolai Alekseevich quickly drank his and began to excuse himself.

"Have a chat, my friend, with Katya! I have to finish one scene...."

And he withdrew to his study.

"Well, Dmitry Petrovich, are you disposed to chatting with me?" asked Katerina Sergeevna with a laugh.

"Of course. You know how to do it so very well.... I consider this a great distinction."

"Thank you. However, you didn't object at all to our proposed trip. That means, you regard it as I described? With horror?"

"Up to now I haven't regarded it at all, but now I'll think about it...."

And he really did think about it a little while, and then said:

"You see, I'm thinking about it from Lizaveta Alekseevna's point of view. She assumes that one must first know Russia. But that's because she's interested in Russia. But, you, Katerina Sergeevna, it seems, can't be accused of that sin.... So, I wish you a good journey. ... As for the fact that it costs a great deal, and that one must have considerable means, which you don't have, I advise you to think about this. Nikolai Alekseevich will have to write a great deal while abroad and send it back here; so what sort of trip will that be for him?"

"Well, it seems that you definitely want to disappoint me!" Katerina Sergeevna remarked in a tone of annoyance.

"Not at all. I merely want you to be honest with yourself. Now Nikolai Alekseevich is writing hurriedly for a publisher named Opukholev; he writes poorly and knows it himself. I didn't say anything to him because I didn't want to offend him, but I'm telling you. I felt very sad to see him and to hear how a person consciously debases his own talent. It's surprising! A cobbler's firm that respects itself at all would never produce even one pair of bad boots. And if by chance such a pair were made, and sold, and returned, just look at how everyone in the shop would be embarrassed; they'd blush, apologize, hasten to put a stop to it, and return the money. . . . But the writer says clearly: here's what I write well, and here's what's inferior, because this is for some serious journal, while that is for Opukholev. It's as if only Opukholev reads his journal, not the public. But his public feels all of this. It's elevated the writer, worships him, values him while he provides works worthy of his talent, but as soon as that public begins to notice that the writer's become careless, it turns away from him. . . . Then only Opukholev will value him, because he's shortsighted and miscalculates. He thinks that one can fool the public with a name. . . . Never! We readers, feel very perceptively a writer's insincerity and we'll never forgive that."

"What conclusion comes from all this?"

"That Nikolai Alekseevich is taking risks. All his considerable fame, all the respect that he's gained over many years of conscientious work, he might lose suddenly, one fine evening, and then it will be difficult for him to regain it. . . ."

As he was saying this, Katerina Sergeevna's face expressed great agitation. Her eyes somehow darkened, and in them appeared that malicious sparkle, which served as a bad omen for Liza.

"I'm hearing this for the thousandth time!" she said in a trembling voice, "and I know that everyone blames me. . . . I know that all too well! But I don't understand, what's so unusual about what I'm demanding. It seems to me that I'm not asking for a pair of trotters, a splendid home, or fine clothing! Besides, why can your Vysotskaya do all of this, while I can't? Ah, no. . . . This is all nonsense! I'm only saying one thing, and have been saying it all the time: Why is my husband a writer? It would have been much better if he were a merchant, or a landowner, or at least a civil servant. . . . You think I don't understand what you're talking about? I've thought about this

for thousands of nights, and I couldn't come up with anything. . . .
One has to live! I can't live in a cellar, I simply can't; what will you
do about it? And we live practically in a cellar as it is. . . ."

"You should wait to go abroad."

All of a sudden, unexpectedly for Racheev, Katerina Sergeevna
flared up. Pale blotches appeared on her flushed cheeks. She stood up.

"Deliberately, just to spite everybody I'm going to go. Let them
think and say whatever they like! I really don't care at all! Not at all!"

She said this in a nervous, hesitant tone of voice, usually followed
by tears. But Racheev didn't get to see that, because she quickly
withdrew to her bedroom, having slammed the door behind her.

Dmitry Petrovich looked questioningly at Liza. She was sitting
still, and her serious face reflected no particular feeling, but it was
clear this was causing her great effort.

Less than a minute passed since Katerina Sergeevna had left;
Liza raised her eyes, which now seemed to reflect a request for indulgence.

"Katerina Sergeevna really needs some sort of change!" said
Racheev, lowering his voice noticeably. He was afraid that their
conversation would be overheard in the bedroom. "She doesn't know
how to control her feelings at all. I've even noticed that at such times
healthy logic seems to desert her. . . . That's unfortunate!"

"Yes, Katya's become completely unhinged. But I don't think a
trip or something like that can improve her for long. . . . Her nerves
are such that there's nothing to be done!" said Liza, also in a low
voice. "You know, it's not fair. I think that such women should be
born with means. They can live only among a constant change of
various impressions. . . . They're not to blame because that's how
they're made. . . . And in Petersburg there are very many such wom-
en. . . . Ninety out of every hundred!"

"Really? What are you saying?" Dmitry Petrovich exclaimed, as
though frightened. "That means human kind is decaying. . . ."

They both fell silent. It was awkward to continue their conversation in low tones—they both felt that. They had to change the
subject.

"And so, Irina Matveevna died!" said Racheev.

"Yes, poor auntie!"

"But she did the right thing to leave her estate to you. What do you intend to do with it?"

"I don't know at all. I hadn't even thought about it, but even when I start thinking, I won't be able to come up with anything. It's not enough to think, one has to know something about the business."

"I'm prepared to assist you in this instance. I know Irina Matveevna's estate very well. It's not large, and she's run it quite badly. It can provide four times the income that it yielded her. I advise you not to sell it now; first it has to be brought into order; then you'll be able to get more from selling it. . . ."

"Why do you think I intend to sell it?" asked Liza.

"It just seemed that way to me. You'd be bored having to deal with running it!" Dmitry Petrovich replied indecisively.

"Bored? And you, Dmitry Petrovich, are you bored?" she asked, without looking at him.

"Me? That's another matter. I've gotten used to it. . . ."

"Perhaps I would, too!"

He looked at her with an expression of incomprehension and inquisitiveness. It couldn't be that this young girl aspired to estate management exclusively for her profit. There must be some hidden reason. But he didn't dare ask about it.

"It's even likely," he said, standing up. "It's not as difficult as one thinks! Good-bye! I'll drop in for a minute to see Nikolai Alekseevich."

She extended her hand, but on her face it was clear that for her this farewell was unexpected. Did she want to have a serious chat with him? That thought occurred to Racheev, but he still said good-bye. He was supposed to see Kalymov at eight o'clock.

He turned and went into the study. Nikolai Alekseevich, leaning over his desk, leaning his chest against it, was writing. His hand moved rapidly from one edge of the paper to the other. "Like an express train at full speed!" thought Racheev.

"Excuse me, I dropped in to say good-bye!" he said, extending his hand to his host.

"What? You're leaving already?" cried Baklanov. "I thought you'd become engrossed in conversation."

"No. And I must ask for your forgiveness. I've spoiled your wife's mood."

"What are you saying, my friend? How?" Nikolai Alekseevich probed anxiously.

"I expressed the opinion that it will be difficult for you to earn money, that abroad you will have to work very hard, and that the trip will be a burden for you. . . ."

Nikolai Alekseevich grew pale.

"My God! Why did you have to say that? What for? Ah, Dmitry Petrovich! You're ruining all my work. I've been trying by all possible means to maintain Katya's good mood. She can only live if her nerves are calm; if she becomes even a little distraught, she falls ill, everything hurts her physically, causing her great suffering. Now what have you done? Why, Dmitry Petrovich?"

His face expressed such torment, that Racheev felt pity for him.

"I myself regret doing this, my friend!" said Racheev, in a soft, compassionate voice.

But Baklanov wasn't appeased. He put down his pen, stood up, and began pacing the room nervously. His voice sounded like a complaint. He said: "But no one wants to understand this! They shout: your wife's to blame for everything! And while it's become everyone's business, no one cares that my wife punishes herself more than any executioner and that she suffers because of it. A writer should behave in a certain way, and not otherwise; he should write this way, but not that way! It is true! Art isn't a grocery shop; it's impossible to sell artistic creations by the pound, as if it were butter, sugar, or tea! True, a thousand times true! But life itself? Where did it go? Mustn't one consider that? You've seen the local women? The way they are? They all have shaky nerves; they all go rushing around like madwomen, not knowing what to undertake, how to fill their lives! We men can overcome grief, and at the same time, think about earning a loaf of bread, and work. . . . But they—if some sadness occurs, they're completely consumed by it; they have no thoughts, no feelings, no other desires; for them the entire world doesn't exist outside that grief. . . . But how are they to blame for having such nerves? You'll say: there are doctors, hospitals, treatments, and so forth, for this. Thank you very much! I love my wife, and I don't want her to be treated; I want her to live and enjoy the richness of life. . . . What? And what about higher goals, and the general well-being? Do you sacrifice them for your personal happiness? Why is that a sacrifice? Why indeed? I simply fulfill my obligation, because the well-being of my wife is my obligation. I married her. When I told her about my love and proposed to her, I didn't limit my feelings to this higher good; I didn't say, 'Madame, I love you, but if anything comes up, I'll sacrifice your happiness for the common good! I accepted a burden and must bear it! No, truth isn't in this, but here's what it consists of: contemporary writer-artists should not get married! If you're alone—then you can sacrifice your own well-being for the sake of art! But if another human being is involved in your life, you don't have the right to sacrifice this creature's well-being for any reason at all. A living person comes before everything else! His or her rights come first, before those of abstract art. . . . Yes, at last, here's the mis-understanding, ladies and gentlemen! If I work hurriedly and poorly, then I will sink in the eyes of the public; and what do you think? Will it spare me? Not in the least! With the same enthusiasm, as it had praised me before, it will hurl stones at me, and forget me. . . . Only I will lose, only me, well . . . and art will, too. . . . Art, which we worry about more than about living people. . . ."

He sat down in exhaustion. His long speech, apparently, was not just a reply to Racheev's words; he also had something else in mind. Dmitry Petrovich understood that several remarks that had been made concerning Baklanov's latest works in print also played a role here. The critics had maintained that Baklanov wrote carelessly and they re-proached him for that. Dmitry Petrovich also saw that his nerves were stretched as a result of his urgent work, from which he almost never rested; he decided to leave his long speech without any objection.

"I advise you to calm down and get some rest!" he said, taking him by the arm. "Will you be free about three days from now?"

"Oh, yes. Absolutely. I'll finish writing this nonsense that I myself despise!" replied Baklanov, still not calmed down from his agitation.

"Well, that's splendid. Evgeniya Konstantinovna misses you. Drop in; we'll meet there."

"I also miss her. I tell you, here's a mollifying principle. When I sit there and chat with her or even remain silent, I feel as if . . . well, what shall I compare it to? As if I were sitting in a warm bath. . . . Such serenity and spiritual quietude!"

"Well, good-bye!"

Racheev was already heading for the door, but Baklanov's voice stopped him.

"And will I still receive Shakespeare? Ah? I'd very much like to!" he said, half-joking. He'd already calmed down, and was now sitting on the sofa in some sort of languor.

"Hardly, and almost certainly—no!" replied Dmitry Petrovich, also joking.

"Ah, almost!"

"But you should ask Evgeniya Konstantinovna about this!"

After Racheev left, Nikolai Alekseevich stood up from the sofa, went over to the desk, and, while standing there, finished writing a phrase that remained incomplete; and, having put down his pen, he headed into the bedroom. He was deeply upset by the thought that Katerina Sergeevna might be seriously distraught. But she met him with a smile.

"It's all silliness!" she said. "Racheev can go back to his countryside, but we'll still go abroad!"

VII

Polzikov became more miserable than ever. One could have thought that the ferocious revenge with which he wanted to gratify and satisfy his soul might improve his mood, but in fact the opposite occurred.

After Zoya Fyodorovna's departure he drank himself into a state of oblivion and fell fast asleep on the sofa. They laid him down comfortably, as best they could; after instructing the maid to watch over him, they left.

Anton Makarych slept until late in the evening; when he opened his eyes, it was completely dark in all his rooms. He got up; his head seemed like some unfamiliar burden. It contained not one thought, not one recollection. He was only vaguely aware that he was in his own apartment, on the sofa, that it was nighttime, and therefore very dark, and that it was time to call the maid or to light a candle. It was just as dark in his brain as it was in the room.

He sat there, leaning back on the sofa, and would have been there longer, had the maid not come from the kitchen carrying a candle. A ray of light shone through the upper glass section of the door and fell across the wall, weakly illuminating the room. Some movement took place in Anton Makarych's brain. He suddenly seemed to recover; he remembered and understood everything; and he shuddered, as if at the onset of some terrible dream.

"What on earth? Did this all happen? Yes, it did! Baklanov, Racheev, and someone else—they were all here. Zoya Fyodorovna arrived with bundles and boxes. . . . Zoya Fyodorovna, here in his apartment? After so many years!! And he'd driven her away. . . . Good Lord!"

Zoya Fyodorovna is a beautiful woman. At one time she'd embraced him, kissed him, belonged to him. . . . He had loved her and was happy; he was a proper human being, like everyone else, and not some twisted, monstrous creature as he was now. Where was it, that distant time? Where had it gone? Was it possible to return it by paying some high price, paying for it even with his life? Eh, his life! Who needed his shameful life? And what value did it have? A half kopeck. A life for which everyone could despise him. Why despise him? Because no one cares about his soul. Why, everyone thinks that he lives contentedly, that his life seems pleasant to him, a jolly game. But in fact—life was a burden to him. If someone had peered into his soul, he would have seen how repulsive he was to himself, how fed up he was, and that he didn't want anything other than to be rid of himself. . . .

All of a sudden he was overcome with a burning feeling of pity for himself, a feeling of orphanhood, of loneliness. . . . At one time it hadn't been like this; at some point there were brilliant plans in his now inebriated brain; and in his heart, which had now turned into an open wound, there had been hopes. Zoya Fyodorovna was a young, graceful, pretty woman. She had a cheerful disposition; she laughed a great deal; and it was such a nice laugh; such purity came from her jokes; her eyes were always so open and clear.

He had been in love and life seemed unusually pleasant; he felt like beginning to live that life together, in a peaceful, friendly, touching manner. Each beat of his heart would be felt, because it was warmed by a deep belief in the future. He had never had too modest an opinion of his own strengths, but now they seemed gigantic to him, able to move mountains. . . . And there was not one doubt, not one dark cloud; he believed in her, and both of them thought that things would always be like that, and that was sufficient to gain happiness.

But what had come of this? Something resembling a vile dream, a dreadful nightmare, in which terrible, ugly monsters appeared without any reason, summoned by no one, stupidly piling up one after another, without any sense or meaning.

Anton Makarych was overcome with a strange feeling. There was a moment when it seemed to him that in his soul he still harbored profound affection for Zoya Fyodorovna, and not the malicious feeling that had dominated him during the recent disgraceful scene, but the previous one, warm and amicable. And then he fell into despair. It had been possible to bring her back and somehow still restore his life. Well, full happiness wouldn't emerge, but there would still be some deceit, something to hold on to in his life. Or else this desolation would swallow him.

Anton Makarych sat down at the table and began some urgent work.

To Zoya Fyodorovna, the scene arranged by Polzikov cost more than it did to him. After Racheev had brought her to her house and had helped her out of the cab, she swiftly entered the gates and almost ran up the stairs. The energy of revenge and rage simmered in her breast. She wanted the staircase to tremble beneath her; she wanted the door that she was unlocking, turning the key with all her might, to crash and spring back; in a word—she wanted to break something, destroy something.

"He made a fool of me! He tricked me! How did I allow it? I believed him! How could I think even for a moment that he was capable of kind feelings? And the way he did it! He invited other people. . . . Racheev, Baklanov, and that other person, what's his name. . . . From *Secret Word*. Oh, he'll trumpet this news everywhere: everyone will talk, shout, and make fun. . . . Can I ever forgive this?"

There was no possibility of forgiving this kind of insult. But what will she do? What could she do? Kill him? Well, if only she could perhaps do it. She was cruelly offended; if she were to have to stand trial, a judge would certainly vindicate her. It was the sort of insult that had never occurred before. . . .

But when she imagined herself going to see him or lying in wait for him on the street with a revolver in her hand, it soon became clear to her that this plan wouldn't work. She—with a revolver— she'd never held any sort of weapon in her hands other than a kitchen knife, or a dentist's pliers . . . No, this was inconceivable.

But what then could she do? It wasn't possible to leave it like this. It was impossible, after such an insult, to allow him to live peacefully on the earth, and to enjoy all the pleasures of life. Could she complain to the court about him? He'd be sentenced, naturally . . . to some sort of meaningless punishment, but what would she gain from it? Reporters would come to the trial, write it all down, and then publish it in the newspapers. . . . The scandal would increase tenfold. . . .

No, that won't do either.

Then a thought flashed through her mind. Yes, that would be the best way. To cut him down at the very root. Matryoshkin at *Secret Word* enjoys great influence. He could do this, and she knows how to accomplish this, whatever the cost.

She took out a piece of letter paper and wrote:

Mikhail Aleksandrovich! Come see me today, immediately, this very minute. It's terribly important. Your service is needed. Nothing should hinder you.

Yours, Z. Polzikova.

The cook raced at once with the note to Matryoshkin who lived on Zakharevskaya Street. All the while Zoya Fyodorovna was wandering in terrible agitation from room to room, changing her position constantly: she lay down, she sat up, she paced, she stood at the window, and gazed without any goal into the street. When the cook returned and said that "Mr. Matryoshkin would come right away," Zoya Fyodorovna thought she needed to prepare herself for the visit. Her hairstyle had been ruined, her eyes were red, her dress was creased. She sat at her small dressing table, covered with pink cotton, and with hurried, customary movements of her hands, she soon restored a decent appearance.

The bell rang. Matryoshkin entered.

"You frightened me, Zoya Fyodorovna!" he said, affectionately looking into her eyes, and shaking her hand with both of his. "What is it? Did you break your leg?"

"No!"

"Do you need money desperately?"

"No, no, that's all nonsense. . . ."

"Oho! So that's how it is! You're talking as if someone encroached upon your honor as a woman!"

"What is my honor as a woman? It's an invention, nothing more! I've been insulted unbearably, terribly, awfully! You must defend me . . . take revenge for me!"

"You do me an honor, delegating such a lofty obligation to me. I'm ready to take revenge. But who's the enemy?"

"Who? Polzikov!"

"Anton Makarych?"

"Yes, indeed!"

"For pity's sake! Was he drunk or something? Perhaps he was beside himself, and in such cases there's one means—avoid him. . . ."

"No, that's not it. Just imagine what a foul deed he committed. . . ."

Zoya Fyodorovna recounted everything that had happened. As she spoke, Matryoshkin's eyes kept growing wider and wider.

"What are you saying? Did he really?" he kept exclaiming. "Is he capable of doing that? Listen," he said, after Zoya Fyodorovna had finished her story. "All of this is so strange, it's hard to believe. . . . It's like a fairy tale. But first of all, how could you succumb and believe him? Ay, ay, ay! And such a clever woman you are. . . ."

"No, please don't try to understand—what, how, and why! You must take revenge!"

"Me? By what means must I do that? Should I marry you, perhaps? But according to Russian law, that's not possible."

"Don't mention such vulgarities! You can take revenge. Listen. He gets seven thousand rubles from you. If he leaves *Secret Word*, he won't receive a kopeck from anyone. . . . You have to make it so that he leaves. . . ."

"You don't say! Only a woman could take revenge in that way! Hit him in the pocketbook. You want to make him poor?"

"I don't know any other way. No, Mikhail Aleksandrovich, my dear friend. Do this for me. I don't know what I'm capable of doing. . . . Any sacrifice. . . . Only do this! This won't cost you a thing. You're the power there. You can have a fight with him; find some pretext. Complain about his article; you'll say, 'This isn't suitable. . . . ' And he, you know, is so proud. . . . He'll begin to use foul language, and then you'll declare: it's him or me. . . . Of course, they'll choose you, and he'll have to leave! Oh, how I'll triumph then!"

"Woman, woman! This is astonishing!" Matryoshkin cried drolly, and clapped his hands. "You subtle, ethereal creature! You pearl of creation! You dream! You're elegance incarnate! A sensitive nervous nature! But I swear by heaven, not one man could conceive of such a crude idea! And it's so insidiously worked out! A whole plan! It's the last word in larcenous cleverness! Yes, you're right, Zoya Fyodorovna; it's easy for me to do this, very easy. Moreover, in our office people are already dissatisfied with Anton Makarych and they're not against seizing an opportunity. . . . But as a human being, I feel sorry for Polzikov. I don't care for him; if you like—I even consider him as my enemy, because in his soul he hates me. But . . . you know, I'm not accustomed to fighting with my personal enemies on such grounds. . . ."

Zoya Fyodorovna looked at him with surprise and an expression of disbelief.

"You want to assure me of your nobility? You, after you've written so many. . . ."

"So many foul things? Is that what you wanted to say? That may be, but this is a very different matter. . . ."

"Listen!" Zoya Fyodorovna said in a decisive tone of voice: "Are you well disposed toward me?"

"Very! With all my heart, Zoya Fyodorovna!"

"You. . . . Well . . . what would you demand from me?"

"What? Demand? I don't dare demand anything. . . . I would like to earn your favor, yes, that's true. . . ."

"Well, what does that mean—favor?" she asked, screwing up her eyes.

"That's the question! When one tries to earn favor from a girl, it means to offer her your hand and heart. When one tries to earn favor from a married woman, it means . . . well, it's obvious what that means. . . ."

"Mikhail Aleksandrovich! Dear, sweet fellow! Anything you want! Anything. . . . Only do it."

She was standing near the armchair on which he was sitting. He liked her and had been courting her persistently for some time. All he had to do was take her hands and draw her to him. He blushed a little and a slight shudder ran down his spine.

He slowly moved his armchair away from her; she looked at him with an embarrassed glance. He stood up, walked over to the window, and was considering something.

"You know what, Zoya Fyodorovna!" he said at last. "Do you want him to understand your vengeance, that is, understand that this is your doing?"

"Yes, yes, yes!"

"Well, you see: Polzikov's fate at our newspaper has been decided long ago. We don't need him. He's become wishy-washy and boring; he doesn't work hard, does everything in a slipshod manner, and he's always drunk. His name, which used to attract readers at one time, has become worthless. But it was proposed that he continue working for another year, and then, one way or another, we'd send him packing. That way, the difference would be only one year, an insignificant amount, I think. . . . Well, so, I'll attempt to. . . ."

"You'll do this?"

She threw herself at him and began to squeeze his hand firmly.

"You know, I never thought, never thought that you were such a gallant man! It's simply as-ton-ish-ing!"

Matryoshkin smiled vaguely, more mockingly than cheerfully. He started to hurry.

"Why are you in such a hurry? Sit here a while!" Zoya Fyodorovna said with sincere emotion. "I'm so distraught, so upset. . . . Sit, Makar Aleksandrovich! I'm afraid to stay here alone. . . ."

"I can't, I can't! They called me away from work, very urgent work. . . . So help me God, I thought you'd broken your leg, but it turned out. . . ."

"Do you really think that breaking a leg is worse than receiving such an insult?"

"It's probably worse. If you had broken your leg, you'd have to stay in bed and you'd groan; but now you receive guests very nicely. . . . Even more graciously than expected! Good-bye."

Matryoshkin smiled ambiguously; after bowing, he withdrew into the hall.

"What a boor!" said Zoya Fyodorovna after him, and replied with a similar smile.

VIII

About four days have passed since Racheev was at the Baklanovs.

He returned home around twelve midnight. He had attended a literary reading in a public hall where he could meet men of letters, artists, and actors. In general they read badly, but there was a great deal of applause. The public attends such events not to listen, but to see what the readers look like. All were people with big names; he attended for the same reason.

He'd hardly approached the entranceway, when the door opened behind him once again and in came a young woman wearing a simple, beige top and a woolen scarf. He turned around instinctively, and recognized the Baklanovs' maid. This startled him.

"You must be looking for me?" he asked.

"Yes. From the lady of the house," replied the maid. Her cheeks were red from the cold; she was breathing heavily from her walk.

"What is it?"

"Something's wrong with the master. . . . It just happened. . . ."

"What is it? Has he fallen ill?"

"Yes. The doctor's there now. He says it's not good. . . . He's been overworking. . . . Here's a note from the lady. . . ."

Racheev grabbed the note. It was a scrap of paper, folded three times, without an envelope. Katerina Sergeevna wrote in pencil:

> Dmitry Petrovich!
>
> For heaven's sake come immediately! Something terrible is happening to Kolya. I've lost my head. The doctor said it was overexertion. I'm in despair. I'm to blame for everything and I curse myself! Don't delay even a minute.
>
> E. Baklanova

Dmitry Petrovich didn't bother going up to his own room.

"Let's go," he said to the maid.

They went outside and got a cab.

"You say it just happened to him?" he kept asking the maid.

"Not more than half an hour ago!"

"But what precisely? What kind of illness?"

"God only knows. He's sobbing, just like a young child. . . . So help me God, I couldn't look at him and started crying myself. He's covering his face with his hands. He was asleep, and was dreaming something. . . . A spider, or else, something enormous. . . . It all began with this spider. . . . He's overworked, that's what. . . ."

"Hmm. . . . And was everything all right before this? Katerina Sergeevna was in good health?"

He didn't want to ask the maid directly if there had been a quarrel between the spouses; but the maid seemed to understand. In the Baklanov household the expression "the lady is unwell" was recognized by everyone to mean that Katerina Sergeevna was upset and would not emerge from her bedroom.

"There was something after dinner. . . . The lady shouted something and wept. . . . The master came running from the bedroom. . . . His hands were in his hair, his eyes ablaze; he ran into the study, threw himself on the sofa, face down, and lay there until nightfall. . . . And then this happened. . . . This often occurs in our house," continued the maid, rejoicing that he was listening to her: the lady gets upset almost every day, the master goes to her room, talks to her, and she calms down. But this is the first time something's happened to the master. He couldn't endure it. . . . One must assume that he's overworked, because for the past two weeks he hasn't stood up from his desk and hasn't put down his pen. . . ."

Dmitry Petrovich could imagine rather clearly the picture of what had occurred at the Baklanovs.

They arrived. The maid darted through the gates, while Racheev walked in through the entrance. When he climbed the stairs, he saw that the door to the Baklanovs' apartment was already open. Liza met him. Her face was red, and her expression one of anxious concern.

She smiled at him instead of greeting him, and without extending her hand, stepped aside to let him pass into the living room. He glanced to the right; the door to the study was closed. Katerina Sergeevna emerged from the dining room wearing a dark housecoat. Her pale face displayed suffering. It seemed to him that she'd even lost weight. Bluish circles had formed under her eyes.

She approached him, took his arm, and led him into the dining room.

"I'm to blame for everything, everything, everything!" she kept saying almost in a whisper. "If something happens, I'll kill myself! I definitely will...."

"Enough of that! What cowardliness! What's wrong with him? Is he asleep now?" asked Racheev, astonished to see how deeply distraught she was.

A hanging lamp was lit in the dining room. A cold samovar stood on the table, a glass of cold tea, and the remains of supper.

"It's awful!" uttered Katerina Sergeevna. "He finished work yesterday.... It was that stupid trip abroad.... Ah, I'll never forgive myself for that.... No, listen; I'm no good for anything. People such as me don't deserve to live; they should kill themselves! We just torment other people! I'll definitely kill myself...."

"We'll discuss that later, Katerina Sergeevna," Racheev said with a smile, "as for now, let's talk about him...."

"Well, but even now I'm not in my right mind.... I'm talking about myself! Yesterday he took his work to the publisher Opukholev and received his money. Fifteen hundred rubles. Just think, in ten days he had earned fifteen hundred rubles! Imagine how much he had to produce! We spent a lovely evening together. We allocated the funds; but even then I noticed that he was somewhat indifferent to what I was saying; he agreed, and kept closing his eyes, as if he were about to nod off. And he should have gone to bed earlier, but I kept on like a chatterbox about how we'd go to Rome and what I would purchase for myself.... In a word, all sorts of nonsense! And, seeing that I was so cheerful and in such a good mood, he was trying to fight off drowsiness. You can't imagine what a marvelous man he is—Nikolai Alekseevich, for me, for me at least.... I don't know what he wouldn't sacrifice to see me healthy and happy.... Ah, but I.... It's awful! I didn't spare him.... No, Why do people like me go on living?"

"Let's talk about him, Katerina Sergeevna!" said Racheev. He noticed that as soon as she shifted the conversation to herself, her anxiety rose to a high level.

"Yes.... So he went to bed at around two o'clock. He suddenly jumped up in the middle of the night.... A nightmare.... Well, that was not unusual. I didn't pay it any attention.... He was complaining that he felt some heaviness in his head and his nerves were upset. He went back to bed and fell asleep. He slept until morning. In the morning he complained again that everything was annoying him. He said that he couldn't even stir his tea with a spoon. The sound of it was unbearable. I thought it was his whim. His nerves were simply overwrought and he was exaggerating everything. He judges others based on himself. I'm often nervous and I have lots of whims. At about five o'clock he received a note from an acquaintance. They were gathering today for a party. They invited him to stop by. Kolya expressed a desire to attend. What for, I asked. Just so, to air out his brain, to fortify himself. I objected to it. Now I understand that this was very foolish and ... unfair. Fresh air? Fortify himself? He sat in his study for two weeks and hardly spoke to me.... Yet he couldn't spend two evenings in a row with his wife! Of course, he was bored.... Previously, when he needed to refresh himself, he would come to me, but now—the love has passed, and it's no longer interesting.... I'm ashamed to recall, Dmitry Petrovich, what I said! But when my nerves are frayed, I sometimes say something against my own will; I know that it's foolish, vulgar, but I keep saying it, I do.... I can't refrain.... I didn't finish dinner and went to my bedroom. He came running after me at once, distraught, and began trying to soothe me.... I became even more upset.... Ah, no, I must kill myself.... You know, that will be all right and no one will lose anything...."

Then Katerina Sergeevna really calmed down noticeably and began speaking in an even voice:

"I'm punishing myself; I'm terribly guilty.... But when I'm like that ... I'm insane! Forgive me for sending for you. But I fear appearing before his eyes.... It seems to me that he'll greet me with reproach.... I think my appearance alone will cause him to recall how guilty I am and he'll once again become distressed.... Ah, I'm so unhappy today, so unhappy! Suddenly I got this idea to go abroad! It's all because of me! No, enough now! I'll take control of myself, strengthen my nerves, and we'll go to the countryside! Life there is five times cheaper, and he'll work less and better there. . . . The doctor said that he has neurasthenia, a very severe case. . . . God knows what that is!"

Dmitry Petrovich listened to her; it seemed to him that he'd fallen into a bewitched circle from which there was no escape. Nikolai Alekseevich is a writer; he lives for literature. Really and truly, to live for literature is a disgraceful thing. That means to trade in inspiration, pure, sacred outpourings of the soul. But this is done all over the world; people got used to it and consider it natural and just. But for a man with a sensitive soul, every time he accepts payment for the creation of his talent, secret pangs of conscience must occur and this alone introduces nervousness into the writer's life. However, he has to accept payment because life makes its own demands. A writer no longer awaits inspiration with baited breath, as previous authors used to do, but he summons it, demands it, harnesses all his strengths, and perhaps deceives himself, mistaking the simple strain of his nervous system as inspiration. . . . All of this consumes his organism by degrees, and leads to some sort of neurasthenia. He's unable to occupy himself with some other pursuit, one more serene and less responsible—he doesn't know how, and even if he did, he would constantly be drawn toward writing anyway; internal division would occur, dissatisfaction with himself. . . . Then Baklanov, in a burst of nervous irritation, came to the conclusion that a writer should not get married. And if one were to go further, then one must say he should refuse all the blessings of the world, everything that contemporary culture offers; he should live alone in a barrel and eat only locusts. But then writing becomes martyrdom and such an ideal writer from his barrel hardly sees and knows the life that interests society. . . .

Dmitry Petrovich proceeded into the study quietly. A candle was burning on the table; a broad blue lampshade filled the room with shadow. Nikolai Alekseevich lay on the sofa face up. He was covered with a blanket up to his neck, and his head was wrapped in a white towel. His eyes were open, and when he saw Racheev, a smile enlivened his pale face. He withdrew his hand from under the blanket and offered it to his friend.

"What an unexpected occurrence, Nikolai Alekseevich?" said Racheev, responding to him with a smile.

"Stupid occurrence!" replied Baklanov in a weakened voice. "I even took to howling. . . . It's never happened to me before! The main thing—my legs feel as if they are falling off. As if they belonged to someone else. That's the worst part. . . . I shouldn't have strained every nerve. . . . Just think, I wrote six sheets of paper in one sitting! Awful!"

Shadows flitted across his sallow face, first here, then there, as if the muscles were trembling. "He's becoming distraught," thought Racheev and hastened to change the subject.

"Let's talk about anything you want, but not about writing, not about literature, not about the pen, paper, or ink. . . . All right?"

"That's true, friend! I can't speak calmly about any of those things! Listen, here's what's weighing on me. My wife is terribly upset. . . . I could see it in her eyes. . . . I know that she's beating herself up; she considers herself to blame and is talking about suicide. . . . Explain to her, please, that this is all nonsense. No one's to blame for anything. . . . What a nuisance! The doctor said I'd be laid up with this rubbish for about two weeks. . . . Our trip's postponed."

"What trip?"

"Abroad, my friend. We'll definitely go. . . . Absolutely. . . . Phew, what an awful headache I have! My eyes are popping out of my head. Wait, let's be quiet for about ten minutes. . . ."

He closed his eyes and without moving, in silence, he lay there for a few minutes.

"Go and calm my wife down, friend. Or else she's capable of God knows what. Ask her to come in to see me for a minute."

Racheev left and a quarter of an hour later returned together with Katerina Sergeevna. She sat down on the edge of the sofa and tried to smile.

"As soon as you get better, Kolya, we'll leave for the countryside immediately, somewhere in the very south. . . . I'll behave myself, you'll see!" she said.

"Nonsense!" he replied serenely. "We'll go abroad!"

"Never! Not for anything!" she cried in horror, but stopped at once, seeing that he was getting upset. "You shouldn't be talking that much. You need peace and quiet!" she added.

He closed his eyes again. His irritability lessened now; he experienced terrible weakness; every sentence exhausted him, and the attacks of severe headaches were tormenting.... But as soon as the spell passed, he felt like talking once more.

He managed to fall asleep around two o'clock; they blew out the candle in the study. Racheev bid farewell and left. Katerina Sergeevna remained alone. It was completely quiet in the study; it was obvious that Nikolai Alekseevich had fallen into a sound sleep. Liza had gone to her room. Katerina Sergeevna walked along the narrow hall and knocked at the low single door.

"Are you still awake? Liza?" she asked.

Liza hurriedly opened the door for her.

She was sitting at her desk before an open book.

"Why don't you get undressed, Liza?" asked Katerina Sergeevna.

"I'll sit here for a while.... Perhaps Kolya will need something.... You should go to bed, Katya!" Liza replied.

"Oh, no! What nonsense! You go to bed, please.... I won't go to bed at all! I couldn't fall asleep!" she said, reclining on the bed. "You know, Liza, I'm having the darkest thoughts!" she uttered in a gloomy voice.

"What are you saying? Why, Kolya's much better. The doctor said there's no danger at all.... He'll be completely well after about two weeks."

"I'm sure of that.... But that's not the point. You know how strong his nerves were, and they've given way.... That's very bad. Now it's difficult to restore them. This will be recurring. And I'm to blame for all of it.... It's terrible!"

"Enough, Katya; why you?" Liza said in a soothing tone.

"Of course it was me.... And you think so, too.... I know you think so, and always have.... I understand things all too well. You conceal it from me because you're afraid to trouble me.... I don't like that, Liza...."

"You don't like that?" Liza asked with a slight trace of surprise.

"No, I don't. That is, I value that in you and in Kolya. You do this for the sake of my tranquility, but. . . . You know, it's even a bit distressing when people treat me as if I were a child. . . . But the main thing is, it's spoiled me. . . . I've grown unaccustomed to restraining myself. And I've driven Kolya to this state. . . . The main thing is for him to get some rest and to write as little as possible. . . . But how to do this? Advise me, Liza!"

"I'd give you advice, Katya, but. . . ."

"Ah, only without the but. . . . You're afraid again that I'll get upset! No, please, say all that you're thinking. Please, Liza! I know that you think a great deal, and, it must be, sensibly. . . . But you keep silent. You're secretive, Liza!"

"Secretive, that's true! But if you want, I'll speak. Only give me your word that you'll hear me out calmly. . . ."

"Ah, why must it be calmly?" cried Katerina Sergeevna anxiously. "You're judging by yourself. You have a healthy, serene nature. But I'm always seething, always agitated. . . . Well, so what comes of this? Get on with it, please, then, without another word!"

"Well, fine!" said Liza calmly and unhurriedly. "I'll speak, if you wish. . . . You need to turn your back on life in Petersburg and live somewhere in the provinces. While Tanya's little, you can live in the countryside; when it comes time for her to go to school, you'll spend winters in some provincial town. I lived for a long time in the provinces and know a great many town residents, but nowhere did I meet such nervous people as you, for example. I think this would be useful not only for Kolya, because then he'll work only when he wants to, and not of necessity—but also for you. For your nerves. A comparison occurred to me: a very bright light—there's nothing harmful or injurious about it, and healthy eyes tolerate it well; but for ailing eyes, one must soften the light with frosted glass. In the provinces life goes on quietly; it's the same life as in the capital, because people are the same everywhere, but it's softened somehow through frosted glass. It's beneficial for your nerves. . . ."

"Tell me please, Liza, is our aunt's house very big?" asked Katerina Sergeevna.

Liza regarded her with mild surprise and distrust.

"There are eight rooms!" she replied.

"Is it warm? Is it suitable in winter?" continued Katerina Sergeevna.

"Oh, yes, of course, it is. . . ."

"And would you relinquish a part of it to us?"

"Katya! Aren't you ashamed to ask? It would be my greatest pleasure to do so!"

Katerina Sergeevna raised herself and sat down again.

"You know what, Liza! Of course, you won't believe me; you'll say it's merely my mood, and that it will change within the hour. But I give you my word of honor, I've made a firm decision: as soon as the first days of spring arrive, we'll move to join you in the countryside and will live there uninterruptedly."

Liza stood up and went over to her.

"Ah, Katya! If only this would work out! I'd be so happy. I'll leave for now, in about two weeks, put the house in order, and make arrangements. You'll be so comfortable there: splendid!"

She took both of Katerina Sergeevna's hands and squeezed them warmly.

"Go to sleep, Liza!" said Katerina Sergeevna, having responded to her handshake. "I won't go to bed! Not for anything!"

IX

A week passed; every day Dmitry Petrovich would spend a few hours at the Baklanovs; he would dine with them; then, in the evening, he would go to see Vysotskaya for half an hour. Evgeniya Konstantinovna carefully followed Nikolai Petrovich's illness and every day Racheev had to fill her in on all the details.

"Well, tell me, how is our friend today?" she asked him, as soon as he entered her study.

Yesterday she'd already received the news that Baklanov was having dinner with everyone in the dining room and would soon be going outside.

"Excellent. He's becoming the same nice man he was previously!"

replied Racheev. "At dinner today he began talking about taking a trip abroad.... He's stubbornly insisting on it. But Katerina Sergeevna categorically refuses! For almost a week he hasn't followed her mood and he didn't know that the idea of this trip has become a sort of punishment for her.... She said to him earnestly: 'If you wish to do me a real favor, then in spring we'll move to the country and stay there until we're fed up with it!' He looked at her in surprise, 'You? To the country? But you hate the countryside and the peasants!' She burst out laughing: 'I'll come to love them, I really will!' she exclaimed. 'For a long time they've provided you with material; they fed us, and I was ungrateful!' The discussion ended peacefully. Nikolai Alekseevich tenderly kissed his wife's hand and didn't say another word about a trip abroad. Lizaveta Alekseevna.... What a wonderful young woman she is! She's prepared to sacrifice everything for them. She'll go there with me, to our part of the world. She wants to renovate the house, make it more comfortable, so it'll be ready for their arrival."

"And you think that this won't change? You think Katerina Sergeevna will remain in this mood for a long time?"

"I think so. She was severely shaken by her husband's illness. She has a generous nature. The whole point is what sort of impulse will control her nerves. Nikolai Alekseevich himself was to blame for a great deal. He constantly tried to adjust to her little whims, to cultivate them; it's only natural that gradually these whims, became larger, grew like trees in good soil and with good care.... In my opinion, if only she seizes upon the idea to go to the countryside, she'll soon see that people are people everywhere, and that there's more fresh air and sunshine there...."

"Do you know what? It just occurred to me, not just now, but two days ago!" said Vysotskaya. "I think our duty—that of Nikolai Alekseevich's friends—is to encourage him somehow ... how to put it? By sympathetic movement, or...."

"What, for example?"

"Say, we organize a dinner for him.... Gather seven or eight people, a small circle.... You'll suggest two, so will I, that's already

six, plus Katerina Sergeevna and him. You'll choose the place. . . .
In a restaurant, of course, but so we could be hidden from view. . . .
Well, in a word—it should be very intimate. By the way, I've never
once in my life had dinner in a restaurant. . . . What do you think,
can we do it?"

"Why not? But whom shall we invite? I'll summon Kalymov,
he's Nikolai Alekseevich's publisher, but I don't have anyone else in
mind!" said Dmitry Alekseevich.

Just not Polzikov. God be with him. . . . He's difficult. Well, then
I'll inform three of them. I've chosen two already. Both are young
writers. . . . I'll think about a third. So you talk to the Baklanovs. . . .
Or perhaps, I myself should go to see Katerina Sergeevna?"

"That wouldn't hurt!"

"Well, I so love Nikolai Alekseevich and his talent, that I'm ready
to make sacrifices!" she said with a laugh. "Or do you think that the
change in Katerina Sergeevna was also related to this?"

"I don't know. She remains a beautiful, clever, and interesting
woman, just as before. . . . It seems there hasn't ever been an example
of such a woman who was able to get along with a another woman—
also beautiful, clever, and interesting!"

"But you've perfectly already acquired the local custom of polite
people."

"Yes, I'm starting to be corrupted. I have to leave as soon as possible."

Racheev had really decided to leave. His wife was sending for
him, and he himself was attracted by the serenity at home. He was
sincerely surprised at how in these two months he could become so
tired, though he wasn't doing anything. In essence, he hadn't done
a thing at all in Petersburg; but he was affected by so many diverse
impressions, that now he wanted peace and quiet.

Baklanov had already gone out twice and walked along Nevsky
Prospect. He was completely recovered; his weakness had passed,
his irritability was replaced by his former good humor; only his
headaches would return at times and were a serious burden to him.
Then he was overcome by an unpleasant feeling of anguish, evil
foreboding, and his state of mind darkened. He would lay down on

his back on the sofa, close his eyes, and remain there for a quarter of an hour in silence, without moving. This method, which he had conceived for himself, proved to be effective; his pain lessened and he would get up good-natured and cheerful again.

Katerina Sergeevna was completely unrecognizable. In her treatment of everyone, her husband in particular, she became unusually even-tempered and gentle. She held herself firmly in hand, looked after herself attentively, with effort suppressed any attempt at a flare-up, and rejoiced in her soul at each and every such victory over herself. Nikolai Alekseevich regarded all this with amazement: at first he even felt apprehension: Was it for the good? Was it, perhaps, an indication of some unexpected reversal? But when he realized that Katerina Sergeevna engaged in a struggle on those few occasions, when those efforts that it had cost her to quench the flare-up at the very beginning were not concealed, he concluded that this was not some painful turning point, but a result of conscious work on herself—and he was happy about it.

On one of those days, when Nikolai Alekseevich was strolling with Racheev before lunch, Vysotskaya appeared in the Baklanovs' living room. At the first moment of their meeting, Katerina Sergeevna blushed deeply and became flustered. This was Vysotskaya's second visit of the season; they were accustomed to visit each other only once, finding that sufficient to maintain good relations.

"I'm very glad to see you!" said Katerina Sergeevna, but added at once: "What a pity. Nikolai Alekseevich has just gone out!"

A light shadow flashed across Vysotskaya's face, but she smiled immediately.

"Yes, I did want to see him.... It seems he's completely recovered. But I've come mainly to see you, Katerina Sergeevna!"

There was a slight expression of bewilderment on Katerina Sergeevna's face.

"Even on business, if you like. We've decided to arrange a small surprise for your husband.... A small circle is organizing a dinner. ... Naturally, if you agree to participate.... We, that is, Dmitry Petrovich and I.... You have nothing against this alliance?

She smiled, as did the hostess.

"Naturally, nothing against it. I agree to attend the dinner. It'll be a small victory. I've never been to such dinners before. It will be interesting. . . ."

"That's splendid. Racheev will tell you when it'll be. . . ."

She stayed another ten minutes or so and then left, expressing the wish to see Katerina Sergeevna at her own place. Not a word was said about the trip to the countryside. . . . Vysotskaya knew about the distressing origin of this decision and feared touching on a sore point.

The dinner took place two days after this meeting. They sought out a separate comfortable room in the restaurant—a small hall with high vaults and completely respectable furnishings. The round table was set for a total of eight people. Racheev arrived first, followed by Kalymov. In a black frock coat fastened up to his neck—he seemed even taller than when he greeted him, standing at his table, leaning slightly forward.

"Do me a favor and seat me next to you; don't leave me among the ladies!" he said to Racheev. "I don't know how to talk to them. . . ."

"Yes," replied Racheev with a laugh; "it's obvious from what you're saying. Knowing how to talk to ladies means first of all being able to give them a chance to talk and to listen to them. They speak so well that a reply is almost unnecessary. . . ."

The ladies arrived together, accompanied by Baklanov, in Vysotskaya's carriage. Then Zebrov appeared; next, a very young man, thin and pale, with fair hair, a simple, open face, not handsome, but appealing. His gray eyes were fixed firmly, but at the same time, trustingly, on the person with whom he was talking. Evgeniya Konstantinovna immediately took him under her wing and introduced him to Racheev and Katerina Sergeevna. He was acquainted with Zebrov and Baklanov; Kalymov approached him and said:

"I've been wanting to meet you for some time. Your small article interested me. . . ."

The young man (who appeared to be no more than twenty-five years old) said little and seemed reticent: apparently, he was somewhat bashful. The piece that Kalymov was referring to, as a matter of fact, was very short; but, after appearing in a certain journal, it immediately called attention to the author. They said that it was fresh, sincere, simple, and powerful, and the name Tomilov was frequently uttered in journalistic circles. But he himself was almost never encountered; very few people were acquainted with him; most thought that he was living in the provinces. Evgeniya Konstantinovna, naturally, had sought him out and he had visited her twice.

The dinner began sluggishly; but then some sort of intricate sweet dish appeared on the table, which, however, turned out to be ordinary ice cream with candied fruit. No one noticed how the goblets were refilled with champagne. Baklanov stood up and uttered a few simple words expressing his gratitude to everyone present for "this kind symbol of their friendship." He added, of course, that it couldn't be explained in any other way except as friendship, since he still didn't have any accomplishment. His toast was—"to everyone seated at this harmonious table."

Evgeniya Konstantinovna replied to his toast. She said she wouldn't dwell on Baklanov's contributions; although they could provide splendid material for a speech, she'd afford other, more qualified people, that pleasure. She herself preferred, to all her accomplishments in the world, genuine friendship, about which Nikolai Alekseevich had proposed a toast to all those who'd gathered here out of genuine friendship—for Katerina Sergeevna and Nikolai Alekseevich. It fell to Katerina Sergeevna to respond. She said simply, that she couldn't accept on her own account any of the kindnesses being mentioned here or that would be; in advance, she attributed them all to her husband. She was glad that he had such genuine friends. She knew that the initiative for this dinner belonged to Evgeniya Konstantinovna, and she would drink to her health with particular delight.

All this was accepted amicably. They would stand, walk over to the person who had been named, clink glasses, and drink; but there still was no real inspiration.

Kalymov rose and asked for attention:

"Ladies and gentlemen," he said. "First of all let me ask for your indulgence. I am not good at public speaking. My profession is a silent one. It sometimes happens that from morning to night I sit alone reading a book or proofreading an article. How could I learn how to speak? But, since I'm here, among you, you have the right to demand that I speak, to require an account. I'm a publisher. Everything that emerges from Nikolai Alekseevich's pen, after the periodical public reads it, passes through my hands and goes to another public, the literary public. Perhaps you didn't even know that these are two separate worlds. The periodical public seeks entertainment in reading, a way to fill its free time. Today a journal has come its way and it's been read; tomorrow, another one will be read and yesterday's will be forgotten. And even in one such journal, article after article, one replaces another, or, better to say, pushes out another; and in the last analysis—everything's grasped hurriedly, precariously, fleetingly, shallowly. Exclusively—the periodical reader is a light reader, like a moth. Success with him is achieved just as easily as oblivion. It's impossible to judge a writer's significance by his periodical success. The literary reader is something completely different. He loves to focus, to hold the book in his hands for a long time, return to it time after time after time; he wants to derive from it not only something pleasant, entertaining, but also something instructive; he wants the book not to encumber, but to adorn his bookshelf. He wants to be able to say to his neighbor: here's a book; I bought it; it's good; read it. And therefore he doesn't buy a book in vain; he examines and ponders it. Especially if the author's already published one book, and this is his second. If the first one was bad, it's better not to publish it. No one will buy it. They'll read it in a magazine because it's printed there in a series of other articles; but as a separate book, no one will buy it. And if you want to know for real if a writer is successful, don't inquire; if his critics praise him, don't listen too carefully to the words of the periodical public. But ask whether the book is selling or not. From this point of view, I, as the regular publisher of Nikolai Alekseevich's books, can boldly state that every one of his books is lively; it already knows the way from the bookstores home to the bookshelves of literary readers, where it is fated to reside. I won't begin to bring forward the numbers; but you can believe me if I say that by this measure, Nikolai Alekseevich's success among the public is solid and deep. His books belong to those that create readers. So, I now propose my publisher's toast to him. We have many fine books in Rus', ladies and gentlemen, but we have few readers. To the health of the author of such books that create readers!"

Zebrov rose. They expected some brilliant speech, but he warned them in advance that he'd say only two dozen or so words.

"If you're expecting a long speech from me, well thought-out, polished, constructed according to a definite plan, rich with conclusions and generalizations, then you're mistaken. We deliver such speeches in court, on the stage, before a curious public, which then disperses to its homes and forgets these speeches.... But here, in this circle of friends—I can speak only simply, as I do with my friend over a cup of tea. Thank heavens that such a competent fellow has borne witness before us to Nikolai Alekseevich's solid and profound success with the public. Personally I belong to the literary public; I love it when a book doesn't burden my bookshelf, but adorns it; therefore, I never purchase a questionable book. And Nikolai Alekseevich's books occupy an honored place on my bookshelf. But... forgive me, ladies and gentlemen, that in this short speech I decided to include this 'but.' But when I pick up a book by Nikolai Alekseevich and attentively turn its pages, together with pleasure I also experience a strange feeling, not quite pity and not quite irritation. I'll explain in a minute; don't make such a stern face, Evgeniya Konstantinovna. I say this because, undoubtedly, my words will be understood in a friendly fashion. Nikolai Alekseevich has some pages that are inspired, pages where the true artist is glimpsed, ready to sacrifice himself to pure art.... But I, ladies and gentlemen, I am guilty of thinking in aesthetic terms; I am of the opinion that artistic truth is only in a work that is free of a goal mentioned in advance, and doesn't serve any interests (however noble they be), besides those of pure art, which has only one God—beauty! And here's what I desire: that Nikolai Alekseevich provide us with more pages of that sort, that his spontaneous inspiration is not diminished by other goals, undeniably noble, but alien to pure art!"

They didn't manage to drink to this toast. At the very moment when Zebrov raised his goblet, and others wished to follow his example, Tomilov rose and roused himself; with his protesting appearance, he invited everyone to focus attention on him. He was pale, as always, but his eyes were shining more than usual. He made a brief negative gesture with his hand and then in an agitated, though not a resonant voice, he said:

"No! I can't agree!"

He paused for a minute, concentrating on some spot on the table.

"I can't agree with this!" he repeated. "We contemporary writers are often accused of tendentiousness. And it's true—we are tendentious. But we're accused of this as if it were an easy thing. . . . No one knows better than we artists do, how pleasant it is to serve pure beauty, how pleasant to devote one's talents to pure art, and how tormenting it is to darken the hours of ecstatic inspiration with life's prose. Yes, to serve pure art—is a noble calling! But one can serve it only when one's surrounded by quiet, rational work, when everyone, without glancing around in fear, marches calmly toward his goal, when the sun rises every day to illuminate people's fraternal work, and when it sets every day to bless their rest. But when mutual hostility reigns on earth, when some are blinded because they're struck by too bright a light, while others can see nothing at all, because thick darkness hangs over them, when the millions of insistent essential questions rain down on you from all sides and shout, demand, howl—then it's not the time to serve pure art, and the artist can't do so if he harbors in his bosom even the slightest trace of a sensitive soul. There's no time, none at all, ladies and gentlemen, to devote ourselves to the ecstasies of pure inspiration! Life impels us, it prompts us to adopt a tendency, it shouts that tendency into our ears; it tears our bosom apart and inserts it into our hearts; and a person whose hand is raised to toss it away from there when it is alive, made of human flesh and blood, trembles, implores, is indignant, sobs! Life before everything! Life with its prose!"

This vehement speech, uttered with passion, sincere feeling, with fiery eyes, elicited an entire storm. Tomilov was applauded. Zebrov was the first to approach him, embrace him, and smother him with kisses.

"You've made a hardened aesthete waver!" he said. Others shook his hand.

From this moment on the general enthusiasm knew no bounds. Everyone was comfortable with each other, felt at home, and lively conversation flowed without toasts.

The wine was consumed. Racheev went to order more. To do so he had to enter the general hall and proceed to the buffet. Just when he was speaking with the manager of the restaurant, a tall figure appeared at the door; as soon as he saw him, Racheev involuntarily broke off the phrase he'd begun. It was Polzikov: but his face expressed such gloomy despair, that Racheev thought at once about some sort of catastrophe. He went to meet him and stopped him.

"What's wrong, Anton Makarych?" he asked anxiously.

"Aha! I've been looking for you. . . . I need you . . . I heard that you were having a dinner here. . . . Let's move over to a corner!"

He said this in an unsteady voice, took Racheev by the arm, and led him into the depths of the hall. There was a small niche, and behind it, a completely separate room.

"I'll tell you briefly: I've been fired from *Secret Word*. . . . Zoya Fyodorovna endeavored and she's right: I did her a foul deed. . . . They've driven me out!"

"How?"

"Just so, they fired me. They said foul things about me and drove me out. . . . However—I brought it on myself! There's no reason to blame others. Now here's the situation: I've spent everything, that is, I've drunk it up. I'm out on the street. I can't go anywhere. There are only two roads open to me: To sink even deeper into the filth—there are such places, but I find that repulsive—or, to go back, return to decency, but no one will ever believe that. . . . It's easy to let myself go, but it's difficult to raise myself up. . . . And there's no decency left in me. . . . There's a third way out. . . . Here it is. . . ."

He pulled out a revolver from his side pocket and placed it on the table.

"What are you saying, Anton Makarych?" cried Racheev, and took a step back.

"You're quite a character! I've thought, and thought, and thought. . . . Just imagine: no one loves me, no one in the whole wide world! Not one dog! I don't intend to grovel. . . . I have no talent left; it's all evaporated. All of my talent was in my honesty. But since I've lost my honesty, I have no talent left, as if my wings had been clipped. In a word, I have nothing, not one chance in life. And the main thing is that it's become loathsome to be a scoundrel. . . . I've decided this definitively; I merely wanted to shake your hand—as a man who . . . felt sorry for me. . . ."

He grabbed Racheev's hand and squeezed it firmly.

"Farewell, friend! Don't think that scoundrels have an easy time of it. . . . One's conscience begins to speak, to cry out. . . . Ooh!"

And he covered his ears with his hands, as if in fact he heard the cries of his conscience.

"You know what? Let's say that you do this, but . . . afterward?" said Racheev. "Let's go in now to Baklanov and Vysotskaya. . . . You know, it sometimes happens that when you talk to people about peripheral matters, it may alter your decision. . . ."

"Oh, no! Not for anything! Not for anything!" replied Polzikov conclusively.

"Well, then, wait a moment; I'll bring Baklanov out here. . . . Why, we're all old friends!"

Polzikov thought for a moment. It was apparent that he was deciding a very important question.

"Well, all right, all right! Go get him, go ahead!" he said, and while doing so, once again grabbed Racheev's hand and squeezed it. "Go on, I'll wait. . . ."

"But hide this!" said Dmitry Petrovich, pointing to the revolver.

"All right, I will. . . ."

He took the revolver and placed it in his pocket. Racheev left and walked through the hall and the narrow corridor. He opened the door to the room where the whole group was gathered, but all of a sudden, he froze on the threshold. The others also exchanged anxious glances. The sound was muffled in the room; nevertheless a shot could clearly be heard.

"It's . . . Polzikov!" announced Racheev.

A deathly pause occurred, then intense movement. The ladies left and went to the Baklanovs' apartment, while the men followed Racheev.

Anton Makarych was sitting at a table; his head and hands had fallen on the marble slab. Blood was streaming onto the floor and forming a puddle. He was absolutely still.

X

It was a frosty day. The streets of the capital were white with snow. At about two thirty in the afternoon at the Nikolaevsky Station on the departure platform, a tall old man wearing a long coat of wolf fur, covered with black cloth, was meeting a young woman in a light fur-lined jacket; a dark blue veil concealed her face. It was Kalymov and Vysotskaya.

"The architects of victory are usually late!" said Kalymov, greeting her.

"Racheev's here. He's dealing with Lizaveta Alekseevna's baggage!" replied Evgeniya Konstantinovna.

"Don't you know her? She's Baklanov's sister. She's a young girl and she's going into voluntary exile."

"Why? Does she have some purpose?"

"Her purpose is to live for others. I've spoken with her. 'I will learn,' she says, 'from Racheev how to live so that my life doesn't pass by in vain!' Besides, she wants to prepare the living space for Nikolai Alekseevich's family. Tell me, did you attend poor Polzikov's funeral?"

"I did. It was a sorry affair. No one came. Racheev, Baklanov, I, and a few curious observers. It was painful to see. . . . But when you think about it, that was how it had to be. . . ."

"Yes, that's how it had to be!" she confirmed sadly.

Just then Baklanov appeared with Katerina Sergeevna and Liza. Everyone was carrying boxes and bundles. Liza had a bag over her shoulder and was wearing a round sheepskin cap: she looked as if she were about to depart on a journey. They deposited their things in the train car and then came back out onto the platform. Baklanov joined Kalymov and Vysotskaya. Liza led Katerina Sergeevna aside.

"Katya, I ask you once again: is your decision final? Are you going to bring him to the country? And not for a month, not for two, but for a long time, so he can do some decent work there?"

"Absolutely, Liza. Don't doubt it for a minute! You've seen how in these past few days I've behaved myself in exemplary fashion. I've become convinced that it's really possible. . . . At first it's difficult, but then it'll become a habit. This nervousness—at least half of it—is lack of discipline! I've come to that conclusion. . . ."

"We'll be fine there. We'll live amicably. Racheev's our neighbor; perhaps others will turn up who're like him! I'm sure you'll come to regard the countryside differently. Perhaps you'll even come to love it. . . . Here's Racheev. There's little time left. That's the second bell, you hear? As soon as it feels like spring, come visit us!"

Racheev was standing with another group. Liza and Katerina Sergeevna went up to them.

"Honestly speaking, ladies and gentlemen, although I do long for home, I'm sorry to part with you!" said Dmitry Petrovich. "Well, we've already enticed Nikolai Alekseevich and Katerina Sergeevna to come to the country. As for you," he said, looking at Vysotskaya and Kalymov. "You're city folk; there's no reason for you to go to the countryside. Everything's here for you. God knows when we'll see each other again. Evgeniya Konstantinovna will write to us, won't she?"

She nodded her head.

"But you'll have no time to write!" he turned to Kalymov. "However, your books will remind us of you. Send more of them!" He shook hands with Kalymov and Vysotskaya and said: "On my arrival here I was fortunate to meet new people. . . . All of this was thanks to Nikolai Alekseevich."

The third bell rang. The ladies kissed Liza; the men kissed Racheev. The train budged.

"Evgeniya Konstantinovna!" Racheev said hurriedly in a whisper to Vysotskaya, who had approached the car's platform: "Do you remember what we talked about? Here's the task for your intelligence, beauty, and energy! We have to move the burden from two ends; it'll go faster. . . . You do it here and we'll do it there! Write in detail. As for how we are and what we are doing, come visit—see for yourself!"

He shook her hand warmly once again. The train started moving.

If we say here that at the beginning of spring the Baklanovs sold all their furnishings and left for the countryside to join Liza; that Kalymov actively kept sending Racheev the books he published for the countryside; that Evgeniya Konstantinovna's salon grew broader, livelier, and that the mistress was appearing no longer with a bored expression, not with a passive, flaccid entrance as before, but lively, energetic, and brilliant, attracting everyone to herself; that her correspondence with Racheev was full of profound interest for them both; then all that will be sufficient to consider our story at an end.